Jo Hanna is an Australian artist and writer. She holds a BA in Media/Public Affairs, majoring in public policy. She has contributed to the Empire Times, Flinders University Emerging Writers Festival 2014, SA Writers Centre Boot Camp, GlamAdelaide, and was shortlisted for the KSP Poetry Prize 2022. *Muckemup* is her first novel. It won't be her last.

'Muckemup was a great read. The manuscript was found to have a clear direction throughout, with strong themes and an important message that readers can relate to.' - Hawkeye Publishing

I0593437

MUCKEMUP

*How to create a water
market by stealth*

JO HANNA

www.muckemup.com

CONTENTS

Dramatis personae (in order of appearance)

Tara Laurel: mid 40s, divorced. Works at the post office.

Ivy Laurel : Tara's eldest daughter, 17 years old.

Chloe Laurel: Tara's youngest daughter, 13 years old.

Yingarda Miro Kalinga (Miro): School bus driver & Tara's friend.

Marion Laurel: Tara's mother. Retired science teacher.

Molly: Coworker at the post office.

Andy: Tara's boss. Owner of Muckemup Post Office.

Cassandra Leason: Newcomer to Muckemup. Artist, early 50s.

Romeo Benito Aconaday Senior (Snake): Mayor of Muckemup. Former State politician, 70 years old.

Liz Calder: Runs Muckemup Op Shop. Late 60s.

Robert Calder (Bob): Liz's husband owns a second-hand bookshop in town. Late 60s.

Signora Aconaday: Mayor Aconaday's mother (deceased)

Matthew Farnham: Local farmer against the Irrigation Scheme.

Brett Farnham: Matthew's brother, a local farmer. Against the Irrigation Scheme.

Dr John Prescott: Serena Benchley's husband. Local Doctor and President Muckemup Business Chamber.

Leonard Reid (Lenny): Apple Farmer, Chairman of the Irrigation Scheme.

Romeo Junior Aconaday (Worm): Mayor's son and a Director of Irrigation Scheme.

Gio Luciano: Friend of Worm. Director of Irrigation Scheme.

Silas Rosetti: Director of Irrigation Scheme, related to Alex Crooks by marriage.

Alex Crooks: Treasurer Irrigation Scheme.

Peter Moriarty: State Politician. Country Party.

Dicky: Federal Politician. Conservative Party.

Charlie "Chuck" Swican: Member of Muckemup Water Security Group. Runs Dont Dam Dilbanup FB page.

Craig: President Friends of the River Association.

Benno: Deputy President Friends of the River Association.

Emily: Benno's wife. Secretary of Friends of the River Association.

Sandra Star Tree: Forest Defender. Mid 60s.

Logan Rovello: Former Mayor of Muckemup.

James Templar: Muckemup Council CEO.

Serena Benchley: Muckemup Councillor and Manager for the Forestry Department.

Minister Julia MacDonald: Agriculture Minister - Workers Party.

Alice Kennedy: Newly elected State Member of Parliament - Workers Party.

Minister Lipshut: Water Minister -Workers Party.

Miko: Former Muckemup Councillor.

Adam Calhoun: Local resident, creator of *A Clear Vote* website.

Chip Smith: Retired mill worker and candidate for local council.

Larry Wolfe: Farmer in favour of the Scheme. President of the Business Chamber.

Jack: Resident of Cockemup, photographer and retired Forest Defender. 80 years old.

Raven: Jacks' wife, textile artist. In her 70 years.

Charlotte Diamante: Farmer against the Scheme. Muckemup Councillor.

Graeme Mantel: Muckemups resident greenie, on numerous boards.

Stanley White: President of Soldiers League.

Big Dave: Farmer, member Water Security Group.

Pat Murphy: Mill tennant.

Sharon and Trevor: Owner of the local linen service.

Viv: Enviro Party State Senator.

Ricco Conti: Wealthy orchardist.

Edward Beauchamp: Former Attorney General.

For Dinika Keeble.
You're right, we all have skin in the game.

'Turn poison into medicine'
-Nichieren Daishonin

'Love your land and you will rediscover yourself'
~ Bacci chocolate wrapper

AUTHORS NOTE

Dear reader, I have tried to write this story as plainly as possible and invite you to hold two concepts in your mind while reading this novel. First, Public Policy is the art of shaping our lives. Second, it takes about twenty years for a new policy to be successfully embedded into the framework of society. Only two decades until we think this is how life has always been.

I'd also like to assert that this writing is a work of fiction. While true life and a mix of places and experiences inspired it, Muckemup is not an actual town; any resemblance to actual events, locales, or persons, living or dead, is entirely coincidental. Muckemup could be any town, every town and no town. It's on no map, for it's in the gaps in between. I encourage you to look and listen and engage with a critical mind, and who knows, you may find yourself in those spaces where everything connects.

JH

PROLOGUE

If one were to describe the entire community of Muckemup, it would be a version of the 1950s social club from which the Country Party of Australia inherited its character. Across the south, the carving back of imposing bush and the need for basic raw materials for mere survival preceded a logging industry that would one day supply local, national and international markets. From Bombay to Belfast, the British Empire laid railroads with sleepers made from the forests of Muckemup. Townsfolk talked about jarrah in the same cultish tones that men in Ballarat once spoke of gold, and if you didn't do the same, you became a persona non grata.

The 1970s mechanised the logging industry, and karri, once regarded as useless because termites loved it, was now clear-felled for wood chips. The industry stripped large swathes of the landscape. Machines removed the close physicality that linked men to the trees, and with that separation went respect for the giants, vanishing them into myth. All that remained were nostalgic sepia-toned photos of brawny men, oversized axes, saws, and trees larger than we can imagine today.

Local authorities managed the collective attitude and promoted anti-intellectualism, prohibiting teachers from discussing logging or forests and even banned recycling paper in the classrooms. They taught children from an early age to support their corporate masters. Expert manipulators encouraged boys out of school early. They squeezed them into prefab identities that made them compliant adults, where everything they did in life was subject to this identity. Blissfully unaware, the men ceased to exist as separate selves. Instead, they became pawns to be moved and a pliant mob for the political elite to use both in and outside of the workplace.

PART ONE: WATER

Wock, wock, wok-a-wok, wock, pjur, weer, weer.'

One's for sorrow. Twos for joy,
Threes for a girl and fours for a boy.
Five for silver, six for gold.
And seven for a secret never told.

CHAPTER 1

Tara listened to the gentle snores of the blue heeler over the warble of Coolbardie claiming its dawn territory. She grabbed her jacket from the back of a chair, knocking the dog's lead to the floor. Just like the magpie had roused her, the canine jerked his furry body upright, bleary-eyed and groggy but ready for action. Even a sleeping dog couldn't ignore the siren's call of the lead's metallic rattle. Tara's shoulders slumped in defeat.

'Okay, Loki! We've time for a quickie. C'mon, boy.' She buttoned up her coat, closing in its tartan warmth. Snatching her phone off the charger, the pair headed towards the karri grove that towered, trunks straight as flagpoles, over the small mill workers' cottage that was home, on the outskirts of town.

The mother of two loved early mornings. It was a hallowed time in the life of a single, working parent when having a spare minute to splash milk into a cup of coffee counted as *me time.* The start of the day offered a liminal space where she could dissect the intrigues of world affairs or gather her feelings for a quick roll call. Her instincts had remained loyal despite the tedious weight of crapitalism trying to evict them as unproductive. She recalled the advice, *Look after your inner child,* in a self-help book a friend had given after her divorce. That was a decade ago.

'Oh! Are you still here?' Tara marvelled as the precious innocent, hearing its name, raised its hand. She marked herself as safe. Jung would've been proud. 'Humpff... No time for crazy!' She told the dog.

Taking in the menthol and honey aromas of the forest, she followed the hound over the frost-covered lawn that stretched across the backyard and into the inky woodland. The Japanesey outline of Banksia ran into wiry clumps of ferns and orchids. Spiders stretched their gossamer webs like fishing nets, bowed heavy with their nightly catch. Instead of fish, they held rain mist, and the damp air was sharp on her tanned skin. Beads of moisture collected on the spikes of blonde-cropped hair that gave her ears no protection. As she wound along the trail, she exhaled soft white clouds of warm breath and brushed her hand against the giants, greeting each one, for she knew them well.

Long ago, Tara Laurel learned the difference between the deep-furrowed grey jarrah and the chequered marri trees, which bled treacly red sap from their wounds. She confirmed the seasons by the elegant pale karri shedding their skins. Her heart counted the creeks by their names before a succession of government departments deleted them from the ordnance maps. Before long, the sun's rosy fingers thickened, pushing away the shadows.

'Shit! Breakfast!' Tara spun, tripping over her boots and a few unlucky webs she'd evaded earlier.

* * *

'Great, you're up!' The wooden screen door slapped behind her as she followed Loki into the kitchen with an armful of logs.

'Yeah, where were you?' asked Ivy. Her eldest daughter was seated at the table eating a bowl of cereal, still in her pyjamas, with a nanna-knitted beanie covering a crown of loose copper curls. The girl's cupid face glowed from the pale blue light of her phone.

'Walking the dog.' It was too late to light the stove. Tara dropped the wood into a basket for later.

'It's cold... Did you go for walkies?' The seventeen-year-old's focus fell from the screen in her hand to pat the hound's age-flecked muzzle resting in her lap.

'Mum, I need to use the laptop tonight. I've got an assignment due on Friday.'

'No problem.' Tara grabbed a mug from the cupboard. Ivy was in her final year of school, and the struggle was real. 'It's brisk out there. You know, mansions with wild vistas of nature. After a while, it just becomes wallpaper. You really need to be out in it....' The kettle whistled, and Tara poured herself a coffee. She swallowed a mouthful. 'Freezing ya tits off!'

'*MUM!*'

Tara grinned. She'd successfully snatched her daughter's attention away from her device and was still laughing at her win as she strode down the narrow hall to poke her other child out of bed.

'Hustle time, Chloe!' she called out, and then her phone vibrated. 'Gahh!' Tara groaned and threw her head back. 'Hi, Mum... Sure, get the jug on. Change of plans, girls!'

* * *

The trio bundled into the ute for the school bus run. Backpacks filled with books, and Chloe, the youngest at twelve, all legs and elbows, having just finished her chores, clambered from the chicken coop to dive headfirst into the backseat.

Tara had attended the same high school as her daughters, as had half the adult population of Muckemup. Whenever she sold a stamp to one of the purple circle, she'd remind herself how she'd seen them shitfaced on passion pop or discreetly picking their noses on the school bus as it sped past vineyards, apple orchards and eucalypt forests draped with the motionless rain of moss.

'Look!' Chloe leaned forward between the front seats, pointing at the sky through the windscreen. A wedgetail eagle flew over the top of them, dipping low in front of the ute. It glided gracefully back and forth across the track, its wingspan almost the width of their wheezy old pickup. Tara tapped the brakes, and the ute yammered to a crawl as the bird led them through the forest before it rose away in a broad circle at the crossroads.

'Waalitj's welcoming someone new to Country.' nodded Miro. The bus driver was also peering upward from his seat while waiting for them.

'Thanks, Miro. Thanks!' Tara watched as the bus creaked off carrying kids of the made-good farming elite and those who worked for them, labourers destined to be sucked as dry as the Darling-Baaka River if the local squirearchy had anything to do with it. The boys made faces against the back window before turning the bend. Some things never change. Her inner child shuddered.

CHAPTER 2

'Hey Ma, I'm here! What's up?' Tara entered the mud-brick kitchen. Her parents hand-built the house in the early 1970s when they were first in love and broke. Seven years later, when Tara was four, her father bought a lotto ticket on the way home from work at the packing shed. He won big and left their lives soon after.

Before the Child Support Agency existed, it was customary for some fathers to do a flit and abdicate their responsibilities. Unfortunately for Mr Laurel, he hadn't checked the expiration date on the new life he'd purchased, and by the time Tara was eight, he was dead.

'Be out in 'alf a mo! The tea's ready,' Marion called from the bathroom.

Tara felt the kettle for warmth before switching it back on. She fussed over the tray her mother had prepared, rinsed and refilled the teapot with boiling water and carried it outside to the porch filled with pot plants and half-finished projects. She rolled herself a cigarette.

Tara had grown up with emus visiting this crooked little house tucked away in the middle of five acres of untouched native forest, surrounded by an envelope of more forest managed by the State. Daddy emus corralled their chicks, and tiny yet bolshie fire-tail finches flitted under the verandah, making nests in mud-caked shoes discarded at the back door. The birds were pretty snake alarms. If one were near, they'd demand with a high-pitched ratcheting that someone remove the intruder immediately.

'There you are!' Tara's mother stumped onto the porch and plunged into a chair, tucking herself in like a hen. 'Thanks, love.' She took the thick mug of tea, strong and heavy on the sugar, and pulled out an old captain's pipe. The two women spent five minutes catching up on local gossip as Marion packed the ebony bowl of her pipe with home-dried tobacco she'd foraged in the bush.

'Have you seen Romeo's got fifty acres of canola along the road into town?' asked Tara.

'Yes, and I've heard all the "*I just love the fields of gold. Cheers me up on a dreary day,* nonsense!" Marion sing-songed before growing serious. 'Odd way of acknowledging a drying climate, don't you think?' she asked archly.

Marion Laurel was a science teacher before her retirement. For years, she'd run *Blue Eddies*, a program where school kids collected samples and recorded the bio health of the many waterways in the region for both the local council and the Water Department.

'I know, I know, climate creep. Never mind avocados, we'll soon be growing mangoes down here!' joked Tara.

'Hey, speaking of lover boy! That's why I called you. Someone's making a helluva racket down the back.'

'Oh?' Tara twisted her neck towards the wilderness at the far corner of the property. Biting her lip, she searched Marion's face for clues. 'I'll have to check it out after work, Ma. I need to run. Who knows what Andy was doing last night, but he sent my pay through at four this morning.' Tara rolled her eyes as she stood and leaned over to kiss her mother.

'Ahh, one of the golden boys,' Marion tilted her head upwards to receive her daughter's affection.

Their characteristics were near enough to identify them as related. Both women were well-rooted in the district. Tara's great-grandfather was a WWI soldier who settled in the area as part of a nationalist scheme where devastated men received just enough land to clear and then starve on. The women had robust, outdoorsy features and soft kid-leather skin the colour of toasted almonds dusted with freckles. Shapely bodies of the maternal and the capable, the elder's more so. Whirling and fluid, as if she was deliberately becoming the broad-hipped healing waters she'd once cared for. In the same way, some people, over time, resemble their pets. But where mother and daughter were most similar was in their powers of observation.

'You know, that boss of yours was a right little arsewipe at school too!'

Tara spat her last mouthful of tea. 'Didn't you get the memo, Mum?' Old women aren't supposed to talk like that!'

'Didn't *you* get the memo? In this town, old women aren't supposed to speak at all!' Marion cracked back, sharp as a bullwhip. 'When we turn fifty, we must go away until we die!'

Tara could feel her mother's gears change. She was about to start up like a chainsaw, and the daughter knew if she didn't flee, she'd not escape a feminist rant.

Placing her empty mug on the tray, Tara gave a cheeky grin. 'Then I've still got a few years left! I'll be back this afternoon. Love ya!' She cried out, dashing for her car.

CHAPTER 3

Tara gripped the key and pushed open the front door of the post office. Molly was finishing up out the back. The postgrad student started early to fit around her studies, organising yesterday's delivery between PO boxes and the canvas bags for Andy's afternoon runs. Most mornings, the two workers crossed over with a quick cuppa, where they straightened out the community, if not the world. Not today; the shop was due to open in fifteen minutes. Tara's keen eye surveyed the worn provincial catch-all. Glancing over the multi-sized envelopes, packing boxes, hardware items, nearly out-of-date calendars, and other whatnots as she made her way to the office.

Grabbing the till out of the safe, she shouted, 'Morning, Molly! Sorry, I had to drop by Mum's place.'

Molly stuck her head around the corner. 'All good. Nothing to report.'

'Phew. I was half expecting to find Andy snoozing behind the front counter. Did you see our pays went through at the witching hour?'

'Witches and degenerates,' Molly grimaced, baring her teeth. 'You'd make a good detective. I doubt he'll be back until late this arvo, so you should have a peaceful day.'

Tara's eyes turned skyward as she pressed her palms together. 'Thank the gods for their small mercies!' She flipped the sign to "OPEN".

Her morning was busy — a steady stream of people sending and collecting parcels. A surprising number of artisans lived in the forest. Selling their wares online in batches, they only needed to visit town periodically. She helped the old-timers who still used passbooks to collect their pensions and buy the weekly paper catering to an ever-dwindling readership.

Muckemup, consisted of multiple eras and industries, lapping over each other. Many Italians and Macedonians arrived after the Second World War. Mostly middle brothers of poor and overcrowded families where the eldest sons inherited the property, the youngest received the education, and daughters needed to marry well because they got bugger all. Mum's right, thought Tara. The district of Muckemup was God's country — the God of men!

Andy, resembling the madness of an ocean squall, blustered through the back door at 3 PM. He blinked hard and fast at Tara and the pouches of mail waiting for him before storming onwards to the bathroom without a *"How'd you do?"* Tara reinforced her mental armour as she listened to the click of the toilet door. She searched for an urgent task to forgo immediate interaction upon his return. He was in a mood.

A middle-aged woman standing empty-handed at the counter rescued her. 'Can I help you?' Tara smiled, concealing her relief and wondering briefly how she had missed the chime of the doorbell.

'Yes, can I have a mail redirect, please?'

'Have you got some ID with you?'

As the woman rummaged through her tote bag, Tara inspected her features. She was a couple of years older, maybe early fifties and, apart from her hair, embodied the polite middle-class beigeness that's the fate of many a washed-up soccer mum. Tara accepted the outstretched driver's licence and started filling in the paperwork.

Andy returned, wiping his nose on the back of his hand. His expression only marginally improved as he leaned over Tara's shoulder to glance at the photo on the licence. Then he peered at the woman, appraising her from the worn hikers over loose-cut, crushed linen slacks and a soft cashmere eco-printed shirt, gum leaves smudged in shades of charcoal as if pulled from the ashes of a bushfire. His gaze stopped on the top of her head, still lowered as she ferreted through the contents of her bag. Her hair was also colourless but striking. She had a silver leonine mane that skimmed her shoulders. She looked up, and Andy served her a bored smile. He inhaled a little taller, letting the newcomer know he was the boss. She stared, her face passive and inscrutable. Only Tara caught the drab grey eyes narrowing as she picked up a copy of the Muckemup Tutelage. The headline read:

"STATE FUNDS $80 MILLION IRRIGATION SCHEME,"

'Sounds like water trading.' the woman swiped her bank card.

Andy interjected. 'Nah, our farmers aren't silly like over east.'

The entire country knew about the tragic fish kill on the Murray River a few summers ago. Australians universally condemned it as a crime against nature

12

committed by corporate farmers taking too much water during the drought. The government then repurchased water for the environment at top dollar. Either way, the water barons won.

The woman weighed the postman with the scales of a stranger's indifference. Andy wasn't one for looking away from a fight. He squared up, and an uncomfortable disquiet grew between them, wanting to be filled with words.

Tara broke the silence by tentatively using the name on the card she was holding. 'Um, here's your licence and box key... Cassandra?'

Given an out, the moment passed. 'I'm going to do the deliveries,' Andy slipped away like the quicksilver of his temperament.

'Thanks, I prefer Cass.'

'Well, Cass, welcome to Muckemup.'

CHAPTER 4

'This water scheme is a no-brainer!' Romeo Aconaday announced in a commanding tone as he took centre stage. Despite his short stature, the mayor was adept at old-fashioned soapbox oratory and understood how to fill a space. He discreetly extended his will beyond his physical frame and impeccably tailored clothes. His homespun guile and charisma were spellbinding, and his dark sense of humour matched the coarse hair growing on the back of his hands. Aconaday scanned the chambers he knew as well as the inside of his eyelids, acknowledging each of his fellow councillors, who were just as predictable. They'd follow his lead as closely as musicians obey the conductor. The Irrigation Scheme was Aconaday's opus, orchestrating a new symphony between his past and a triumphant future. It didn't bother him that the audience was small — a young couple wanting development approval to breed dogs, and Liz and Bob Calder, both in their late sixties.

The older pair were regulars who'd settled in the area thirty years ago. They were originally from Melbourne; growing up when progressive, city schools drummed into their students that *"Democracy is government by the people, for the people, and of the people."* The sense of civic duty stuck. They were no threat. Aconaday nodded a friendly hello. They bobbed back in unison.

Romeo Benito Aconaday, born in Muckemup, was the eldest son of Italian immigrants who'd made a new start in an old land. His parents carried the legacy of surviving a war with only a few meagre belongings. They sailed for eight harrowing weeks across the Indian Ocean until disembarking in Fremantle. They were not alone. Together, the battle-weary refugees headed south to sow their miseries into the soil of their new home, where the collective trauma continued to self-seed like wild tobacco.

Romeo's mother was homely and uneducated, but intuitively agile. She apprenticed all her children with Calabresi mind tricks that could have disarmed a Jedi Knight.

'Listen to me, Picciotto. The wolf will eat whoever makes himself a sheep.' Every afternoon she would instruct her boy with a string of Sicilian proverbs, drying her hands on her apron as he sidled into the kitchen after school — hoping to extract a snack for his troubles.

'Don't tell your friend all your secrets; remember you may have him for an enemy one day.' she'd wag her finger in his small, moon-shaped face. The sayings tumbled over her thick accent.

'Sssi Mama.' Young Romeo would softly lisp, nodding his round head while trying to sneak a biscuit into his pocket.

Occasionally she'd halt her pointing midway and make an OK sign, her three remaining fingers stretched towards the boy. Signora Aconaday would then squint, returning her son's gaze. Her tired face intently searched his before knitting her brows together. 'Porco!' her hand was a guillotine. Bang! It would drop. Crushing the stolen treat in his soft, damp palm.

A steady diet of country air, well-peppered with Machiavellian wisdom, saw Romeo "Snake" Aconaday overgrow into a political animal that dug his way downwards from being a potato farmer. By his mid-twenties, he was married with young kids and cutting his teeth on the local council, gaining trust in a place city folk thought didn't matter. From there, he moved into State politics by presenting himself as the saviour to a fatigued local population looking for someone to promise them a better life. Country people blindly supported him. It didn't make a difference if it was all lies. They simply wished for one of their own to succeed. Who cared if he gained a little more for himself?

Romeo joined the political class. Wizards who practised the finer art of deceit so well that even they believed their own forked tongues. Lying was a survival skill for any politician. Aconaday held the provincial seat with various portfolios for almost three decades. Now here he was, full circle, celebrating his 70th birthday, once again presiding as mayor of the district he felt was his kingdom in every sense of the word.

CHAPTER 5

Matthew and Brett Farnham were also farmers. The brothers inherited large tracts of fertile land with freshwater springs and havens of virgin forest skirting their paddocks. They could trace their forefathers back to when the colonists hunted the local Aboriginal tribes across the sandy banks of Lake Dyer for sport after Sunday Mass. Few people now knew that 15 miles down the road were thousands of red kangaroo paw wildflowers giving rise to a living vigil. The massacred souls left their link where they fell, and Boodja never forgets.

The siblings' avocado plantation backed into wilderness that necklaced the Dilbanup River. One of the last freshwater tributaries which soaked into Lake Dyer before meandering another ninety kilometres to reach the ocean. Down south was full of locations ending in ~*up*. In the local indigenous language, it was a root word that meant *meeting place*, and *Dilba* was a bag for carrying bush medicine. Since the dawn of time, the Dilbanup River has been a place of fresh water. A birthing place, a food and medicine source — one of the world's first hospitals. Until 2010, the river had always flowed, even in the driest summers. However, things had changed, and you didn't need a hydrology degree to see it.

'Brett! Did'n yer say Snake's Irrigation Scheme is gunna pull 13 gigs outta here? Matthew called out to his brother as they pushed through a dense track ending on a gentle rise with breathtaking views across a bend in the river. The forest sweated a fine silver curtain of mist across the water. Karak, the red-tailed black cockatoos, screeched. Norne, an ancient yellow-bellied tiger snake almost two metres long and thick as a man's hand, woke from hibernation, wrapping itself around a dead log overhanging the shallows to admire its reflection in the surface shared with the sun.

'So he reckons,' the younger puffed as he pulled himself clear of the undergrowth.

'Nah,' Matt shook his head, his voice twanging. 'Romeo's dreamin'. By Christmas, she's gunna be dry as a root without foreplay!'

* * *

The Farnham boys took it upon themselves to examine the Irrigation Scheme closer.

'I don't get it.' Matthew rubbed the bristles on his jaw. 'Why would yer spend eighty million to take non-existent water from a half-empty river and sell it to farmers forty k's away?'

'Farmers who already have water.' Brett pointed to the crux of the question.

The brothers see-sawed between the Irrigation Co-op and the Water Department's websites. Double-handling water versus the price farmers could sell avocados for was not economically viable. The Water Department, not investing $25,000 on flow devices to measure any new unallocated water in the river, didn't add up either. They could smell a rat.

* * *

'Aconaday and Co plan to increase their property values by taking water from the Dilbanup.' Matthew explained calmly to the eight men that gathered on his patio after work one evening. Half of them were his extended family. The others included the local publican and a couple of hobby farmers, one a psychologist and the other an accountant.

'Yeah, so what, Matty?'

'Soo... go have a look. There's no water!'

His brother cut in, 'With changes expected to the spring rights legislation, it means they're gonna be taking *OUR* water. Transferring the wealth from here...' he jerked his thumb wide, 'To there!'

The penny gradually dropped.

'That's... stealing,' said one of their cousins.

'Well then, we won't be having it,' affirmed another.

All the men solemnly nodded in agreement and drained their beers in companionable silence. Then they formed an official collective to protect their interests — The Muckemup Water Security Group.

CHAPTER 6

The mayor could have been a sleeper agent who'd received the call to duty a decade ago. For since then, he'd quietly busied himself, methodically laying the groundwork for the Irrigation Scheme.

After a few years' hiatus following his departure from State Parliament, Aconaday got back onto the local council and ushered various new organisations into the district; the Southern Foods Group, the Muckemup Water Steering Committee, the Dilbanup River Rural Strategy Group and the Muckemup-Dilbanup Water Users Coalition were all formed to appear to represent different local interests. Their real purpose was to legitimise the need for an irrigation scheme and gently nudge the project forward. The groups sat allied with the Departments of Agriculture and Water and the town's existing clubs that limped along.

That the list of committees read straight out of a Monty Python skit was irrelevant. The trick was for them to hold the same key players. The government would approve the well-practised ruse — tick and flick. No one from outside would inspect too closely. Aconaday's lips twitched as he suggested the town's new physician, Dr Prescott, become President of the Business Chamber.

* * *

'It's simple, Lenny. We pitch to Julia MacDonald the need for water security in a drying climate.' Aconaday referred to the State Ag Minister as he splayed his hands before him. He was sitting in the office of his friend Leonard Reid amongst invoices, sample juice bottles, and towers of apple crates stamped with "Lens's Orchards" on the side. 'Thanks to all this climate change nonsense, we've got the peer-reviewed evidence to leverage off,' he said with a beguiling smile.

'Go on, tell me more.' Reid and Snake were prominent men in the town. They went way back, connected before entering this world, as families from agricultural communities often are. Born only months apart, they had been good friends all their lives. Sharing school, football, roo shooting and girls. Unruly and headstrong, they measured their youth by what they could get away with. When Romeo Aconaday entered State politics, they started getting away with plenty. Understanding incoming legislation and being prepared for upcoming grants was always valuable.

'We need to form a co-op to receive the federal funding. I can't be on it and be on the council. Junior can be one of the Directors, along with Gio Luciano and Silas Rosetti; Alex Crooks has agreed to be Treasurer. You've got to spearhead the Board for us, mate. It's twenty thousand sitting fees plus water shares... Also, you should buy the old Ruskin farm.' Snake tilted his head and gave his comrade an enigmatic nod. Lenny slid back in the bravo-red leather chair behind his desk. He stared out the window, watching the Pacific Islanders working amongst the lines of espaliered trees as he toyed with the idea.

Finally, he spoke, his voice rasping but quiet. 'How? I'm stretched tight as a drum.'

Like most things in a small town, Reid's financial difficulties were a poorly kept secret. On the surface, it appeared to be beer and skittles for the man who married into the apple-growing business years ago. Meanwhile, underneath, old Lenny's legs were peddling double time, and his body screamed at him every morning that it had had enough.

Romeo glowed. 'I'll introduce you to some prospective partners interested in water assets. Then we're ready to roll. I've spoken to Dicky. It's an election year; the feds will bring $40 million. You and I are going to retire rich as Cronus.' he reached over and patted his friend's knee.

'When a rich man caresses a poor man, he will take advantage of him.' Whispered his mother's voice in his ear, for she had died without realising it and often reminded him of her adages. Aconaday withdrew his hand as if he'd touched fire.

'Who?' Financial anxieties had made Lenny vague.

'No one that matters, mate. I must go. I've got a seasonal labour meeting in half an hour.' Romeo's wink was full of innuendo as he rose to leave.

CHAPTER 7

'We need more traction.' Brett concluded when Matthew relayed that both the Federal and State Parliamentary Members had stonewalled the handful of farmers who'd gone to see them to voice their concerns.

'Moriarty rubber-eared us. He kept repeating, *"Everything's in hand, nothing to worry about,"* and Dick, well, that was bizarre. He started losing his shirt, shouting and carrying on.' Matthew pulled a stool up to the kitchen bench and plopped himself down, burying his face in his hands. What a week!

'Oh yeah?' Brett fetched two beers from the fridge and sat beside his older brother, sliding a cold can across the countertop. 'That's living dangerously! He's lucky Big Dave didn't plant him one.'

'Nearly,' chuckled Matthew as he dragged back the aluminium tab and listened to the sweet sound of gas escaping. 'They've hired a CEO from the city. The plan is to pump the water from the Dilbanup into Regent Brook.'

'What? Dam the valley?'

'Yer, to hold 15 gigalitres, then pipe it all over the bloody district.'

'I dunno, bro. Chuck's started a Facebook page, Don't Dam the Dilbanup.'

'Charlie Swican did?' asked Matthew, taking a sip of lager.

'Yeah. Catchy name, don't yer think?'

'Sure. What else can we do?'

'You need the tree huggers, babe,' said Brett's wife as she breezed into the kitchen to check on dinner. 'Shall I set you a plate, Matty?' Both men stared at her, their jaws slack. The farmer's wife had suggested they get into bed with their natural enemy.

CHAPTER 8

Cassandra Leason lay on the dark jarrah wood floor as if in a fugue state. The house was dingy and void of furniture. She stared sedately at the possum piss-stained ceiling. She lived a semi-nomadic existence passed down from a long line of travelling folk — the story tellers and the story collectors. Over time, she'd learnt to manage the anxiety that accompanied each move and reviewed her life as a series of ten-year cycles. Rotating through like a bushfire, cleaning up the excesses of the past decade, purified to start the next ten years from scratch. Every place she landed, she viewed new stories with fresh eyes and triggered her inner adventurer to declare, *'Ah, sure, we'll work it out!'* Now her fifth cycle looked to be defined by the land of trees.

The fringe-dweller was tired and needed to find a job. Intuitively, she knew something had drawn her to this service town surrounded by temperate forest. But what? She'd intended to head north. In the emerging burgundy twilight, Nietzsche came to her; *The snake that does not shed its skin will die...*

Cass yawned and shivered. 'Not warm enough for snakes yet.' The last dregs of Makuru pressed its cold grey face at the kitchen window as she heated a saucepan of milk for a hot chocolate. She would sleep in her swag; tomorrow, she'd trawl through Facebook Marketplace to furnish what was to become her home and greet whatever awaited on the horizon.

CHAPTER 9

Like attracts like, Benno recognised Craig as one of his own soon after meeting each other in Wiregrass in the late 1990s. Back then, people knew the outback town as where the spinifex and fine red pindan dirt began. Too far north for city day-trippers, young bucks were free to run wild. Together, the pair thrived as small-time bandits, and if you'd told them to their faces, they'd have taken it as a great compliment. There were regular road trips between the city and their illicit marijuana crops hidden up there in the bush. They partied hard while offloading their harvests to several dealers. Decades on, they had honed their trade.

'Are you blokes' oright?'

Benno and Craig looked at each other. Help had arrived. The Farnham brothers were calling out to them from about eighty feet away in a clearing that overlooked a wide bend in the Dilbanup River.

'Nah, we're not!' Craig yelled back.

'Mate, are we glad to see youse? We're bogged, eh?' shouted Benno.

Brett and Matthew glanced at each other before carefully approaching on a slippery, moss-smothered track by the river's edge. They knew enough about the local dope growers to be cautious. With the wild pig population, bodies could disappear forever in the forest.

As they clambered over a fallen trunk studded with stripes of lime green lichen and grey tufts of usnea hanging on like Spanish moss, they could see the ute's rear wheels were indeed half buried in a mud-filled rut. The brothers assessed the situation as all farmers are accustomed to because agriculture is nothing if not fixing broken things with a bit of wire and ingenuity.

Matthew finally announced. 'She'll be right. With the three of us, we'll push her out. No worries!'

'What yer guys doin' out here, anyway? Looking for somewhere to plant a crop?' joked Brett. They all laughed with guarded unease.

'Nah, mate...' Benno relaxed. These farmboys were harmless. He slid into the driver's seat and put the ute in neutral. 'I've got a shack up the river. We wanted to find the Star Tree.'

'One, two, three. Push!'

'It's around here somewhere.' grunted Craig as they all ploughed their weight against the tailgate.

'Brett, do you remember the old man talking about the fire spotter trees, like Big Ben, when we were kids?' asked Matthew.

'Yeah... sorta.' Brett dropped his arms down by his sides as the ute lunged free.

'Woo-hoo!' cheered Benno. He switched the ignition off and jumped out to thank the brothers.

* * *

Benno was always on the scout for an opportunity and the next nubile young thing. Back in the days after his first divorce, he'd bought his river shack for almost nothing. Since then, it had remained his feral interpretation of a Playboy mansion. Over the years, a steady stream of European backpackers passed through his bed while they completed their 88 days of compulsory farm work to meet their visa requirements.

Benno grinned, remembering his current wife's first visit to the shack when they'd been dating for about a year. He'd unlocked the house to find a message left for him by a pretty German girl with whom he'd had a brief interlude. She'd broken in and spray-painted *"BETRÜGER"* across his lounge room wall. Luckily, Emily was busy unloading the car. Go figure that all that womanly playing house crap she'd insisted on packing delayed her long enough to save him from accusatory tears and drama. He hastily rearranged the furniture, dragging a bookshelf to cover the offending graffiti. His fiancé noticed nothing amiss, and they'd now been married for five years. Women inhabit a parallel but very different universe to men, and much sneaks under the radar.

* * *

'We'll set it up here,' said Craig, checking out a disused trail close to the greenies forest camp.

'Yeah, that'll work.' Benno grabbed his axe off the backseat while Craig started clearing the area. They were attempting to catch themselves some tree-hugger-loving.

Forest Defender groups were often a motley crew, consisting of university students, the unemployed and self-funded retirees. Within those demographics is a blend of the naïve, the zealous, and the predators. Nine times out of ten, there's a hierarchy and a megalomaniac near the top with delusions of grandeur.

It took a little while for the bait to work. By lunchtime, a faint sheen of sweat filmed their faces and stained their armpits, and the heavily scented air was alive and buzzing with insects. Their creation was complete. Catching sight of three activists wandering toward them along the track, they quickly signalled each other a warning look — *Game time!*

'Whaddya doin?' asked a plain, square-built woman in her mid-sixties. Two younger, scrawny men in dirty jeans and expensive hiking boots flanked her.

Benno and Craig wore their best *"respect for old people"* disguises.

'Hullo there! Oh, we're just keeping our skills tuned up.' Craig wiped his brow with a clean white extra-large handkerchief, his olive skin glistening.

'You never know when you'll need to respond quickly,' added Benno, his face pink from exertion and a touch of the sun. Benno liked to regard himself as 21st century Ned Kelly, a strong man's hero rather than a thug and a thief. He sported a Che Guevara tattoo to express he was a romantic revolutionary despite having never read Marx.

'Impressive barricade,' murmured one boy, circling the strategically positioned logs. The woman folded her arms across her barrel chest. She was as defensive as antiseptic and sized them up with a sour look. The second guy remained beside her, his eyes dead as a cod in the fish markets. Craig noted the irony of the words *"Nature Is The Cure"* emblazoned across the youth's filthy t-shirt. He bore all the hallmarks of having been in the forest for too long, unwashed, living on a sustenance diet of two-minute noodles and out of Xanax.

Some gatekeepers! These three couldn't punch their way out of a paper bag. Benno's assessment echoed his partner's, but he kept his baritone voice hypnotically smooth. 'Thanks. Should keep an enemy at bay for at least a few days.'

'What enemy?' The woman was still suspicious and unaccommodating.

Hags were such a pain in the arse, thought the two liars for hire, but they didn't dare exchange glances should she catch the sentiment passing between them. Crones had a knack for doing that.

'No one in particular.' Craig drawled, light and easy.

'We learnt this in the army, and ya know the saying "use it or lose it," winked Benno, squeezing his waistline cheekily.

The woman appeared to be determining why anyone would be out in the forest building a makeshift fortress, then slowly lowered her guard as she grudgingly applauded their morning's work.

Finally, she yielded, ' You look like you could both do with a cold drink of water.'

'That'd be great!' Benno visibly crumpled as if he hadn't had a sip of fluids in days.

'Thank you — Sorry, what's your name?' asked Craig, in his super-polite voice.

'I'm Sandra. This is Simon and Ekko.' The crone waved towards the boys. 'Follow me!' And just like that, the Forest Defenders gave the two duplicitous rogues the keys to the city, or in this case, the base camp. It was easier than expected, and they couldn't help but flash sideways at each other — *Gonna drive it like we stole it!*

CHAPTER 10

As often happens with evil, it originates from well-meaning people. The Howard administration established the blueprint for a nationwide private-sector water market in 1993. Water trading started with farmers sharing what they could spare during the 1979-83 east coast drought.

New South Wales took the first steps, trading water allocations in 1983. By 1989 they'd introduced entitlement trading among private diverters, allowing water ownership to be separated from the land. Then, in 1991, the State enabled trading across different catchments. In 1994, water trading was put onto the COAG agenda for nationwide reforms.

The public servants in Canberra took the farmers' generosity and ruthlessly applied reform. They were like obstetricians scheduling caesareans to suit their golf dates, delivering the reborn National Water Initiative to the hedge fund managers and the Cabinet of Water Ministers to be further polished to make it as lucrative as possible before enshrining it into law.

By then, Aconaday had been a legislator for five years. Being from Muckemup, where the long, wet winters flung torrential rain sideways, Snake persuaded the Conservative Party heavyweights he was an expert on Adam's ale. They assigned him to the joint Ministries of Water and Forestry.

He and his collaborators set to work on privatising water. Separating the ownership of water from land allowed them to create and legislate a water market sans the pesky mechanisms of the ASX that prevented insider trading. They mandated that each State Premier sign the agreement before releasing any funding.

Aconaday went on the record, quoting another of his mother's utterances. *Mio Cucciolo,* 'Public money is like holy water; everyone helps himself to it....' He added his own ending while rolling his thick, well-upholstered shoulders. 'Why not get something for it in return?'

That was a long time ago. Aconaday's life had since twisted like a wild river with many treacherous shoals. But Romeo resembled the snake his surname suggested. The Anaconda python was a biological swimmer with no natural predator except for the fear held in men's hearts.

Romeo identified with that vampiric confidence as he slithered through parliament's murky waters. He knew to keep his counsel to himself lest his enemies try to devour him. His mother's lessons came into their own.

'Acqua in bocca! Say nothing!'

However, the whitewater of politics can crush even the strongest of minds. Aconaday was fortunate; when the vortex eventually dragged him under, it didn't hold him for long. Instead, it spat him out, ego-scarred and exhausted but unharmed, at the entrance of the Lobbyist's darker realm.

Snake had waited patiently for the water traders to look beyond the golden goose of the Murray River. They were like foxes in the henhouse, aiming for as many livers as possible before escaping the shower of devastation with their hides intact while their victims bled out. He, too, had profited from his water shares, but what do you give the man who has everything?

More. Romeo's truth was, 'I want more!' Because as the old Sicilian saying goes, t*he more you have, the more you want.*

CHAPTER 11

You're a strange place, Muckemup, thought Cass, standing outside the laundromat on Main Street at 10 PM, absorbed with her surroundings. Someone had recently pumped a lot of money into the town's public infrastructure. She was alone on a school night, and the street was lit up like Kings Cross. Row upon row of multi-coloured lights reached across the entire road, covered by a transparent perspex roof. For what? The shopfronts below comprised a butcher, accountant, fish and chips, and one of the grottiest laundries she'd ever had the misfortune to use. The lights varied into a Mexican wave.

'I guess if you build it, *THEY WILL COME!'* She shouted down the empty street, listening to her voice reverberating off the empty buildings then break-danced an arm wave back at the winking lights before pirouetting inside to empty the dryer.

It took Cass a fortnight to collect the basics: bed, table and TV. Her books and art materials would arrive out of storage any day now. She could tide things over with a few miserable cleaning jobs. Cass needed just enough income to pay for rent and canvases. Every morning, she packed her sketchbook for dawn hikes. She used a pot of black Indian ink and "nib" sticks found on her walks to re-imagine the forest on paper before heading off to clean holidaymakers' bathrooms.

She was getting her head around the place and often visited a 500-year-old tree seeded long before colonisation.

It had survived storms and the red bull of fire and even avoided the foresters' axe in 1910 when a young settler recognised the giant as extraordinary and marked it *"To Be Protected"* the day before it was due to be felled.

While loggers sharpened their axes in anticipation and the billy boiled for tea, the boy jumped on his push bike. He rode the 30 km corduroy track to the warden's office to successfully petition for its pardon. Standing 120 feet high with a trunk so broad that it would require four, if not five men holding hands to encircle her. The locals called it King Jarrah, but Cass didn't like that name for the grand old behemoth and dubbed her "Mother Jarrah."

'You're a Queen.' she whispered, pressing her cheek against the rough fissures of the enormous, dark bole.

CHAPTER 12

'Sorry, Mum! Things have been hectic. Andy's in Perth, and this election has got everyone crazier than my ex!' Tara looped her index finger in small circles by the side of her head.

'That's okay, hun. Nuthin' urgent. What's everyone worked up over?' Marion was at her carpentry bench under the verandah, chiselling into a thick, arthritically misshapen branch.

'Oh, just this water bizzo. The farmers out in Dilbanup are pretty pissed about it all. But you know how it is; farmers always want more for themselves — that looks good! Going to be one of your garden chairs?' Tara asked, pointing at her mum's handiwork.

'Yes. Do you like it?' Marion held up the piece she was working on, and both women admired the twisted wood transforming under her deft hands.

'I do!' Anyway, what will they do?' Peter Moriarty has held that seat for how long now?'

'Oh, only about 15 years.' Marion drifted back to when the Country Party member first won the seat. 'Yeah, he's going nowhere! Well, not unless he gets accused of child pornography or a charismatic Conservative candidate emerges from the woodwork, and they're pretty thin on the ground around here.'

'Ha! Indeed they are. Just ask Wally from Tollie!' snorted Tara.

'Oh dear, that's right!' Marion shook her head as she recollected when the former local mayor, Logan Rovello, had taken a run at the State seat soon after Aconaday departed from Parliament. Rovello had gone off script and got busted, using an alias to attack the incumbent Premier on talk-back radio. The show's producer blew his cover, and the hapless candidate ended his immediate political aspirations before he'd hung up the phone.

'That's what I want you to investigate. Machinery noises are coming from down along the creek. I don't know what the Forestry boys are doing, but it's too slippery to risk exploring by myself.'

'No probs, I'll check it. Then we can have a coffee before I collect the girls.' Tara ambled past the house dam and through the main gate, moving with her purposeful swinging stride. She was in her mid-forties and still a tomboy at heart.

A narrow strip of State Forest surrounded Marion's property. Trees buffered her place from the highway and the farm next door — Aconaday's place, the family farm his son Romeo Junior now managed. The path Tara took was a disused train track. One of the many crisscrossing the bush to transport logs in the 1940s. It ran parallel to Sapphire Brook, a small creek veining through a ditch from the other side of the road at the top of the block.

The cold water meandered deep through prehistoric zamia palms, their cones getting ready to turn bright red to attract animals to spread their seeds. It then splashed past black granite outcrops before cutting between the two neighbours and a sliver of pristine old-growth forest about half a mile wide. The further Tara walked, the thicker the undergrowth became. She was glad to wear her wellies; the ground turned from sponge to swamp.

'What have we got here?' Tara set foot on the cleared fire trail that doubled as her mum's property line. The dirt track now bridged over the creek thanks to a large concrete culvert marked as belonging to the Forest Bureau and continued towards Aconaday's place. This was new. Tara could see a cutaway diverting water from the stream into a small holding pool, a pump and a pipeline following the extended roadway. Her nostrils flared. 'No prizes for guessing where that is going,' she muttered curses, pulling her phone from her pocket to record the scene. When finished, she backtracked to her mother's. 'Get the kettle on, Ma. We're gonna need that cuppa!' Tara could feel a fire burning her throat and flames of annoyance spreading to her cheekbones.

CHAPTER 13

'We'll list it under "Urgent Late Business" and wait until a day before the next meeting to include it on the Agenda.' Aconaday and Lenny Reid sat across from the Town Clerk, who snickered.

James Templar was a small-town public servant success story, with the mediocrity awards in his pool room to prove it. He entered the workforce as a graduate trainee for the Muckemup Council straight from university and stayed. He spent 15 years working his way up to Chief Executive Officer and held that position for almost a decade.

'The next meeting is at Walker Beach,' said Templar.

'Exactly!' replied Lenny. 'There's less chance of trouble. No farmer wants to drive a 200-click round trip after working all day for a "Rubbish and Roads" meeting and chance hitting a roo on the way home.'

'This will be easy.' assured Aconaday. 'As Chairman of the Irrigation Scheme, Lenny gives us a presentation. We'll pass a motion and provide a letter of support for the Federal funding. Dicky is sitting on the paperwork. It's all approved; just need the documentation, and that's half of the $80 million sorted. Moriarty has already squeezed twenty out of the State. We are nearly there!' Romeo smirked as he thought about the $10 million committed by the local farmers, like driving pigs to the abattoir.

'We've got the numbers. Six of you need to abstain... conflict of interest. Which of you will convince the doctor's wife she's out?' asked Lenny.

Aconaday volunteered, 'I'll tell her. Pecuniary interest with her Forest Department job that'll leave five councillors. They'll vote unanimously in favour.'

It took one misstep for the Fates to change direction and start weaving a different story. The local farmers were familiar with the mayor's tricks. The Farnham brothers accepted Chuck's offer to regularly monitor the council website. After all, he was online daily managing their Facebook page.

* * *

Despite the distance, councillors and the proponents of the Irrigation Scheme watched with escalating discomfort as fifty farmers trooped into the makeshift gallery at the Walker Beach Dance Hall. Aconaday's deep-set eyes shifted nervously. They were all there to say their piece or view it play out first-hand under the ornately framed portrait of a young and dignified Queen Elizabeth II.

The meeting was a full house, with standing room only. Aconaday realised too late to implement any countermeasures. He'd need more time to tune everyone else up, even if he had a backup plan. Instead, he flickered his tongue over dry lips. There was little he could do except keep Question Time to the legal minimum of three minutes and disallow further input after the presentation.

As Chairman, Lenny Reid gave a speech advocating for the Irrigation Scheme. He raised his tired but wily blue eyes to look into the face of each councillor as if he was directing his words to each of them individually rather than as a group.

'The concept behind this is to ensure water security. That we farmers are facing a drier future is irrefutable.' It was at the mayor that Reid looked the last and the longest. 'This Irrigation Scheme will improve water efficiency, for as a co-operative we'll utilise allocated, but unused water.'

Despite vociferous opposition from the gallery, the motion passed. Snake purred his relief and focused on brushing an imaginary dust speck off his blazer to control his glee. Time to shine. This many local growers at one event was an opportunity not to be missed.

'Batti lu ferru mentri è càudu—Strike while the iron is hot.'

Farmers milled about the ute-filled carpark following the meeting, catching up with rural and inter-family news. As Matthew Farnham stepped out of the hall and shook hands with his colleagues in solace, he spotted Benno and Craig from their Dilbanup River encounter. As a ratepayer, Benno had lined up to speak during public question time, asking about the legalities of installing a *"Don't Dam the Dilbanup"* banner out the front of his shack. Matthew sauntered over to greet them as an idea started forming.

CHAPTER 14

Tara and Cass both missed the Walker Beach meeting. However, they followed the fallout across the various social media groups over the next few days. Tara, mainly after work while preparing dinner as a menagerie of teenagers, dogs and chickens, scampered through her small jarrah-clad kitchen. Camouflaged behind a jungle of pot plants were mint-green painted cabinets from the peak Baby Boomer era when Holdens, student politics and vinyl records were the norm. Taylor Swift now shook the thin walls of her house wi-fi'd to the speakers from her daughters' phones.

In contrast, Cass's house was quiet. She poured herself a wine in comfortable solitude, squinting at a painting drying on the easel before flopping onto her couch to check her phone.

'Aye, it's water trading.' She pushed her nose into the wine glass, smelling rustic notes of blackcurrant while trying to distinguish who was who among the players commenting online.

Both sides had several key stakeholders. Supporting the Irrigation Scheme were the old family elites and their flunkeys, the Muckemup Council, the avocado plant nursery, local trucking and earthmoving companies and seventy early-registered subscribers to the Scheme. Many farmers had forked out a couple of grand for deposits to hedge their bets and keep in the mayor's good books.

Against the Scheme stood a group of farmers headed by the Farnham brothers, a woman from a nearby town whose interest revolved around the Star Tree and the Friends of the Dilbanup River Association, a newly formed environmental group. According to a Facebook debate, the Star Tree was the tallest karri tree in the world. Unfortunately, it grew in the valley designated for the Scheme's dam. Facebook was the town square. Plenty of argy-bargees and even more spectators were coming online to cheer and jeer from the sidelines. Cass could sense the suppressed tensions of the community as she read through the commentary.

'Magicians perform to please people, and politicians perform to fool them!' She felt something was decidedly off about this whole water business.

CHAPTER 15

Authentic country thrift shops, run by village matriarchs, are rare birds, and Muckemup's was particularly remarkable. Housed in an old bungalow with a wrap-around verandah covered with a prolific yellow climbing rose that greeted every customer with a bright nod as they entered the store.

Sadly, fast fashion and shoddy rip-offs were swamping it, too. Modernity was the future, devouring every moment of the present faster and faster.

'Gobble, gobble.' Cass said quietly to no one as she surveyed the colourful installation of plastic kitchen utensils and tuned her ears into the surrounding conversations. She'd dropped the casual *"This looks like water trading"* comment here and there online and was getting noticed.

'Hi...Cass?'

She spun around. 'Yes?' A woman stood before her. 'You're from the...Post office!' Cass pointed at Tara's uniform as it clicked they'd met before.

'Yes. Good guess! I'm Tara. But my name badge already tells you that. Silly me!' Tara became flustered at their awkward introduction. Why did you talk to a stranger? Her "gobble, gobble" wasn't a personal invitation for you, yer turkey! Cringing, the Postmistress wanted the rack of clothes behind her to slink forward and swallow her up.

The corners of the artist's eyes crinkled as she placed her basket of purchases on the counter. 'Nice to meet you again.' Cass looked at the uniformed woman. A few inches shorter and a few years younger than herself, with almost Scandinavian features. Skin tanned to rosy gold, cat-shaped blue eyes that could flash hot and cold in equal measure. Freya, the Norse Goddess of love, war, and the ability to influence the future sprang to Cass's mind.

The shop assistant had watched the exchange between the two women with curiosity. 'Are you new to town?' Liz Calder asked, as she fished out each trinket and rang them up on an ancient pressed metal till, polished to a gleam. 'Where are you from?'

'Don't scare her off, Liz!' Look at us jumping on you like fresh meat.' Tara teased her fellow Muckamite, who wasn't always diplomatic.

'That's okay. I'm from over east,' said Cass, which could have meant anywhere from Adelaide to Brisbane. She picked up a small black bible leaning against the till and flicked through its fine rice paper pages, contemplating its potential for use as collage.

'That's for sale. Might give you some divine guidance.' Liz was the consummate salesperson. A stylish woman with vintage Hollywood glamour that was out of place in these backwoods. She had an ultramarine silk turban wrapped around her head.

Cass half giggled and returned the leather-bound book. 'No thanks, I don't need it. I'm exactly where I should be!' The words spurted forth from somewhere outside herself, but through her like a premonition. All three women recognised the weird cadence of preternatural knowledge as the words skipped from her mouth and out the front door like an unbridled fart, leaving an embarrassing silence.

'Umm, does anyone know about that Friends of the River meeting?' asked Cass, doing a poor job of hiding her discomfort.

Liz broke the spell. 'I think they'll have it at the pub.' She knew most things in town, 'Are you a greenie?'

'Not as green as cabbage-looking.' quipped Cass, feeling normalcy return to her voice. 'I'm interested in what's happening with the Irrigation Scheme. It looks like water trading.' The two local women locked eyes and again fell quiet. They agreed with the newcomer but knew better than to say it publicly.

Cass immediately noticed the tension and pulled a face. Perhaps the book I need is *"How to Make Friends and Influence People?"* I seem to be killing conversation faster than a speeding ticket.'

'I'll keep an eye out for a copy for you,' Liz, threw a sympathetic smile from her velvet-red painted lips.

CHAPTER 16

'We're an enviro group without being an *Enviro Group.*'
The President stressed the last two words. A dozen or
more people congregated in the pub's roomy vine-covered
beer garden — a couple of burly farmers, trout anglers
and concerned townsfolk. They were discussing the
possibility of paid radio advertising during the upcoming
State election.

'Our aim is to put pressure where we can, to stop this
insanity from going ahead—' stated Matthew Farnham.

His brother interrupted. 'They're going to spend
$80 million and are still $11 million short! Even after the
government funding and subscribers buy-in.'

'That Water Department's bent as a banana!' cried
another farmer.

'They've reduced our winter take for this!'

You're doing okay working yourselves into a lather
without water! Thought Cass, groaning at her soundless
pun.

'Hey, everyone! Let's remain focused on the
environmental impact.' pointed out the Secretary, who
was also married to the Vice President, or Sergeant in
Arms, as he preferred to be called.

'Yes. *Thank you!* We must protect the Star Tree and
its valley at all costs.'

Cass registered the last speaker as the tree enthusiast
as her eyes darted from one person to another, trying to
place the principal actors she'd seen online.

'Here, here!' said the farmers, back on course.

'Excuse me, are you an incorporated association?' Cass asked from the back of the group. They all turned to gauge her with interest.

'No. We don't need that kind of thing yet.' the President's tone was brusque.

'We're just a group of concerned citizens,' the Sergeant in Arms smoothed. Cass had lifted an eyebrow when she read his title on their website. Like Bikies, she'd thought. Watching them now further confirmed her suspicions. These guys have a script, she thought as she sat back to observe.

The President thanked the farmers for donating $15,000, and they debated the benefits of hiring a helicopter to film over the Star Tree and Regent Brook. Cass bit her tongue. An Enviro Party Senator had helped form the organisation. Despite this, everyone decided it would be best to remain apolitical. Muckemup was a logging town, and greenies were traditionally unwelcome. As per most community meetings, it closed with plenty of talking but not much commitment to action.

Cass filled out a membership form and took thirty dollars from her purse.

'It will keep you in the loop.' the Secretary smiled and wrote a receipt.

Sandra Star Tree fell into pace with Cass as they left. 'Have you just moved here?'

'About six weeks ago. What do you think's going on with the water?'

'I don't know about that side of things. The best person to ask is Matthew Farnham,' said Sandra. 'I'm more interested in the area's ecology. Did you know the valley has remained untouched since the 1950s?'

'No, I didn't,' said Cass.

They emerged from the pub into a half-decent afternoon. It was coming to the end of Djilba or First Spring, and a weak white sun was throwing mottled light through specks of cloud. Sandra stopped and assessed Cass, who sensed the appraisal and was doing her own evaluations.

'I'll take you to see it one day if you like. I'm documenting it.'

'Sure, thanks, that would be great. Here, I'll give you my number.' Sandra took out her phone and began typing as Cass recited her contact details.

'Okay, I'll be in touch. Nice meeting you,' Sandra headed off towards her car.

Cass stood alone on the pavement; she'd walked to town. 'I think I passed that test.' She waved at Sandra's white sedan, then turned on her heel back into the pub. 'Matthew Farnham next!' It took a moment to readjust to the gloom of the front bar. She spotted the farmer standing at a table with a few others from the meeting. He was 6'4", overweight with broad shoulders, short brown hair and a farmer's open face, kissed by a life in the elements.

She introduced herself and got straight to business. 'Looking at the map for the Irrigation Scheme, what are the chances they also intend to take water from other rivers?'

'Where did you see that?' The President was leaning forward to listen with his hands shoved deep in his pockets and his muscular chest pushed out. Cass took in that they were both big boys in their late forties, but she guessed Matt's size came from sitting on a tractor all day, whereas Craig indulged in the gym.

'It's online.' she replied.

Matthew choked on his beer and shot a look at his brother and Chuck, who rolled their eyes. 'They're never gunna do that! All the farmers would lose the plot.' and with that he easily dismissed her.

As the group lost interest, Cass read their faces; who is this mad cow to be making such implausible suggestions? 'Okay, good to know.' she gave a wry nod of resignation and said farewell.

* * *

When she got home, she poured herself a wine and studied two Constitutions, neither impressed her. The first belonged to the Irrigation Scheme. 'Don't farmers read fine print, down here?' she wondered out loud, scanning the website. According to their documents, page two stated a water market with no supply guarantee, and required no justification to cut members off. The second document was that of the Friends of the Dilbanup River Association. 'Huh? They don't have to provide minutes of their meetings to members. What the hell is this?' The President's quote "...without being an *Enviro Group*" echoed in her head.

CHAPTER 17

Tara quite enjoyed her job at the local post office. Her days were a series of brief interactions, enough to stop her from getting bored without becoming irritated. Most importantly, the hours worked around the school week. The only real downside was her boss. How Andy kept the service contract was a local mystery. Before Tara's employment, the shop opened whenever he turned up, 10 AM or 2 PM or not at all.

'Hey, Miro! It's been a while.' She joked with the man she'd seen earlier that morning when he picked up her daughters. 'How's your sanity coping today, bussing all those kids?'

Miro gave a large smile, showing his dimples. 'They're good. A funny bunch this year.' The bus driver had once been a farmhand and rodeo star, but injuries forced early retirement. The dark, rangy cowboy helped the Education Department meet its indigenous equity employment quota by driving the school bus for the last 12 years. Nothing phased him and he carried his precious cargo as coolly as the space between the stars as he flew along Muckemup's back roads. The kids loved him.

'Whad'ya make of this ginnin with the water?' His grin was gone.

Tara did a double take. She examined her friend's face while crafting her words. 'Are you seeing stuff out there in the forest?'

Miro gave the slightest nod.

'Like what?' Tara knew the main reason Miro stuck at his job for so long was it freed up the middle of his days. He spent most of his downtime amongst the trees doing god-knows-what.

'I forgot my box key!' His sudden change of conversation bewildered her. Then the doorbell chimed.

Tara looked up and then quizzically back at Miro as Romeo Aconaday's eldest son Romeo Junior swaggered into the shop. 'No problem. I'll grab the spare key.' She walked out the back swearing to herself 'Shit! Damn! He's all I need.'

Anyone who has spent time working in an orchard knows the apple doesn't fall far from the tree. Romeo *"Worm"* Junior Aconaday had gone to school with Tara. She remembered him switching from oblivious of her existence to an over-the-top charm offensive for about a week before he asked her out. When she declined, he turned nasty calling her *"frigid"* and *"lezzo"*. Despite looking delicate back in her youth with a trim body that could be scooped up in one hand, she had always taken after her mother and didn't suffer fools. She hit back at his taunts by suggesting he was more of a worm than an anaconda. Their classmates overheard the quarrel, and the insult fastened itself to him like prickles to a sock.

Tara returned to the counter to find more customers had entered the shop. Feeling relieved she wouldn't be alone with the mayor's son, she gave Miro the key. 'Just bring it back when you're done, mate.'

Worm was next in line. Tara met his subterranean misogyny with an icy stare thick enough to skate on. He smirked and passed his collection note across the counter. Junior's anger at Tara's rejection all those years ago had contorted until he'd convinced himself that she was intrinsically flawed. Her divorce and subsequent single status reinforced this distortion. It was unthinkable that a woman wouldn't need a man. Back in the old country, the church had, for a time, successfully argued witchcraft. A couple of continents and centuries away, here in the Deep South, many men still suspiciously regarded single women as damaged fruit. And everyone knew that it only took one rotten apple to spoil the barrel.

Tara could read his face; they both knew the backstory. 'Sign here.' She placed his parcel on the counter.

Ten minutes later, with the rush over, Tara realised Miro hadn't returned. She grabbed her tobacco pouch, flipped the shop sign to *"Back in 5"* and locked the front door behind her.

Miro was still outside. But so was Worm, talking to him with his back to her. Eyes wide, she quickly skipped out of sight, holding her breath. Phew! Close call! Creeping away, Tara leaned against the building and concentrated on rolling a couple of cigarettes. The thin, dry paper crinkled under her fingers.

Before long, Miro swung around the corner. 'Grrr, sorry Tara. That man has more front than Davy Jones!'

Tara smiled at his mix-up between the Scottish pirate who fell in love with the harsh and untameable sea Goddess Calypso and the chain of department stores. 'That's okay. Was starting to worry about you. What did

Worm have to say for himself?' she opened her palm to swap the key for a durrie.

'Nah, thanks, I quit. They'll kill yer.' Miro dropped the keys into her hand. 'He's one of them dodgy brothers' team, humbugging about water and Native Title. To my understanding, they registered all water courses as Indigenous Sacred Sites, Section 18 of the Act. First, they abolish Native Title, then this mob brings it back refurbished with those dodgy brothers.' Miro shook his head in contempt.

Tara put the spare ciggy in her top pocket as she listened to the sinewy old bushie.

'I told a few people, but it's ego city of those environmental groups, along with the usual inner clashes. So pointless.'

'Told a few people what?' asked Tara.

'That they removed three tribal areas just like that!' Miro snapped his mahogany, age-polished fingers. He was angry. 'Now this joker is telling me they're going to use a government-sponsored anthropologist when it should be a Traditional Owner. All are working to make things happen for money. They are not to be trusted and do not control our Lore. They're triggering hostilities by going around things.'

'What's Junior got to do with it?'

'He's a Director of that Irrigation Scheme. Making sure I keep quiet. They've contaminated enough of our people. The blackfella traitors will do what they're told. Coconutters~' Miro spat his bitterness onto the ground.

'Oh, right. I'm sorry mate.'

They stood in shared pathos.

'Muckemup? More like Fuck 'em up! Who needs water, anyway?'

CHAPTER 18

Cass followed behind Sandra. There was hardly a discernible path through the replanted forest. Guide markers only recognisable to those informed. The women were a mile inland from the Dilbanup River. The night before, Sandra had called the newcomer and offered to show her the Star Tree.

'Wear sturdy shoes and long sleeves, navy blue if you've got it,' Sandra recommended after they'd arranged to meet at the Town Park. Cass now knew why; the march flies were an infantry dedicated to stalking them, and the colour navy was supposedly a deterrent.

Sandra halted. They'd come to the edge of the rise they'd been tracing. Below them opened up a valley that could have been straight off the set of Jurassic Park, exuberant with complex plant life uninterrupted for millennia. She thundered. 'I SEE YOUR POSTS KEEP GETTING DUMPED OFF THE COMMUNITY FACEBOOK.'

Cass soaked up the view. 'You noticed?... This is magnificent!'

'SORRY, I'M DEAF IN THE RIGHT EAR.' Sandra tapped her head.' 'Yes, it's STUNNING!' she shouted. 'IMAGINE THIS WAS ALL THE SOUTH BEFORE LOGGING AND SO-CALLED "REGEN" FORESTS' The older woman emphasised the word by using her fingers to make bunny ears.

'What's regen?' asked Cass.

'WE JUST CAME THROUGH SOME. THEY TEAR DOWN THE OLD TREES AND THEN REPLANT THEM.'

Cass waved her hand, showing for Sandra to lower her voice.

'Sorry...That's the argument for wood being a sustainable resource. But, the natural stem density of karri in virgin bush sits around 20 to 50 stems per hectare, even less where large canopied trees have taken dominance, like down here.' Sandra pointed towards the valley. 'Whereas areas of karri planted by the industry can be 1000 stems per hectare, 20 times the natural density.'

'How's that work for biodiversity?' asked Cass. She looked behind at the dense copse they had struggled through compared to the basin below.

'FOR WHAT?' roared Sandra.

Cass turned so the woman could see her mouth move. 'BIODIVERSITY?'

'It doesn't. When we alter the landscape of flora so severely, it impacts the animals. You can see for yourself. The current situation is a monoculture of single species and same-aged trees. It may as well be a suburban lawn! The marri, sheoak, wattle, zamia palm and peppermints are all destroyed during the clearing process and then smothered out by dense replanting. Hence my visits to get it all documented before it's gone.'

'Shit!' Cass processed what Sandra was saying while assessing the curtain of trees they had pushed through.

'Come on, let's go down; watch your step. Best I go first. I want to check if there's been any new animal action,' said Sandra.

Cass assumed any nearby wildlife would have surely fled after hearing their shouting. But she was content to bring up the rear, soaking it all in as she entered the gully. Nature rushed to bottleneck at the entrance of her pupils; the visual overflow sat on the rims of her eyes with a glassy tension. Sandra stopped often, taking the lens cover off the digital SLR camera hanging around her neck. She took close-up photos of flowers, tracks and wildlife scat hidden in the undergrowth. It just looked like dirt to Cass.

The Star Tree had two sisters, shorter than their magnificent 85-metre sibling. Yet, they appeared as tall because they were slightly further up the valley. The crowns of the three giants formed a triangular awning, protecting delicate-coloured orchids and sundews sparkling like fairy wishes on the forest floor. On reaching them, the grey-haired duo sat to rest in their secret garden.

'I can't believe they want to dam all of this?' Cass peered at the abundance of flowers growing at the base of the tallest karri tree in the world, swatting the flies needle-biting through her trousers.

'They're called Forest Mantis.' Sandra nodded at the cluster of orchids. 'Why are you interested in the water?'

'Oh, yeah, I can see it! They *do* look like they are praying, and the Star Tree is their Buddhist shrine. Umm... ' Cass felt mesmerised by the fragile blooms' spiritual beauty and had to drag herself back to the conversation, 'I've been following the water shitfuckery over east for a few years. Sorry, that's the only word for it. When I moved to town, I had no idea there were issues here. What about you?'

'Retired. I've been coming down here for decades to save the forests. I bought a house in the next district.'

'Are you helping to make that film with Friends of Dilbanup?' asked Cass.

'No. Those guys are a pair of Walter Mitty's,' said Sandra, with a superior little curl of her lip. 'A helicopter would chew through their money in no time. I think they're a shield for the farmers. It's hard to pretend that you now care for the forest after years of tearing down trees for pastures.'

'Oh, okay. So, what's your plan?'

'Pretty simple,' said Sandra. 'While waiting for the Environmental Protection Agency to open for public submissions, we need to get the wider community onboard. The Star Tree has historical appeal. It was one of the original fire lookouts before technology took over. About nine across the region had small cabins built on their tops, manned by volunteers during the summers for about thirty-odd years. They used lanterns and mirrors to signal the location of fire breakouts.'

'Wow! That sounds like a Terry Pratchett novel with the Clackers... So, what's the go with my Facebook posts getting censored? Is the community predominately pro-scheme?' Cass squinted as she watched Sandra stand. Her seat had exposed roots that reached up from the earth like kraken tentacles rising from the ocean.

Sandra swatted at her arms. 'We better get going. The flies are vicious this year because the marri trees are flowering. It only happens once every seven years... My knees are shot; climbing up the hill always takes much longer than coming down.' She stretched her legs as if to prove they were indeed stuffed. "Regarding your posts, maybe the page admin is pro-scheme, or maybe they are just pro whatever Aconaday tells them!'

Cass copied the older woman, brushing the forest debris from her backside. 'Oh right, the mayor. He has that much power?'

Sandra pivoted and met Cass head-on as she slowly articulated in her loud, forceful voice, 'The mayor, Snake, he *owns* this town. Be warned, the term "Muckemup Mafia" is no joke.'

CHAPTER 19

Regen is just corporate spin! Another word for plantation, thought Cass with her laptop open on her knees and a glass of red wine balancing on the bookshelf next to her. The outsider spent her evenings painting and researching the Irrigation Scheme. After visiting the Star Tree, she studied how the high density of shallow-rooted, thirsty, and growing trees soaked up a higher percentage of the rain runoff that was once destined for creeks and rivers. She chewed her lip.

'Hmm, interesting. According to the Ag Department, rainfall has dropped by thirty percent in this region in the last fifty years... How's that fit with their planned Irrigation Scheme? Why the Ag Department? Where are the Water Department stats?' Cass was full of questions as she searched through the government website. Nothing. She compiled a query for the online community noticeboard, hoping local knowledge could shed some light. She then put aside the computer and returned to her painting; exhibition deadlines were creeping closer.

An hour later, she checked her phone to find that, once again, the admins had deleted her post.'Really? Muckemup Mafia? ... Christ on a bike! Where have I landed?' Emboldened by her third glass of wine, Cass pulled the paintbrush from her mouth and emptied the bottle into her fourth glass in a singular tipsy move. She threw herself onto the sofa, pushed her reading glasses onto her nose, and opened her laptop again. She pulled up her Facebook page and stabbed at the keys. "Create Group" 'Right... "Name Group" What's a good name?' She wiped her paint-smeared chin, the drunken brain cogs whirring haphazardly for a few minutes. 'Hmm...Muckemup, Muck... Uncensored? Unrivalled?' She tried the words for size. "Muck Unrivalled" That sounds low-rent enough!' As she typed, Cassandra heard a high-pitched cackle escape from her lips. But instead of closing her mouth, she embraced the sound. 'Oh, hail to thee, Thane of Muckemup...All hail, thou shalt be a Water Baron — Oh Shit! Hang on...' she hiccuped. "Invite Friends", 'Eeek!' Besides chatting with the supermarket staff, Cass only knew about three people in town. 'Don't bore me with... details, Facebook. C'mon, Cass! You know God is in the details...Yeah, but as Steinem pointed out... the *Goddess* is in the questions! And once we ask, there is no-*NO* turn...turning back,' half cut, Cass slurred while writing the introduction to her newly formed group.

"Welcome to Muck Unrivalled. Created to share information of interest to the residents of Muckemup, particularly WATER."

'Now for the hook, and then... then b-b.... Bed for you, girl!' She raised her glass in a wobbly salute and prepared her first post.

* * *

Tara studied the notifications on her phone. A late-night friend request from Cass Leason and an invitation to join her group, *Muck Unrivalled*. The corners of her mouth drew downwards, and she frowned with concern.

'Tut-tut. Lady, don't lick the lawnmower,' said Tara. The group was public and had only five members. But, in her first post, Cass published the Irrigation Scheme's map showing where the 250 km of pipeline extended across the region. 'What have we got here?' Tara read the post with interest, for she was sober and knew which properties the Irrigation Scheme reached and who lived there.

CHAPTER 20

'We've got a problem.' the CEO lounged on Aconaday's terrace. He'd finished work and made a detour to the mayor's place on his way home. Whiskeys in hand, the colleagues watched the sun drop to sizzle and hiss behind a line of truffle oaks.

Sitting together, the men appeared comical. Aconaday was short and, in his youth, husky enough to cut a tree with a hatchet. He'd lived a long, glutted life, and it showed. His skin was pink, and glowing jowls gave him the look of an end-of-season pumpkin on top of a thick bull neck. His hair was luxurious and a dark salt and pepper, worn in the same utilitarian style since the age of ten. Yet, neither time nor the physical wear of excesses had slowed his unquenchable thirst for power.

The mayor was a shrewd one-man show, forever chasing an audience. He regularly invited himself to the meetings of various community groups he wasn't an active member of, knowing they would always defer to his expertise. He attended any funeral he could speak at, shaking hands with the grieving and buttonholing the unwary. Aconaday's aura dazzled like an Angler fish's lure, wiggling to mimic good fortune. His prey, often too late in recognising the cut-throat ambition, either became indebted, strapped to his side by their own trivial corruption, or he crushed them. Envy was a punishment devised by Sicilian tyrants. From a safe distance, Romeo took savage delight in ruining the careers of his opponents, destroying their businesses and organising their relatives to be fired with the help of a hoard of bootlickers who did his bidding without question. Resistance in this community meant being ruthlessly cut from social standing while watching your peers get ahead.

In contrast, James Templar's slim body created long shadows. Dark thinning hair, which he camouflaged by wearing it cut close to his bullet-shaped head, accentuated the pasty complexion of a bureaucrat who spent most of their time indoors. Deficient in fibre — both moral and dietary. While Templar looked incapable of cutting his way out of a fog, he recognised which side his bread was buttered on. Initially, he disguised his apathy for Romeo Aconaday so well that he'd almost forgotten his loyalties to his former boss. James felt partially responsible for Rovello's misfire; how could they have known the radio producer would recognise Logan's phone number?

'What problem?' Aconaday stretched back. He was due to preside over the local School Board meeting in an hour. When he was young, Snake's father taught him to hunt and to be successful at it; one must know his ground and quarry. Applying this rule to his political career and life in general, Romeo gained the loyalty of thousands of people, including teachers and police officers. He remembered when he first met Serena Benchley five years ago. She'd attended a school meeting and impressed him with that rare mix of ladylike etiquette and business smarts. Serena was a divorced professional in middle management at the Forest Bureau. In her late twenties, she still possessed the malleability of youth. She was attractive, but Aconaday had been more enthused in mentoring her than seducing her.

'*Mio Figlio, Cumannari è megghiu i futtiri Giving orders is better than making love.*'

'Si Mamma.' He remembered thinking Serena would make the perfect wife for the new doctor in town. Meanwhile, he would groom her into his support base for the future.

'Hey, Snake!'

Hearing his name, Romeo opened his eyes directly into Templar's anaemic gaze.

'Are you with me? How is your mother connected to this?'

'Huh, what—what's the problem?' Romeo was dazed and annoyed at being interrupted. He had wrapped himself like a taco in the reverie of his handiwork and hadn't realised he had spoken aloud.

'I was saying we've had a formal complaint about you chairing the Walker Beach meeting last month.'

'From who?' The mayor pulled himself together.

'The Farnham brothers. They've formed their own water security group and suited up by the looks of it.'

Aconaday snorted. 'Ha! I doubt those boys got a lawyer. They're tighter than a gnat's fanny!'

The CEO's mouth was a bitter line above a stubborn jaw, hinting at how miserable his outlook was. The body can only lie for so long before it wears our state of mind on the outside for everyone to see, should they care to look close enough.

'Romeo, listen to me. They've highlighted critical governance oversights, including pulling Serena out of the vote on the Irrigation Scheme. I didn't think they'd push back on that, but they have, and we'll need to redress it. It's a pain, but we need legal advice. Now's not the time to be careless.'

Aconaday cocked his head. 'Is there something else?'

'Yes. Some woman has created a new Facebook group.' Templar glanced at his notes, fixing a thin sneer, 'Muck... Unrivalled.'

'Dio Mio! How is that a problem?' asked Snake, shaking his head in disbelief. 'She probably got dumped from *"Have a Whinge"* or whatever forum the locals of Hicksville are using this week.' Romeo disapproved of the incontinent discourse on social media. He preferred radio. Uni-directional, one way — him to the masses and thanks to budget cuts at the national broadcaster, no recordings were kept on file. He could almost say anything without impunity. He looked at his watch. 'Set up a conference with the solicitor and let me know.' The farmers' obstacle was merely an inconvenience. With a dismissive wave, he drained his glass. 'I've got to go! Are we done?'

CHAPTER 21

'Ma. Ma! Listen, have you still got those old district maps?' Tara asked Marion, for three hundred people had joined Cass's group within two days.

'What the...?' Tara had kept the friend request on hold, trying to figure out what she wanted to do.

After a soft launch, the town's newest resident entered the public arena as if she'd drunk a can of Redbull before cutting sugar cane with a machete. She wasn't only online. The local rag had also published a letter she'd penned to the editor in which she poked holes in the Irrigation Scheme and the ineptitude of the Ag Minister, Julia MacDonald. If you didn't know better, her timing looked almost deliberate.

MacDonald exercised her right of reply with a condescending response. But Cass's calculated risk had paid off; the ruling Workers Party produced a candidate to run against Peter Moriarty at the eleventh hour. The contender, Alice Kennedy, had no chance of winning the long-held Conservative seat.

Tara detected the vibration of war drums on the wind. This undercurrent defied reason but quickened her pulse in time with the beat. She waited until Sunday afternoon to send Cassandra Leason a message suggesting they catch up.

"Sure, come on over!" was the immediate reply.

* * *

'Take a seat. I'll make coffee. Sorry, I've only got Instant.' Cass cleared the paint tubes off one end of the table before disappearing into the kitchen.

'That's fine, thanks. Nice letter in the *Tutelage*.' Tara raised her voice as she looked around with interest. The room was more of an art studio than a lounge. A table and two chairs were in front of a large paint-filled canvas sitting on an easel.

'Thanks, I liked the Minister's return volley. I shared that everywhere online!' Cass called back, reciting Julia MacDonald's reply with an upper-crust accent. *"Unfortunately, Ms Leason's understanding of the proposed Irrigation Scheme is limited, and her concerns about water trading are misplaced."* The artist followed with her analysis. 'Those words will return to haunt that woman! But you only get one chance to be underestimated.' She paced the kitchen, opening and closing cupboards.

'Uh-huh, sure. I've been looking at your Irrigation Scheme map. Do you think they intend to take water from elsewhere too?' A red bookshelf overflowed with tomes on history, art and politics, next to an old black vinyl sofa was graffitied with the words "Carpe diem" and three drip-filled question marks in white paint. Its arms split, bursting with stuffing and a messy rainbow of brush wipes.

'I call it my *crying couch*.' Cass nodded at the two-seater as she set their mugs on the table and pulled up a small stool on wheels, like those hairdressers used, except this one was covered in paint. 'But back to your question;

I asked Matthew Farnham about that, and his answer was, *"Ho-ho, little lady, that's never gonna happen. The farmers would all lose their shit!"* She pushed her chest out and swayed her shoulders side to side, mimicking Matt's broad ocker accent. 'So, I don't know? I've only been here five minutes. You tell me!'

Tara nodded coolly. 'Well, I think water can come from both ends of a hose. Check it out. That map of yours goes to multiple waterways.'

'Yeah, I saw. I've also been looking at the Water Department's register of licences. For example, the arm that extends south to the Proja River. According to the register, there's only one farm down that way. That's some costly pipeline for supplying a single property that's not even that big, by the looks of it.'

'Uh-huh, and did you notice it stops before it reaches there? It comes to a dead-end on the other side of the highway!'

'I did. But then the river can become the conduit. You release the water on one side of the bridge and suck it out on the other, further downstream.' Cass swivelled on her seat as she spoke.

Tara laughed. 'Do you know what Pro-*Ya* means?'

'Oh, is that how it's pronounced? No, no idea.'

'It's Macedonian for *"salty"*. You wouldn't be dumping clean water into it. Not even in the middle of winter, and that's not when you need the water. But if you *took* water *from* there in the height of winter, when it's less saline and mixed small quantities into dams full of freshwater...' Tara prompted, watching Cass's face as her voice peeled off.

'Ah, mix your flea powder with the good gear, and increase your profits.' Cass clicked her fingers.

'Exactly!' Tara saw a glimmer of promise in this Johnny-come-lately and was relieved her afternoon visit would not be a waste of time. 'How well do you know the area?'

'About as good as I pronounce names of rivers... Then what was Farnham's game the other day?'

'The farmers' *only* concern would be that they're missing out!'

'Right. So, that explains the setting up of that green group.'

Tara fidgeted. 'Can we sit outside? I do my best thinking when I'm rolling a cigarette.'

'Ha-ha. Sure, no problem. I'm reformed... about seven years now, so you have my empathy.'

The two women stood in unison.

'Oh, that's right, you went to that Friends of Dilbanup meeting. How'd it go?' Tara stepped onto the back deck.

Cass retracted her head, giving herself a double chin. 'I'm not convinced. Not being incorporated is dangerous. It puts all the financial responsibility on the members. Big business doesn't mess around. They'll do whatever it takes to remove obstacles, including bankrupting people. Look at what mining companies like Adani have done over east.'

Tara lit her cigarette, blowing a thin line of smoke out of the side of her mouth. 'Who was running it? Farnham?'

'No. He was there, though, with a bunch of farmers. It's confusing, but I think they've got a different group called "Don't Dam the Dilbanup". Friends of the Dilbanup River is headed by a couple of guys... Craig and Binno, something?' Cass scrunched her face, trying to remember.

'Craig and *BENNO?* Are you joking?' Tara's eyebrows shot up.

'No. I'm pretty sure that was their names; let me check my notes.'

Tara detoured home via her favourite section of the forest. Slender white trunked karri's fringed the goat track that passed for a road, forming a skeletal guard of honour. She wondered how those two miscreants got involved.

'Bloody *Matthew Farnham*, that's how!' She pulled over, slammed the car door and tramped into the woods, obsessively clenching and unclenching her fists again and again. Tara had taken a risk in divulging to Cass the framework in which the Friends of the River committee was likely to operate.

'Ugh, Cass, those boys have form. Here's a taste of their brand. Years ago, they were growing and dealing pot up north, living a boom-bust lifestyle. Whenever they ran out of money, their regular fallback was to "live off the vadge", and that's their term for it!' Tara wrinkled her nose in disgust.

Cass's eyes widened.

'Benno's standard line around the campfire of the Wiregrass chapter of *Blokes, Beers and Bitches* was, *"Sure, she's not pretty that'd you'd want to rape her, but the plumbing works!"*

'Beers and *Bitches?* For real? Cass pulled a face that women of a certain age do when they hear them fighting words.

'Oh yeah! We have a chapter here, too; probably every country town does. Like the Freemasons without the dib-dib, dob-dob crap. Lowbrow, but just as dangerous.' Tara pulled her pinky under her thumb as she spoke, showing the universal Scout's sign. 'Eventually, Benno came unstuck and went down for beating a Yamatji man within an inch of his life.; She nodded emphatically as Cass recoiled in horror. 'That's right, but it's not all!' she jabbed the air with her glowing cigarette. It incensed Tara that those deviants were Muckemup's presumed hope against what she could foresee unfolding. 'Not waiting to be implicated, Craig high-tailed it to the United States. Six months later, he gets arrested for running drugs across State borders. He then skips his bail and flees back here via Mexico!' she took a deep breath, almost shaking with fury. 'His warrants are still outstanding. And that's just for starters!'

Cass sat back and silently regarded Tara as she processed the current ramifications of her story. After a few minutes, she said, 'I believe you.'

Tara now exhaled as she moved far enough into the scrub to be screened from the road. She shook her arms downwards to rid herself of bad juju and picked up a large stick. Standing for five minutes in what yogis would call the mountain pose, her head back, eyes held shut, and her palms turned open to the heavens like empty abalone shells. Only when her breathing calmed to a soft silence, and she felt the forest reply in communion, did she use the twig for scratching large arcs across the dirt. She slowly wrote, T-H-A-N-K—Y-O-U.

CHAPTER 22

Neoliberalism got a foothold in Australia in the early 1990s. Farmers began working for subsidies, the planting and ripping out of crops, dependent on wherever the money came from. Government handouts made many farmers overnight Socialists without a second thought. So, the local farmers watched with interest when Lenny Reid bought the Ruskin property for $1.5 million. The river that supplied that farm had even more salinity issues than the Proja. Rumours soon circulated he would plant avocados, keeping them well watered for the initial few years, then sell up a year before the first harvest. Preferably to a city farmer who would pay top dollar and enthusiastically keep watering for another 12 months while scratching their head at an orchard full of dying trees, ignorant that irrigation was raising a water table full of salt. It was an old Cocky trick. But the farmers were wrong.

Reid and his new partners had other plans. They applied to increase their dam size, including a permit request to clear the riparian zone of the river that fed into it. This was universally understood as illegal. Only the law and difficulty for machinery to access waterways saved the big old trees along the streams from certain death. Tara had shown Cass how to tell the difference between untouched native forests and regen plantations via Google Maps.

'Oh, I can see it!' The forest canopy along creek lines and the edge of main roads is different density and a darker green,' exclaimed Cass with excitement.

'*Visual Amenity*. Is the term the government spin doctors give to the narrow band of trees that hides the loggers' truth from tourists driving through the south.' Tara's words dripped with sarcasm. 'They've classified the road reserve as a National Park. I mean, how is that habitat for native animals? Stray a hundred metres in the wrong direction, and you're roadkill!'

* * *

'What a crock!' sighed Cass as she lay in bed, following the pipeline map along those road reserves. Interestingly, the pipeline was missing from the Irrigation Scheme's EPA submission for Regent Brook. She started putting together a post for Muck Unrivalled.

CHAPTER 23

Cass had pulled into the post office to get her mail. She looked up from her PO box to see Tara strolling towards her with a wide green. 'Well, that escalated!'

'Oh, hey! Are you talking about Facebook? Umm... yeah.' She pushed her sunglasses onto the top of her head. 'The group is reaching an average of four thousand people. How many live down here, in the district?'

'Almost nine. I'm on my lunch break. Do you have time for a coffee?'

'Sounds good. I've just finished cleaning toilets.' Cass pulled a face.

'Ah, poo-scrubbing. That's where I used to do some of my best thinking!' exclaimed Tara, laughter crinkling the golden skin around her sharp blue eyes.

The two women entered the local bakery. It was lunchtime, and the dining area was busy.

'Come on. It's quieter out the back.'

A sudden hush fell over the shop as customers recognised the latest local controversy. Every eye in the room centred on Cass.

'Yikes,' she whispered, lowering her sunglasses.

'It's your hair Samson.' said Tara, matter-of-fact. 'Two cappuccinos, please, Bazza!' She hollered as they passed the service counter to an outside table reserved for staff and smokes.

'What's happening? I noticed you published that Regent Brook is a Trojan horse, and they intend to take all the water.'

'Yeah, I think that's the plan...*ALL* the water.' Cass leaned across the table using a loud conspiratorial whisper while fishing for a hair tie in her bag. She scooped her pearl-coloured mop away from her face and twisted it into a low ponytail. The women tried to read each other's thoughts. Looking at Cass's grey eyes, Tara caught the flecks that sunlight made on the river, where every ripple shimmers.

'Hmm, maybe...You'll need help to convince people here, though. I mean, look at Farnham. He's researched this better than anyone, and even he doesn't believe you!'

'I know,' said Cass, 'I'm new. But that just means I've got no bias. No ties that bind me, to blind me.'

'I dunno, Cass, be careful. They can be nasty down here. Real ugly, rabid dog mean.'

'Yeah, I've seen. Have you read some responses to my posts? They're pretty wound up. One guy even made a stand-alone Miss Piggy post of me, picture'n all, then tagged me to be sure I saw it.' Cass gave a derisive Miss Piggy snort.

'I missed that one. What did you do?' Tara felt a knot forming in her stomach.

'What could I do? I shared it on my personal page and tagged him so he could own it.' the artist giggled. 'Juvenile, I know, but effective. He didn't like that quite so much.'

Tara's anxiety also dissolved into cautious laughter. The town needed this new arrival. Like most of the community, she'd followed the online banter. First, watching in silent pity as the hardcore knuckle-draggers pounded on Cass, belittling her while showing off to their mates. They were enjoying themselves and teaching this mouthy blow-in a lesson, or so they thought. But Cass was no amateur at the verbal blood sports of the Patriarchy. She focused on unpacking the water issue while she goaded the loud boys into conversation with what looked like a wide-eyed repartee. They missed the cues. Their debating skills were equivalent to a P-Plate driver, overconfident and underqualified. When she got them in nice and close, Cass strategically slowed the conversation by juggling comments and waited for her opportunity to take the kill shot. Her punchlines were sharp, funny and unmissable. She hogtied them with their own arguments. She transmogrified their hostility into an evening's worth of entertainment, whether for herself or the wider audience was yet unclear.

Initially, the rednecks responded by jumping in to back each other like a pack of hounds chasing a fox. But Cass saw them coming and picked them off one at a time. She was polarising, confronting for some, and refreshing for others. But mostly, she was gladiatorial and unapologetic. No one likes to be made a fool of, not even those capable of gaining the status under their own steam. The humiliated attack dogs didn't take long to skulk back into the shadows and wait.

'Oh, dear. That post will make you the subject of this month's BBB club!' Tara wiped away tears, whether of merriment or relief; she wasn't sure which.

'Ugh... What? A bunch of grown-arse blokes standing around the bonfire crying into their cups, Boo-hoo. She's so mean to me!' wailed Cass, pretending to sob before growing serious. 'I overheard a couple of workers at the Town Park confirm a meeting was coming up; supposedly, the mayor is attending the next one.'

'Ahh, slumming it with the peasants under the guise of men's health. You're definitely on the radar. Watch your back, girlfriend.' Tara's face became grave.

'I reckon he is trying to shore up support for the Country Party guy. What's his name again?'

'Peter Moriarty. Yeah, maybe? That, and damage control. Telling them you're an interloper with no idea what you're talking about. They don't want the natives getting restless and to start paying attention.'

Cass scraped the foam off her coffee, sucking on the teaspoon. 'I met Moriarty the other day at the polls.' she paused, searching for the words to best describe the interaction. 'He feels... almost like a hollow man to me. He's screwed when his base dies; they were all in their eighties. Old ladies patting his hand. *"Thanks for the fuel vouchers, Pete!"* Cass mocked, 'That's how cheaply their votes were bought, the price of a carton of beer.'

'What were you doing at the polls?' asked Tara, mildly surprised.

'Reconnaissance... and handing out how-to-vote cards for the Enviro Party.'

'Oh, gawd!' said Tara.

* * *

"No Group Rules does not mean a free-for-all. We'll adhere to the accepted conventions of society." Was enough for most members of Muck Unrivalled to engage civilly. The greenies, despised in the loggers' dominion, had found themselves a virtual sanctuary. Key players included the leaders of peak environmental groups, members of the various Forest Defender organisations, and an apiarist who wrote like he'd swallowed Google Scholar.

The local publican joined the group and soon learned that the Irrigation Scheme was a boiling hot topic. He was also a lifelong unionist and a paid-up Worker Party member. He organised a political debate in his beer garden a week before election day. All the candidates took part. It was a popular, robust evening with a motley crew vying for the State seat and an even more colourful audience.

The Legalise Marijuana Party candidate drew the short straw to present first. He hit upon the farcical tone of the Australian political landscape by stating, 'I'm not against a bit of pork barrelling, and as I am dying of cancer, my mandate is simple. Whatever anyone else on this panel offers you, I will add ten percent!' With that, he sat back down and remained silent for the rest of the evening.

As expected, Moriarty spoke well, but it was a tough crowd. Recently recruited for the Workers Party, Alice Kennedy lived about 300 kilometres southeast of Muckemup, in the same well-heeled coastal town as Moriarty. A world away from this crowd of mullet haircuts and chequered flannel shirts. The new candidate could see that any hint of privatising water gravely concerned the residents of Muckemup. The Enviro Party candidate didn't live locally either, and he appeared about as comfortable as an Aboriginal in an arena full of crow-bar toting coppers from north Queensland. Cass scanned the space out the back of the Cattleman Hotel. She reviewed the lineup and concluded handing out how-to-vote cards had been a waste of time.

The Friends of the River boys had made a special trip from the city and were sitting with Matt Farnham's crew. Sandra Star Tree was near the front so she could hear better, and like royalty, Mayor Aconaday and his wife sat in the front row.

After the candidates had introduced themselves and given speeches along their respective party lines, there was a brief interval to allow the locals to refresh their drinks before taking questions from the floor. Alice Kennedy raced out to her car for privacy to call her mentor. She relayed to the Minister of Agriculture how upset the fine folk of Muckemup were about the proposed Irrigation Scheme.

'Honestly, Julia, this water business could sink Moriarty. These people are not happy!'

Julia MacDonald had been in politics for twenty years. She had been a fresh-faced newbie when Aconaday was a minister. During his tenure, they had ridiculed each other so much that no love was lost between them. As far as Julia was concerned, Moriarty was cut from the same cloth as her former adversary.

She was at home enjoying a few glasses of port. 'Okay, tell them we will commission a CSIRO review into how much water is available in the river. I'll follow up with a press conference tomorrow morning. We can't offer any higher authority than that!' The Ag Minister was also up for re-election in the Upper House. The party had dumped a colleague in pre-selection to accommodate her changing regional seats. A lot was at stake.

Alice Kennedy may have been new to public affairs, but she was no dummy. Questions about each candidate's position on the Irrigation Scheme came thick and fast. The Hunters' Party hopeful was a local chap. For anyone politically astute, it was clear he was all froth and no beer. His role was to split the vote. When asked, he agreed with the Scheme, albeit with a caveat to investigate the Water Department. As a farmer, he was privy to the local bush telegraph. He knew which buttons to press about the double standards and inadequacies farmers faced with the Water Department's regional management.

The raucous event ended without degenerating into fist-a-cuffs and therefore qualified as a success. Cass wore a woollen cap against the cool night air. She entered the pub unnoticed and left just as discreetly. She quickly voice-recorded her impressions of the evening into her phone while walking home under a clear sky. Stars light-years away hinted at endless possibilities. Tomorrow morning, she would tidy her notes into something publishable. Tonight she'd just reflect on the group dynamics she'd observed.

CHAPTER 24

The digital age was infiltrating the Deep South. Muckemup's residents were waking up to the notion that social media could be used for more than just a Pinboard for lost dogs. Cass stepped her group through what happened with water trading over east. She also pushed the concept that it was okay to vote on a single issue, in this case, water. Each candidate's official position on the Irrigation Scheme was published, clearly identifying those for and against.

Cass looked down at her phone. It was flashing "Craig Dilbanup."

'Hmm... What could you want?' She hadn't spoken of Tara's revelation to anyone, not that she knew anyone to share it with. But she'd been too busy for more than cursory glances at what the farmers and these boys were doing online. She accepted the call.

'Hey Cass, I thought chatting would be easier than writing you a message.' Craig's voice was slick. He was priming her; she could hear it and thought it was interesting how one notices the small things when you don't need to fill in the blanks.

'What's up?' she played cool, remembering he'd dismissed her as a halfwit not long ago.

'I just wanted to correct you. You've listed the Hunters' candidate as supporting the Irrigation Scheme. He's actually against it.'

Cass took a deep breath. Her voice mirrored Craig's calm. 'I was at the pub. I heard what he said. With a caveat, he was for it.'

'You were there?' Craig hesitated for a second. 'Oh, I didn't see you. You should have come and said hullo. Anyway, yeah, the caveat means he is really *against* the Scheme. We caught up with him last weekend, took him out on the river, and he assured us he is against it.'

Cass rolled her eyes and peered into her empty coffee mug. 'With respect, sharing beers around the campfire with interest groups is known as lobbying. He gave his mandate to a hundred people in the pub. I'll change my post when he publishes that he is against the Scheme on his official page.'

There was a long pause.

She added. 'I don't understand why you're championing him, anyway. Aren't you supposed to be apolitical? His preferences will go to the Country Party, and Moriarty is definitely *for* the Scheme. Do you guys understand how politics works?'

Her last sentence raised Craig's hackles. With the speakerphone on, he looked at Benno. His expression said, *Who the fuck does this lady think she is?*

His partner responded with his hand jerking across his throat. *Abort mission!*

'Yes!' Craig snapped. 'Of course, I know how politics works! What you've posted is incorrect and misleading!' He abruptly hung up.

'Ooft. Good try, mate. But I can see the Emperor is naked.' She shrugged and returned to working on a large canvas inspired by her visit to the Star Tree.

Right on cue, as if tuned in to pick up all astral thoughts of that splendid giant, a message came from Sandra. "Call me!"

'Guess what we got on the trail cam?' The Forest Defender's excitement was palpable.

'I didn't even know you had a trail cam,' said Cass.

'A local volunteer borrowed a couple from the Forest Department. Only she and I know about it.'

'Is that allowed?'

'Probably not. But begging for forgiveness is easier than asking for permission, don't you think?'

'Oh, for sure, straight out of the book of mining approvals. So, what have you got?'

'A quokka! A beautiful, cheeky, tree-saving quokka is cheesing right into the camera like his cousins on Rottnest! They won't be able to flood Regent Brook now that we have evidence that the valley is home to an endangered species. *Everyone* loves quokkas. They're the poster child for Western Australia!'

'Oh right.' Cass was Googling "Quokka" as she listened to Sandra gush like a burbling book.

"The quokka is a small macropod (such as kangaroos and wallabies) about the size of a cat…Like other marsupials, it is herbivorous and mainly nocturnal. Conservation status: Vulnerable." She scrolled through the first few images online and agreed they were adorable.

'I've sent film stills to the local paper and am putting together a pitch for all the TV news programs. This is perfect with the election around the corner! I'll also send you the pic for Muck Unrivalled later if you wouldn't mind posting about it?' asked Sandra, coming up for breath.

'No probs. Tomorrow morning will catch a bigger audience; let me know if you get on the telly.'

The rest of Cass's day passed uneventfully. A few hours later, Sandra forwarded another message. The regional news had picked up the story and would air it in two days. They'd scheduled a journo and cameraman to meet with the volunteer, making the Irrigation Scheme central to the article. Cass set a reminder and made herself a peanut butter sandwich for dinner.

CHAPTER 25

Timing is everything. Cass agonised for days over the state of play, deliberating when to publish for the most significant impact, meditating on what the dark side could counteract with. Tara was right. With a toilet brush in her rubber-gloved hand, the cleaner agreed that the upside of her menial jobs was that they were so mindless that she had the headspace to visualise the situation like manoeuvres on a chessboard. She could see that the farmers were at least three moves behind what was really happening.

Sandra forwarded the quokka picture as promised, and Cass agreed to keep it on hold until after the news aired on TV. The tree enthusiast confirmed they were interviewing the volunteer and Craig from Friends of the Dilbanup Association. Cass sent Tara a message as she switched on the telly. She wasn't a fan of mainstream media and got all her current affairs via the internet. The overt consumerist offensive with no fast-forward button was now alien to her. Remote control in hand, she caught the teaser for the quokka segment.

'Coming up in half an hour... controversial irrigation scheme...down south,' the newsreader reminded Cass of an air hostess, polished and in control while potential and actual emergencies unfolded around her. Sandra's trail cam footage was in the clip before being interrupted by adverts.

'Great stuff,' Cass said aloud to herself, and she went to make a quick coffee before it began.

* * *

'Woah! Did you see that?' Sandra rang forty minutes later. She was still excited but without the enthusiasm of a few days prior.

'Yes. What *was* that? They didn't show any of the quokka. And your volunteer chickee? She made no sense!'

'I've just got off the phone with her. She's devastated and says that wasn't her interview but part of a conversation with the journo afterwards. It looks like someone has done a last-minute cut and paste to the story.'

'Oh? That's interesting! Who has the power to chop a piece on such short notice?' Asked Cass.

'I don't know. Peter Moriarty, maybe?' Sandra walked Cass through the intricacies of television news production. 'If you have 2.18 minutes allotted for footage, you must fill it to the nanosecond. We should be grateful they didn't dump it altogether.' she felt defeated.

'Oh, you're right. This tells us so much more! If they dropped it, we could argue media bias towards the Scheme, but we would never be sure. There'd always be a doubt you got bumped for something legitimate. This?... This was just white noise! And unless you were paying close attention with knowledge of the backstory, you wouldn't even register what you'd watched.' said Cass. ' I noticed they didn't cut Craig's part. Do you know why?'

'He wasn't talking about the quokka?'

'That too. But Craig's schtick sounds good while saying nothing. Jargon. Just blah-blah-blah words; go back and listen... And your friend? This is a classic example of how greenies are seen as flaky. Sorry, but I doubt this was an accident.'

'What should we do?' asked Sandra, still coming to grips with the fact that her quokka story wouldn't achieve all she had dreamed it could. She'd made plans for that valley.

'Nothing we can do. I'll post it properly tomorrow on Muck Unrivalled,' said Cass.

CHAPTER 26

Tara had invited Cass to her mum's place after voting in the State election on Saturday. She hoped to introduce her to Marion and take another look at the little stream with Worm's pump setup. They met at the entrance to the track circling the property, so they could first walk down to check out Sapphire Brook. Tara knew that time would slip away once the three women settled in with tea, cake and politics. She also wanted to show Cass close-up the splendour of the untouched native forest. Treetop clearance was ample for horse riding, as pioneers recorded in their journals. She was pulling her gumboots out from the backseat of her ute as her guest arrived.

'Heya!' called Cass, waving; she, too, had brought a pair of wellies.

As they strolled through the woods, Tara gave Cass a rundown of the wildlife in this little pocket of Eden.'There are numbats, phascogale and antechinus. Antechinus is interesting; they look like small rats with enormous eyes,' she explained, for Cass's expression told her she'd never heard of them. 'The males only live for a year. The *James Dean* of the forest — they mature fast and die young after the first mating season. They literally fuck themselves to death!'

Cass rubbernecked in shock. 'What a way to go!'

'True story.' Tara raised her eyebrows sardonically. 'Sadly, it makes their existence precarious. It only takes one cataclysmic event to wipe out the boys, be it fire, flood, or a new predator, and they are all done for!'

'Reminds me of when cane toads entered Kakadu National Park a few years back. Killed almost everything... of course, there was the usual government coverup "It's all fine" bullshit. A friend of mine worked out there. David Attenborough even did a show; they were training quolls to avoid eating the toads by feeding them cane toad sausages laced with something like Antabuse. They tagged and released about seven and helicoptered them in. Within 24 hours, six were dead.'

'Should rename it *Kaka-Don't*,' joked Tara. 'Did you know scientists with the then CSIRO told the Queensland Government that introducing cane toads was a bad idea?'

'No, I didn't. But that doesn't surprise me.'

'Unfortunately, sugar growers had more political clout.' Tara sighed.

Cass joined her. 'Farmers certainly have a lot to answer for.'

'There's a book about it. If you ever come across it in your travels, grab it. Very rare...' Tara's voice trailed off as they reached the section of creek where black granite cliffs extended from a narrow bank on the other side of the stream.

'Wow! That's gothic.' Cass stared in wonder at the forbidding ebony rock face just out of reach. 'Have you ever crossed over to it?'

'As kids, my brother and I did once. He tried to climb up and fell, knocking himself unconscious. I had to run home to help. Mum went apeshit and told us to never go there again. She scared the bejeezus out of us, saying it's a sacred Aboriginal site with evil spirits. I don't know whether that's true, but it worked. I can imagine the local Kurdaitcha men coming here.'

Cass nodded in agreement, staring at the impressive black granite in wonder.

Tara backtracked to the left. 'Come on; the road isn't much further.'

Since Tara's first border exploration, Worm had drilled a *"Keep out. This site is under video surveillance."* sign into a tree opposite the fire trail. A wall of rocks formed a small weir on the stream.

'That's new! And the rocks... like a goddamn beaver!' Tara pointed at the warning notice.

'How many people come down here?'

'No-one. Some trail bikers, possibly firefighters, during the season or for back-burning. But it's been years — we are overdue.'

Cass had her phone out and was taking photos of the sign, the Forestry Department's culvert, the sump and the white PVC pipeline threading away from them through the forest. She raised her middle finger to an unseen camera and then linked her arm through Tara's. 'Let's go meet your mum and have that cuppa!'

CHAPTER 27

It took the Electoral Commission two weeks to declare political newcomer Alice Kennedy as the winner. Moriarty was gone, and not even the professional pundits picked it. But the locals had.

Cass received messages relaying that for the first time in their adult lives, locals had voted against the Country Party. The other surprise was that the Legalise Marijuana Party gained two seats, including the satirical and cancer-riddled candidate from the pub. The achievement was nominal, for the election returned the Workers Party with a landslide win. Western Australia was now a State with no effective opposition. But the folks of Muckemup were satisfied. They would get the promised CSIRO inquiry into the modelling used to justify taking 13 gigs from the Dilbanup River.

While everyone waited for the results, Cass focused part of her research on the recently formed group claiming to save the river. During election mode, she'd kept quiet about Craig's phone call, not wanting to throw a lifeline to Moriarty via her commentary. Instead, she threw some money at getting a copy of Craig's criminal record from the United States. She also discovered that the group was not an association; they'd just included the word *"Association"* as part of their name to make it look legitimate. The Securities Commission identified the group as an *"Other Entity."*

'That's a clever way to open a bank account, Cass thought. Thanks to Tara, she was familiar with the leaders' history but not how they became the local environmental voice without residing in Muckemup. As she dug, she uncovered that Benno's wife was a senior public servant and former staffer of Ag Minister MacDonald.

'Just happens to be the same minister who tried to denigrate me with her response in the local paper.'

'Oh, it gets better!' said Tara late one evening when Cass rang with a list of questions. 'Emily's father runs an environmental consultancy that has worked for most of the major mining companies in the State. But it's a small industry.'

'You don't say? Water and mining' mused Cass.

'Oh yeah, Benno hit the jackpot with Emily. She'd been married before and lost the house her dad bought them in the divorce settlement. Her old man wasn't happy; he helped her buy another place and said, "We put this one in our joint names. No more marriages!" Then Benno came along.'

'How do you know all this?'

'I'm friends with his first wife. Tell me how someone who claims to earn under ten thousand dollars, the minimum before child support kicks in, does so little paid work yet is so skilled that he not only gets nominated as Western Australia's Stonemason of the Year. It was submitted by Muckemup's own builder slash councillor four years after the job, mind you. But he wins it!'

'Whaat?'

'Oh, yeah... and with the win comes five grand prize money. Ta-da! Half of his supposed annual income. But the prize money is exempt from assessment.' Tara clicked her fingers. 'He paid the equivalent of a cup of coffee a week towards the welfare of his kids. Riddle me that one?'

'That sounds like a job for the boys, but why now? What's the favour?' Cass could visualise Tara sitting on her back porch, blue eyes snapping with sarcasm through puffs of smoke.

'He's a fifty-cent man!'

'What's the go with the councillor?' Cass was trying to connect the dots.

'Who, Miko? Go back and read some of the council minutes during his time. That should give you a flavour.'

'So, Benno married Emily for her money?'

'Emily had diabetes,' said Tara, 'Knowing Benno, his life won't have changed much from when he was a bachelor. He probably thinks he'll outlive her and get the lot!'

'Good grief. But if she was a staffer in a ministerial office, she's a loyal Worker Party drone through and through. Yet they hooked up with an Enviro Party Senator to create their river group. That's weird.'

CHAPTER 28

A growing list of concerns began nagging Cass. One of them was Sandra; she'd become obsessed with the Star Tree and considered herself its unofficial gatekeeper. People wanted to see the giant and messaged Cass with their grievances, thinking she had influence. Eventually, she'd had enough of trying to appease strangers and broached it with the activist. Sandra could be bombastic at the best of times and already had her nose out of joint because Cass had refused to use Muck Unrivalled to endorse Alice Kennedy for the local seat.

'But, I gave you the quokka story!' argued Sandra, stunned at the newcomer's refusal.

'Oh, I didn't realise that it came with strings.' Cass said dangerously. Sandra heeded the warning and backed off. She sat on Cass's sofa, sulking. Fit for the *crying couch*, Cass thought. Outwardly, she softened. 'All I'm saying is chillout. You have my support, but you don't want to alienate people. It's a State Forest and belongs to everyone, that's all.'

* * *

Cass had a rudimentary understanding of the logging industry and displayed her ignorance the first time she entered the fray online. She remembered Sandra cautioning that she risked losing any ground she'd gained with her knowledge of water.

'Stick to what you know.' was Sandra's sound advice.

'Water, water, water. What do I know... about water? I know this makes no sense at all!' she groaned with frustration and exhaustion. She barely slept, spending her nights combing through parliamentary documents, thinking of the freshwater stream out the back of Marion's place. When she closed her eyes, Cass often dreamt of ebony cliffs, chest-deep in a river gloaming with tannins so dark she couldn't tell where the water finished and the stone began. Water gurgling in a tongue only the seers understand.

The universe communicates in strange ways. Ultimately, Sandra's hyper-vigilance towards the Star Tree provided clues for where to look. It was two in the morning. Cass rubbed her face and crunched her neck from side to side, listening to the bones crack with relief. She was bent over the water register for hours with many questions in her head. Why would Worm install a sign and a video camera where nobody goes? ....and when it's not his land. Is he trying to make it appear lawful?

'You can't own a State Forest... Can you? She asked the empty room, bowing her weary head onto the table. She quietly reset for a moment, counting. 'Three, two, one,' then rose, giving her arms a quick stretch, and typed into the search bar: "State Forest Lease."

'Fucking Bingo!'

CHAPTER 29

A loud knocking woke Cass. Moaning, she struggled to unfold herself from the crying couch. She'd fallen asleep there in the wee hours of the morning.

'Yeah, yeah, hang on!' She called, reaching for the front door.

Tara stood on her porch, resembling the Goddess Kali. Her arms overflowed with cardboard tubes, and her expression was as fierce as a forest fire. 'Well?' she asked impatiently. 'You've gone and kicked a bull ants' nest this time... Are you going to let me in?'

'Oh, sure. Sorry, come in. I feel like Marie Kondo packed me into a drawer. Let me get the coffee on.' Cass stumbled away towards the kitchen, still trying to wake up. Her hair was a bird's nest.

Tara had risen soon after Cass had fallen asleep to discover the mad artist had speared Romeo Aconaday Junior to the wall of her Facebook group for everyone to see. It was all there, legal and backed up with the documentation, including a 15-year State Forest lease for only $600 annually. She couldn't get her daughters packed to her mother's place fast enough.

'Can I dump these here?' Tara dropped the tubes onto the sofa. She started clearing the table as Cass moved around in the kitchen. 'Mum loaned me all her old maps. Before everything went online, you could get them from the Forest Bureau for free. When digital came in, stuff began to vanish, like that little stream you sprayed Junior with this morning.

Sapphire Brook no longer exists on paper. The road used to have a sign just before the bridge. I can't remember when they removed it, but that shows intent.'

'Here, let me.' Cass grabbed a milk crate and swept all the paint tubes into it. 'I need caffeine! Let's sit outside so you can smoke; you look like you need one.'

'Good idea!' Tara pulled out her pouch of tobacco as she followed.

Cass sat and tried to push a hand through her wild hair before giving up to sip her coffee while watching her new friend expertly run her tongue along the thin paper's edge between her fingers. Tara then pressed it down to close the seam before lighting up. She leaned back and blew out a smoke ring. Melting away in contemplation as the vapours rippled outwards, followed by another puff of blue smoke piercing through the centre.

'I never could do that.' Cass watched the smoke disperse. 'Tried when I was young. We used to sneak ciggies behind the school lunch shed.'

'The trick is to click your jaw,' said Tara. 'Please fill me in on Worm's lease,'

'Why do you call him that?' asked Cass.

'Aconaday Senior, our *illustrious* mayor, is nicknamed Snake, as in anaconda, because supposedly he used to have a lisp. Worm is a diminutive.'

'Oh, right? I would have thought, "A-Con-A-Day", but Snake works too.'

'Yeah. It does.' Tara leaned forward and took a swig of coffee. 'Well?'

'Well, what?' Cass's face was blank. 'Oh, the lease!' She shook herself as she remembered what they were talking about. 'It pieces together just as I posted it. Worm applied to the council to increase his dam size back whenever. The size struck me; it's precisely listed on the water register at 608,142 mega-litres. Usually, they round licences off to 600 or 400, or 250.'

'Aconaday would've had an engineer in and measured it to the last cupful.'

Cass grunted. 'Right... council approved his application in April last year. In the meantime, legislation is going through Parliament for the Water Department to charge for licences. The costs go from a big fat zero...' she looped her forefinger to her thumb, 'To a tiered system. But it doesn't get gazetted as law until October; Worm receives his water licence six weeks beforehand.'

'That's some coincidence..' Tara's head swung like a metronome as she processed the information.

'Fits nicely, huh? And if you examine the date on that lease I posted this morning, it started on the 1st of July, the start of the new financial year. Real tidy.' she pursed her lips. 'They knew exactly what they were doing, and he is not the only Irrigation Scheme director with such a lease.'

'Ooh? Do tell.'

'Gio Luciano has one, too, on Crown land.'

'Hmpff, Gio! He's one of the football set; he and Worm are the same age, same social group.' Tara rolled her hand with a red-carpet flourish. '*Same* male privilege!'

'Ah, *of course* they are... I looked at the Tasmanian Scheme that's supposedly the blueprint for ours. Once a market is established, Worm could pull $1.8 million annually at today's prices just by switching on the pump. He got the water for free and has a $600 per year lease to suck from that little stream at his back door, and according to their maps, the Scheme's pipeline conveniently comes directly to his front door.'

Tara pulled out her phone and opened the calculator. 'Um, that's 27 million dollars over the fifteen years.'

'At today's prices... and every farmer knows scarcity sets the price. Who knows exactly what the future holds, but it's definitely looking dryer — even the knuckleheads in the Ag Department can see that.'

'For sure. Look at the bottom falling out of Avos because of all those greedy bastards wanting in on the act!' said Tara.

'Yeah, that's what the Scheme's planning to leverage off. Hear me out..' Cass calmly laid her suspicions bare. The objective is to build a dam on Regent Brook to hold water from the Dilbanup River. The farmers invest in the Scheme, thinking it's a traditional Cooperative. The State and Fed's fork out the money; therefore, with all the hype, farmers plant wall-to-wall avos believing they'll have access to more water without issues and will be retiring as millionaires. Fast forward three years, the trees are nearing maturity, and there's insufficient water. What happens?'

'Everyone wrings their hands in despair', said Tara.

'Exactly! A few farmers could even top themselves... and we are now almost due for the next election cycle. Remember, everyone thought Moriarty's seat was safe and didn't expect a handful of farmers to actually check how much water was in the river.'

'Gawd! So it was to become an election issue, and there's the political impetus to extend the Scheme to take water elsewhere.'

'Uh-huh.' Cass nodded. 'From *everywhere*... No matter which side of the political fence you sit on, you gotta do it! The pipeline's already in pace; we are $80 million plus in the hole, and farmers are against the wall screaming like banshees. Viola! Fait accompli' she flipped her hands out like Marcel Marceau and then fell silent. Both women sat quietly in their own worlds, each evaluating the rickety bridge swinging precariously above the public policy quicksand they could see surrounding the small community of Muckemup.

Cass abruptly stood up. 'Come, show me these maps!'

As Tara followed her inside, she grabbed the artist's arm, the local woman's face moving close to search Cass's features. Again she saw the sunlight on the water in the grey eyes, a pale glass-green-gold flickering atop depths that revealed nothing. 'You don't know Snake like I do. He's held this town under his boot for forty years. You either need to shut up about this and never speak of it again, or you must see it through to the end. No matter what. Anything less, and he *will* destroy you!' Tara intoned the words so that there was no misunderstanding.

Cass looked at the concerned face before her, then she lifted Tara's hand from her arm and held it. 'I'm going nowhere, and I will *never* shut up.' She promised.

They both took a deep breath.

Tara exhaled. 'Good. I've been waiting a long time for you.'

'Yeah, sorry about that; it took me a while to find the place.' Cass squeezed her hand and grinned.

PART TWO—AIR

The woods are lovely, dark and deep,
But I have promises to keep,
And miles to go before I sleep,
And miles to go before I sleep.
~Robert Frost

CHAPTER 30

Romeo listened to the arrogant music of the wind rustling in the karri branches above as he shimmied down the path to the back of his property and Sapphire Creek humming 'Let's go to Rio.'

He called the stream his rio of liquid gold. Snake had worked hard to set up the wealth stream for the next generation of his family and would not stand by watching it wash away. He glanced across the fire track towards Marion's unused acreage. What a waste! One day soon, he would add her block to his portfolio. His eyes followed the ancient trees upwards. Djeran was chasing the heels of Summer. It was the season for dry winds, flying ants and, this year, voting. This time, it was local elections and the mayor's four-year term was over. He needed to get back in. Templar had been right; the Leason woman was a problem. He fretted as loose clouds puffed their cheeks and shawl'd themselves over the sky. The sun-speckled shadows all at once became ominous.

'Burrasca furiusa presta passa. A furious storm passes quickly.'

'I hope so, Mama.' Snake could smell the ozone as he walked. Karri forests were hazardous places during thunderstorms, and his flesh shivered with doubts. He turned back towards his house.

* * *

Serena Benchley was also vying for re-election. Aconoday had suggested they share a ticket, but Serena declined. The Women in Government Lobby advised her that incumbents did better standing on their own record. With social media firing mayor-seeking missiles over Snake's bow, she thought it politically prudent to distance herself from him. The meeting at Walker Beach was exposing itself as a sham. She'd received the council's legal advice from Templar; apparently, she could have voted on the motion for the Irrigation Scheme. Displeased, she replayed in her mind's eye the mayor and the CEO, initially informing her it was a financial conflict of interest because of her job. She was no one's puppet and decided to visit Matthew Farnham.

* * *

Cass read through all the council minutes back until 2011. 'Seriously, Tara. Thank God for Liz Calder asking questions for all those years! If it weren't for her, there'd be nothing to follow.'

'I wonder if she knows what's happening?'

'I'd say she's more away than most, but I don't think she *knows*, knows. Heck, half the councillors don't have a clue, and they're voting on it,' said Cass.

'I heard the Calders bought shares in the Scheme.'

'Who wouldn't? Unless, like Matt Farnham, you have a spring on your property. They sold it to everyone as an insurance policy of sorts. Except, it really is like one, and you need to read the fine print. Because when you need it, the company will say sorry, but you've built it in a fire risk zone or on a floodplain.'

'Or an act of God!' said Tara.

'Ha, yes! An act of God! That's what *we* need. I'm going to the thrift later this week to pick Liz's brain,' said Cass.

CHAPTER 31

Molly finished the morning mail as Tara sat on a stool at the sorting table, drinking tea. She said, 'I found a crack pipe on the windowsill in the toilet yesterday.'

Shocked, Molly looked up at her colleague. 'It wasn't me!'

'No, it wasn't you, yer duffer. We both know who it was... who it is! Our high-functioning addict is fast becoming more of the *high* and less of the *functioning*. Customers are noticing.'

'Oh,' said Molly.

'Yep. Noticed the mood swings.' It was barely a question. '... Kay Gill out by Gnomesville was chasing down a parcel.' Tara referred to a shaded grove twenty kilometres out of town, home to thousands of garden gnome statues — a farmer's folly in the forest. The tracking number has it as delivered weeks ago, but it never arrived. I left Andy a note. He denied it was in the van for over a week. I turned the place upside down, and it's not like we're disorganised. I mean, look around! You have the sorting down to military precision.'

'You reckon he left it in the van?'

Tara frowned. 'Or took it home. But yesterday, I found it sitting there.' she pointed to the wire shelving behind Molly. 'What wigged me out was how he watched me find it from the edge of his eyes. Like a crocodile calculating who is the weakest in the dinghy if you don't have a dead chook to mollify it with.'

'He blamed you?'

'Oh, he'd already done that. This was outright gaslighting.' Tara paused. '*Raggedy-Andy* forgets I went to school with him. He was sly then. Add a drug habit into the mix, and he is now dangerous.' Tara grabbed her empty mug and stood up. 'Nine o'clock! Better get this party started... before I turn into a pumpkin!' She whispered the last line under her breath as she walked through the shopfront to unlock the door.

The day was busy. Before any local election, the Electoral Commission provided a mail-out summary of the enrolled candidates with a 150-word sales pitch to everyone on the electoral roll in their prospective councils.

Tara opened the letter addressed to her. 'Would you look at that? Snake had written his blurb in a **bold typeface**, so it stood out against the other candidates. 'Every trick in the book!' she muttered, screwing the paper into a ball and slam-dunking it into the bin.

CHAPTER 32

When he first met Cassandra Leason, Miro had just finished the morning school run and was on an enduring personal quest into the forest. She was sitting shut-eye in the lotus position upon a giant moss-covered stump sheared long ago three feet above the ground. Her feet were bare and dirty. Her hands extended over her knees, were long and strong, with dried paint clogged underneath her fingernails. A pair of old trainers splattered with colour and socks shoved into them and waited for her at the base of the trunk.

He watched for a moment before loudly snapping a twig. Cass opened one jaundiced eye to peer down at the Aboriginal man standing on the trail a short distance from her. He was dark as bush honey, average height, fit looking in a wiry sort of way, with thick black stringy hair and high cheekbones sharp enough to cut butter. The brim of an ancient leather Akubra shadowed his eyes.

'Don't be doing women's business here. This is mens country,' said Miro, his voice mild but firm.

Cass raised an eyebrow. 'And how much magic do you think a middle-aged white woman can conjure?'

Her response threw him. She shifted a fraction to view him better. A hint of a smile played at the corner of her mouth as a single bleary eye watched him search around for a reply.

'That's not respectful. You need—' His mouth was open, shaping the next syllable, when a swish of reddish-brown flashed in the undergrowth, grabbing both their attention.

'A long way from home,' said Cass.

Miro pressed his mouth shut; he gave her a deeply sceptical look. But Cass was correct.

The native cuckoo was found north from the Pilbara to the east coast. Not down here. Miro knew the spirit of this bird was an excellent problem-solver and could invent a way out of any trouble. He wondered if it had had to make a quick escape. Standing still, he considered Cass with a fresh lens; he'd need more time to appraise this stranger. Birds are messengers. He didn't know the Noongar word for the pheasant but remembered his granny's Ngadjon name, *"Bunbunbu"*.

Symbolising clairvoyance, the cuckoos' keen sense of perceiving their surroundings kept them safe from any lurking threat. Miro knew if the bird was showing itself, then what he was looking for wasn't around. He observed Cass ungainly climb down from her stump like a fifty-year-old white woman watching a bird. Miro mocked her for a minute before stopping himself, confused. The woman's lack of poise conflicted with the greater awareness she revealed moments earlier. It baffled him, for he never dismissed the magnitude of first appearances.

As she came to stand on the ground, she panted. 'Too much toxic men's business may be where Muckemup's problems lie... Hi, I'm Cass.'

He looked at her naked feet and then into her pink face, framed by a cloud of white hair. The Trickster Spirit came to mind. He tipped his stockman's hat. 'I'm Miro. Are you local?'

    'Like the cuckoo. I am now!'

CHAPTER 33

Matthew Farnham stood on the verandah of his farmhouse, an arm angled across his face to shield himself from the late afternoon sun. Serena Benchley was coming down the track. Thick blooms of gravel dust lifted and followed her four-wheel drive a short way before giving up and floating back down to settle on the road.

'Let's sit outside. It's cooler,' said Matthew. It was an Indian Summer, and everything showed fatigue. Curled gum leaves dizzied in waves falling to Earth. To the unaware, what looked like a spectacular autumn leaf fall was, in fact, the trees suffering from heat stress. He retrieved a jug of chilled water from the old fridge on the deck's end. Two glasses sat in the middle of the table with a thick stack of A4 papers, bulldog clipped and marked with fluorescent sticky notes, waving from the top of the pages like Himalayan prayer flags.

'That's a copy of the State water legislation,' said Matthew as he turned the glasses upright, pouring them both a drink. Serena put one hand on the paperwork while accepting the outstretched glass. She took a seat in the shade.

'We've been monitoring stream-flow at key locations the last couple of winters 'cause the Water Department is doing less than nuthin," said Matthew.

'Oh, okay. What numbers are you getting?'

'About half a gig... total flow. They're gonna git nowhere near the eleven or twelve that Snake's boys are spruiking. Regent Brook doesn't even have enough to meet the environmental flow. We've all had our winter takes cancelled. It's not "new" water, but *our* water... that they intend to sell back to us!'

'They're some scary figures, Matthew.'

'They sure are.' He sipped his water. 'Some daft buggers have been jumpin' the gun' n ordering avo trees early... gonna go broke.' He shook his head, 'The Water Department's a law unto itself. Operatin' outside of the legislation... needs an investigation.' His face flushed with anger and heat. 'It's "about interpretation", my arse! Sorry, my foot.'

Serena smiled, ignoring the rough language. 'I've also been doing some research,' she offered. 'I see they didn't like the *High Uncertainty* feedback on the modelling by the first consultants they engaged.'

'Tell me more,' said Matthew. He had wondered about Serena when she initially contacted him. Politics was a dirty game, and he would take every opportunity he could.

'So, the Department hired another firm to review the original report in what appears to be an attempt to override the initial consultants' professional advice.' Serena clarified, mirroring Matt's head shake, hers also contemptuous.

'I see you've done your homework.'

'Yes. That new woman's Facebook posts fascinated me, and then Templar produced the revised legal advice about the Walker-Beach fiasco. He'd only do that if he'd done something wrong.'

'True. With James, if you can smell smoke, better pull out yer leave plan and start the car. That Facebook page is a cracker!'

'She's certainly upset the applecart. Templar was ropeable. Talked about the council paying for legal fees. Going after her for defamation.'

'Bit hard when she's attached Parliamentary documents.'

'It's certainly ridiculous wanting to bill it to the ratepayer!' Serena pursed her lips and then broached the real purpose of her visit. 'There is one more council meeting before we go into caretaker mode. What are your thoughts on me tabling a motion that withdraws council support for the Irrigation Scheme?'

Matthew Farnham stared blankly at the young woman, calm as ice water, waiting expectantly. Then, as he realised what she was saying, he hollered to his feet. 'Councillor Benchley, I could kiss yer!' He slammed on the brakes. 'But I won't mind, yer is married to the Doc'n I don't want him making any accusations at my next prostate exam!' Trying to contain himself, he shuffled his feet and waved his hands before dropping them awkwardly. This left him nodding enthusiastically like a dashboard Elvis. He had Aconaday on the ropes.

CHAPTER 34

Tara and Cass had already begun their campaign to unseat Aconaday. Tara more covertly than the artist who worked alone and didn't seem perturbed by public opinion.

'The secret is to care about people without caring about what they think.' said Cass.

'Easy for you here, working alone. I've got two-thirds of the town passing through my office. And while blood is thicker than water, there's nothing like the hint of money to bond people like shit to a blanket.' Tara needed to be cautious. Living alone with two daughters, the last thing she wanted was to invoke a Muckemup-style warning that involved shadowy figures wandering around the yard at night and waking to find her dog baited.

'Okay, grasshopper, there are only three rules. Number one, don't make it personal. Attack the issue, not the person.'

'Okay.' said Tara.

'Number two. If you accidentally post misinformation, don't stress too much. Guaranteed, someone will pull you up, even when your info is correct.' Cass rolled her eyes. 'But if you get it wrong, politely acknowledge the person who pinged you and edit it as an add-on note. Try not to change the original post... It looks suspicious, and credibility is all we've got.'

'Okay. I'm nervous.' Tara felt a sense of apprehension rising.

'Don't be,' said Cass.

'What's the third rule?'

'Number three is, it's social media. Within 24 hours, it's old news, and everyone has moved on. That works *for* us if we make a mistake. But it also makes it challenging to grab the target's attention long enough to transmute into any tangible action.'

'Hmm...' Tara digested the information. What action did they want? Aconaday booted out for sure. Although, after forty years, his influence would still linger, even if he dropped dead tomorrow.

'I got some good news,' said Cass.

'Oh, yeah? Do share.' Tara wiped the vision of *"End of an Era"* headlines breaking newspaper sales records.

'A local contacted me. He and his wife live down here and work remotely. A young couple, they work in IT. Anyway, they've put together a bunch of questions about the water for each candidate to answer.

'Yeah, so?'

'They've also created a flash-looking website and will publish the candidates' answers verbatim.'

'What? Woah, that's huge! That's the 21st century officially having arrived in Muckemup. What are they calling it?' asked Tara.

'I thought you'd like that! *"A Clear Vote"*, clever, huh? We got this; people are stepping up. He's a goner.'

Cass should have known better. The next day, she returned from her cleaning job to find a waitlist of local loggers wanting approval to join Muck Unrivalled. The

Premier had released a media release, "As of 2024, we shall cease Native Forest Logging."

She messaged Tara at work and made herself a coffee. It was going to be a busy day. After re-watching the press conference twice and gathering her thoughts, Cass muttered, 'When the elite conspire against you, and circumstances seem to join them. High time to visit Mrs Calder.'

* * *

'I've been waiting for you!' Liz's powdered face lit up with recognition as Cass entered the shop. 'I found you something.'

'Is it that book on How to Make Friends?'

'Ha! No. At your age, you don't need any more friends.' Liz rummaged beneath the till, only the top of her crown and squirming plump backside visible. Today she was wearing a gold Lurex scarf wrapped around her head.

'You remind me of a caramel sweetie wrapper,' said Cass.

Liz hadn't heard her. 'Here it is!' she came to the front of the counter to thrust the small folded parcel of white t-shirt fabric at Cass.

The artist unfolded it slowly. It was a white t-shirt embellished with black font *"TROUBLEMAKER"* Cass grinned.

'It's for you to wear to the council meeting tonight,'

'How did you know?... It's perfect. Thank you!'

'Oh, you're not the only one who knows things, dear.'

'Ha-ha! Touché. I have been reviewing the council minutes and am indebted to you, Madame Calder.' Cass bowed dramatically.

'How so?' asked Liz.

'Well, you either *do* know stuff, or you've been inadvertently relaying cosmic injustices like an army comms operator transmits morse code.'

A gush of tears rose behind blinking lashes. Eyes suddenly bright. 'Don't make my mascara run!' Liz Calder knew that for decades, she'd almost single-handedly held together the tattered threads of democracy in this tumultuous place. Suddenly, she felt tired. Oh, so tired, and there was little left of the fragile garment that so many men worldwide had died just for the idea of it.

* * *

Tara debriefed at Cass's place after the council meeting. Part of their strategy was to not be seen together in public too often.

Cass chuckled as she poured two glasses of wine. 'It feels like we're clandestine lovers.'

'Give it time. If we're linked, that'll become the story!'

'I'm sure it's already half of one. Today I discovered I have a fan club. A few online copycat groups, including *"Muck Diesel Dykes Unrivalled."*

Tara spat her wine. 'Oh, heavens! Seriously?' she laughed. ' Ugh, I've seen the villagers carrying pitchforks before. They once ran a manager out of town for being openly gay.'

'Meh, I'm not worried; they've got four members.' Cass scoffed. 'They're like dim little moons revolving around me. Male or female?'

'The manager? He was male?'

'Don't threaten that fragile masculinity, huh? I'm pretty sure they'd see lesbians as a challenge. I can hear it now, *"You just need some good dick!"* Cass aped.

Tara grew sober. 'Fragile is one thing; we've also got sadistic. A toxic element down here would happily rape you with a star dropper just to teach you that men are the boss, even if they're dumb as a box of hats,'

Cass shuddered. 'That Neanderthal logic would turn you off, men forever!'

'It's happened.... And while most men wouldn't dream of committing such a heinous crime, there is a silent acceptance amongst the brotherhood.'

'Ugh. Silence is violence. It's shock collar training. Women become socialised to stay within the boundaries because we expect to be punished if we don't toe the line.'

They both sipped on their pinot grigio, quietly sending two brief prayers to keep women safe.

Cass switched the subject. 'Talking about logging. The public gallery was pretty full tonight. How many towns will the Premier's native forest logging ban impact?'

'Us and maybe one other — Bellenup. The logging heyday is long gone. The taxpayer has propped up the industry since the mid-90s. Did you know Snake was the Forestry Minister back in the day?'

'Yeah, I read his bio. That in itself is interesting. I now have to do a crash course in forest policy...Gahh! I had a few years head start on the water.' wailed Cass.

Tara lifted her glass. 'There's two of us now, remember? Salute.'

They tapped their glasses.

'Here's to smashing the Patriarchy.'

CHAPTER 35

Tara sat at her kitchen table. She'd woken early to study the current Regional Forestry Agreement before going to work, laptop open and a cup of tea to strengthen her fortitude. As the soft grey morning light approached, two magpies appeared on the open windowsill. The birds strutted like only magpies can, yodelling for the brekkie.

'Morning, guys!' Tara took some mealworms from the fridge. 'What are your flight plans for today?' She handed each one a grub. Generations of the Coolbardie family had visited Tara's weatherbeaten cottage on the forest's edge. Years ago, the birds had taught Loki the difference between a magpie's distress call for an eagle and a fox. The dog knew when to look up or down from their cues. Their warning cries sounded the same to Tara and her girls, but the canine knew the difference. He was now lying under the table, hoping for a walk.

'Hang on a sec—' Tara turned up the volume, Aconaday was on the radio.

'The announcement has blindsided us, Pippa! Without logging, Muckemup is a dying town. I am the only one with the experience to save us....' The spiel was a broken record trotted out for the elections, along with his best blue blazer, and visits to the local aged-care facility to drum up votes.

'He's pouring on the fear marinade.' Tara explained to the birds. They agreed with her, for magpies are familiar with opportunism.

Snake continued, 'Our CEO has received a death threat and is now on stress leave. Having such a reprehensible element amongst us is very worrying... a new danger in our wonderful community.'

Tara grabbed her phone. 'Did you hear that?'

'Aconaday? Yep, I heard it.' Cass was looking for her sketchbook. She was dressed for exploring the forest, old trackies, vintage Nick Cave t-shirt and hiking boots. 'Do you think it's real?'

'Did you see a cop or extra security at the council meeting?'

'Nope. Nothing.'

'Exactly.' Tara's voice was deadpan.

CHAPTER 36

What remained of the State's Opposition party rallied together and arranged a demonstration at the Town Park. Liz, Tara and Cass watched from a log bench. Liz was wearing a dark juniper-green pantsuit with a deep purple faux-fur stole, Cass in jeans and an indigo shirt, her hair tucked under a black Nike cap, and Tara in her uniform, black slacks and shirt with the company logo. Three of them sat together, like crows on a fence, observing the activity in a brightly-coloured field. They erected a stage and delivered two busloads of mill workers from Bellenup. The local journalist and a television team moved amongst the crowd.

'Have you ladies looked at the forestry details announced by our State Daddy?' asked Liz.

'Researching MacGovern's latest stuff now,' Tara squeezed the fashionista's hand.

'Gosh, listen to Snake! I'm pretty sure I read this speech on his parliamentary media releases from 93,' marvelled Cass.

'And try again in 98, 03, 08 and 2012. He probably went out to the garage last night and dusted off the Commodore 64 to pull it from!' Tara sarcastically sucked the air through her teeth as she watched the mayor twirl his hands above his head. The deputy mayor followed Snake with a speech. Then Logan Rovello, the former mayor, hunched like a boxer waiting for the bell to ring. He was hoping for a political comeback.

'Serena's making too many of the mummy statements,' said Tara.

'That's because she is a mummy, dear.'

'Yes, but not to these men, Liz! If she keeps it up, she'll lose votes.' Tara countered.

'Hmm... it doesn't seem to have the same foaming-at-the-mouth savagery that I remember,' said Liz, scanning the crowd.

Cass agreed, 'I'm surprised too. The only one close to preaching fire and brimstone like an evangelist is Rovello.'

'Maybe Snake has something else lined up? Like an ambassadorship?' suggested Liz.

'Hmpf. He wishes! Anyway, I'm done. Fill me in later if it gets interesting.' Tara stood and waved goodbye as she headed back to work.

Cass surveyed the men standing near them. Most wore bewildered expressions as the politicians droned about transitioning to pine plantations and government payouts. 'Look at them, Liz. They've been doing this for over 20 years and are not angry. They look confused. Why is that? I need to get hold of a logger and ask some questions.'

'Liz nodded as a deep, melodious voice behind them said, Maybe I can help you?'

The women both turned around.

'Chippy! It's you!' Liz beamed and patted the space next to her, vacated by Tara. 'Come sit! I'd like you to meet Cass Leason of Facebook infamy and Muckemup's newest resident!'

'Oh, ho. Yes, please! Nice to meet you. I'm Chip Smith. You don't appear too unstable.' He extended his hand and looked closely at Cass as she took it in hers.

His palm felt cool, dry and solid, and his face spoke of a man with integrity. 'Hardly Liz!' Cass grinned at Chip, 'Of course I'm crazy. But that doesn't mean I'm wrong!' You're running for the East Ward, aren't you?'

'Ha! I am. Some of these guys and I worked at the mill, where I was a logger and Shop Steward. Now I'm a retired numbat enthusiast.'

'I've seen some of your photos online. Nice work.'

Chip's chest puffed out a fraction. He was proud of his ability to get close to the little numbat colony next door to his bush block and enjoyed sharing them with the world. 'Oh, really? Thank you.'

Cass smiled. 'Don't underestimate the reach of social media, Chip.' What's the go with the pine trees?'

'We're all scratching our heads because it takes at least 11 to 15 years of growth until the pine is harvest-ready. Also, it's a softwood, and we fit our mills for processing hardwoods like jarrah. So, something is going on.'

'Okay, let me get this straight. The Premier says, "We're stopping native forest logging, except mining's exempt and ecological thinning." whatever that means! Then the Forest Bureau plans to purchase 500,000 hectares of farmland from here to Newport for pine trees that won't be useful for 15 years? And we would need to refit our mills to process them anyway?... riiight!' she drawled.

'I think you've just given yourself the answer for where to look,' Chip Smith gave a conspiratorial smile, raising his eyebrows a fraction.

Liz sagely tapped her nose. 'Always follow the money.'

CHAPTER 37

'Off the record, the CEO's death threat looks like bullshit.' The local journo met Cass in a neighbouring town for a drink.

'Tell me something we don't know!' She passed a cold pint to the young scribe. 'You and I were both at that council meeting. Thirty people in the gallery, staff and councillors. Unless you were mentally deficient, you'd report a death threat to the police on a duty-of-care basis... even if you didn't think it was a genuine threat. And why is he on stress leave if he didn't believe it to be true? Of course, it's all bullshit!'

'Agreed. I'd say Snake wants him to lie low for a bit.'

'Hmm, political leverage, maybe? Romeo insinuating he's wrangling with the great unwashed down here,' said Cass.

'Did you see the Business Chamber almost folded?'

'Yeah, I read about the doctor closing it down. Interesting timing, just before the announcement to end native forest logging.' Cass sized up the university graduate. He was smart; it was a shame mentors no longer existed in the newspaper industry.

'What are you thinking?' The journo took a mouthful of beer, wiping the foam from his moustache. His facial hair grew in uneven patches, characterising the transition from adolescence to adulthood. He wore a Hawaiian shirt and had a young Hunter S. Thompson vibe.

'I think it's odd. There's about to be $80 million floated to transition business, and you suddenly lose your peak business representation?' Cass pulled a face full, her mouth twisting in disbelief.

'They rescued it. Larry Wolfe put his hand up for President.' said the journo.

'I bet he did! That sounds like an appointment by the mayor. What are the chances we've got some internal factionalism going on?'

'They're all for show. Behind the scenes. Aconaday and Rovello despise each other.'

'Yeah? What, Templar's Rovello's boy?' Cass gave a dry laugh. 'That's politics, baby.'

'Dwight from *The Office*?'

Cass nodded with admiration. 'I'm impressed! I think it's a hybrid. Dwight meets Humphrey Bogart.' she chuckled at the questioning face before her as she skolled her last mouthful of wine. 'Before your time!'

'Bogart's gotta be before yours, too!'

A few days later, the logging rally made it to the front page of the local newspaper. But it received a similar bemused reception as the event itself had. Page five gazumped the sham protest, for somebody had anonymously written a full-page open letter urging locals to wake up about the Irrigation Scheme.

'Booya! Check this out!' Tara laid the page flat on the table at the back of Bazza's bakery. The three women huddled together bent over to see. They'd made a date for coffee with Tara on her break, Cass had just finished cleaning after a wedding party, and Liz had come to town especially.

'Woah! That must have been expensive.' whistled Cass, tilting her head to read the headline. 'Good on' em!' She smiled as Tara ran her finger down the page, picking juicy tidbits to read aloud:

"TIME FOR REAL CHANGE IN MUCKEMUP."

"Will our children and grandchildren thank us for destroying this pristine part of the world?.... The Irrigation Scheme appears to be another example of raping our natural assets to benefit the vested interests of a select few... This coming election, arguably the most important in decades, gives you a significant opportunity to have your say in choosing the right leaders with a real vision for this beautiful part of Australia. It's over to you.... A Concerned Ratepayer."

'Well, that's something!' Liz's emerald satin-clad head bounced in approval.

'Someone will be pissed!' said Tara.

'Adam's website for *A Clear Vote* should be up in a week. I think they're just waiting for a few candidate replies,' said Cass.

'Will the CSIRO review be ready?'

'I doubt it. The elite will hold off until after the local election before releasing that. Which reminds me, has anyone heard from Farnham?'

'Nup, their Facebook page is pretty quiet,' replied Tara.

'Thick as thieves with the Friends of the River,' said Liz, still reading the paper. Cass and Tara exchanged looks over the top of her head.

CHAPTER 38

The mayor's opinion of wedlock was old-school catholic. Gays were an abomination, and when in government, he'd openly supported the archaic legislation that denied marriage equality. He'd spoken the usual rhetoric of matrimony as being a sacred covenant when, in reality, it was only a practical arrangement for comfort. After half a century of living within that constitution of convenience and nearly as long in politics, Snake was adept at sliding out from underneath feminine mischief. The Leason woman's wickedness was foreign to him. How dare she! Romeo genuinely believed that the world's natural order was to please him. Still, his mother had taught him to be a strategist who understood the logic of people.

'Du Su i putenti, cu avi assa e cu nun avi nenti. The most dangerous were those with everything to lose and those with nothing.

'This *putana* is surely the latter.' He involuntarily clenched his jaw, grinding the words. Life had changed for the man who thought of himself above mixing with the hoi polloi on social media. The Leason woman had him in the gutter with everyone else, checking Facebook each morning. She liked to post early, almost as if to dictate which direction the wind would blow for the rest of his day. It further infuriated him to think she was intentionally living rent-free in his mind. His wife wasn't online and was unaware of the cause of his perpetual bad mood. But half a century had taught her not to ask questions. She'd become accomplished at staying out of his way. Her life was busy with her grandchildren, and she often stayed in the city to be closer to them, leaving her husband to his own devices.

Aconaday racked his brains to scour why Cass suddenly appeared in Muckemup. Now of all times! She knew too much to be a coincidence. Have we met before? Has one of my old enemies sent her? You don't get within a bee's dick from the top job without some collateral damage.

'But who?' Snake dug deep into the thickets of memory. Engrossed, he gazed through the kitchen window. Below him, cradled in the bottom paddock, was the new dam, swollen with water and drowning half a dozen karri trees. As if in sorrow, the sky pressed down like fresh concrete, gentle rain pattered and a thin Djeran mist hung low, waiting for the sun to burn it away. Snake realised he, too, was hanging about. Waiting. He shook himself as the smell of charred toast pervaded the kitchen, and the smoke alarm beeped.

'Oh, merda!' the bread was rendered inedible. He threw it in the bin and gave the smoke alarm a few frantic waves with a tea towel before returning to Facebook. With increased annoyance, he noted the names of those foolhardy enough to openly support the woman. Like clockwork, she'd posted.

"According to Hansard 2014, the past local government and/or farming representatives on the Muckemup Water Futures Steering Group were Mr Romeo Aconaday, Mr Gio

Luciano, Mr Larry Wolfe, and Mr Leonard Reid. Would y'all look here! The same crew that are now directors of the Irrigation Scheme were working on water efficiency... *OR* were they really measuring it to the last drop to see how much water is being used by farmers in Muckemup so they know how little it will cost to squeeze them out in the future?"

Anger flooded Romeo's face. He was sinking in her words, drowning in them, as surely as his kari trees in the paddock. Did she know what she was doing? How does she know? She tied his mind in knots and was a clear and present danger to him, keeping his seat on the council.

He picked up the phone. 'Get someone into that bloody Facebook group. Their job is to follow and report on every move that woman makes. Find out her story! Is her arrival here premeditated, and if so, by whom?'

'Good morning... The Snake sounds unhappy today.' Templar's tone was trite as if he was soothing an upset child.

'Yes. The Snake is fucking furious! Just do it.' Aconaday hissed and hung up. 'Ssstupido!' He took a swig of coffee and burnt his tongue.

* * *

The number of people searching for the truth in Muckemup started catching up with those frantically trying to conceal it. Revelations crept into people's skulls like water. Cass received daily tip-offs. Bolstered by the defeat of Moriarty, townsfolk offered pieces of the puzzle they'd meticulously collected over the years as welcome gifts to their resident enigmatologist, and the greenies flexed a newfound confidence.

~ "They are clearing the forest by Railings Road. Go check it out. Ignore the CLOSED road signs. There's nothing wrong with the road."

~ "The Water Department manager has locked himself in his office for a week now with the blinds shut tight. If it weren't for hearing the shredder going, yer wouldn't know he was in."

~ "I thought you might like to know that the local manager for the Water Department also ran for council in the last elections."

~ "Look at Giovanni Luciano's dam size versus his allocation. The Water Department is acting illegally. Licences must equal the amount your dam can hold."

~ "The one you want to watch is Snake's brother, Angelo; he works for the Water Department and has a block out in the forest."

CHAPTER 39

'Do you believe there is such a thing as the lesser of two evils?' It was a Sunday mid-morning, and Cass sat at Tara's kitchen table, surrounded by Ivy's massive collection of greenery. Tara's eldest was an indoor plant fanatic, and the kitchen was a jungle of foliage in every shade of green. Plants sat on shelves, hung from the ceiling in macrame slings and climbed the walls.

Tara gave the artist a quizzical look. 'This isn't gonna be a sermon, is it? You saw the sign on your way through the gate?'

Cass chucked. 'Yeah, I saw it. "No Hawkers or Preachers" hanging next to a dead fox. Don't worry; no preacher will waste his time coming here! It's a genuine question.'

Tara was making focaccia from scratch for next week's school lunches. She kneaded the dough with the rhythm of someone who had cooked every day for nearly twenty years. 'Caught it sniffing around the chooks. Evil is just evil, not better or worse. Why?'

'I've been watching the greenies and that beekeeper. Viewing people through a political lens puts them in two classes: either tools or the enemy. Something isn't sitting right.'

'He's in deep with the Forest Defender mob. I warned him to be careful with Craig and Benno a while ago. Pretty sure he would have taken that information straight back to the inner circle.'

'Hmm...' Cass sipped her tea. 'Is it appropriate for a peak enviro group to be associated with an introduced agricultural species? Feral bees are a thing?'

'Noble cause corruption?'

'Exactly! Self-interest. He contacted me after I published the Irrigation Scheme map. Supposedly, the pipeline went through his property, but now it doesn't. What strings do you reckon need to be pulled for that to happen?'

'Or is the Irrigation Scheme just placating him?' asked Tara. The two women often challenged each other's ideas by taking turns in playing the devil's advocate.

'Who knows? But they're all acting shifty. Nearly as much as those Dilbanup boys.'

'There's evidence that stupidity is worse than evil,' said Tara, still kneading.

'Oh, for sure, stupidity has far greater potential to fuck up our lives. And every time you compromise a little, you adjust the moral lines—'

'Until...' Tara sprinkled flour from her fingers onto the dough ball and then pounded it into the table. 'There is no line left!'

CHAPTER 40

'Hullo?' a voice called from the front door.

'Is that you, Sandra? Come in.' Cass was deep into her painting.

Sandra entered the lounge and sat on the other side of the table. She watched Cass quietly for a minute before blurting, 'I thought I told you to stay in your own lane!'

The hostile tone surprised Cass, and she momentarily turned from her work to examine the Star Tree woman with interest.

'You know nothing about forestry or silviculture.'

'What's your problem?' asked Cass vaguely. Her mind was on her work.

'You look like an idiot! But do you listen? No! You don't listen to anyone. You just do *WHATEVER* YOU WANT!' Sandra's pitch rose with each snarl.

It took Cass a moment to realise the older woman was seriously pissed off. She slowly laid down her brushes, wondering why would the article she posted about BlackMore Investments and carbon credits upset her so?

But instead of asking, Cass nodded. 'Yep, you got it! I do, do *exactly* what I want!'

Sandra remained seated. Sudden sparks of malice glowed and lit into a rage. Cass saw it flashing, wanting to smack her face. The unadulterated hatred took her by surprise, and then it was gone! Sandra's face hardened into a stiff mask as she slammed the door shut and was back in control of herself. However, both women knew that a dark secret had shown itself. They glared at each other. Sandra was unwilling to leave of her own accord but didn't know what further action to take, so she just sat at the table like an angry potato.

Eventually, Cass said, 'You can go.' That she'd issued an order was clear, and with curiosity, she watched the forest activist depart. Thanks to Sandra's outburst, she now knew the native forest logging situation was the path to follow.

Sandra wasn't the only person upset by the carbon credits article Cass had shared. The former mayor also took a bite.

'Are you drunk?' she questioned as she read Rovello's comment under the article.

"Why don't you crawl back under the rock you came from? You act like you're some Keyboard Worrier, but we're all laughing at you,"

Cass cracked her knuckles. 'Take the biggest ones down first. She punched back hard.'

"LOL Rovello, you got me! I am a Keyboard Worrier. I am *WORRIED* about this sham of a water scheme. I'm *WORRIED* about the water assets company partnered with Lenny Reid. And last but not least, I'm *WORRIED* about what's happening with Acheron Avocados. Do you think I haven't noticed that mega-dam project? You don't build 12 gig dams for only 50 hectares of avos. So instead of attacking me with your poor grammar, why don't you fuck off back to Tollie!"

Rovello fell silent. The rest of the town also said nothing, but she could feel them all watching the exchange with bated breath and buckets of popcorn. Her concentration to keep working was gone, so she washed her brushes and prepped a board with gesso, waiting for a response. Half an hour later, still nothing.

'Don't wanna come back for another round, Rocky from Tollie?... That's right, you just be quiet now!' Cass polished her nails on an imaginary lapel and hummed Eye of the Tiger to herself as she pottered, putting away clean clothes that were sitting in the laundry basket for a week.

CHAPTER 41

'And what do you do?'

'Huh?' Cass looked up. A wafer-thin elderly man gingerly lowered himself onto the bench next to her. She slipped her phone away. 'I paint.'

'Does it pay well?' Age had clearly worn his body to a stick but had not diminished his mind.

Cass half-laughed. 'A cocaine habit would've been cheaper.' They were waiting for the post office to open; it was quarter to nine. 'What do you do?' She returned the question, more out of social convention than genuine interest. Her brain was spilling over with local Muckemup anecdotes.

'Retired potato farmer.'

'Oh, right?' Cass didn't know what to ask about potatoes. She was thankful he required no prompting.'

'That's what it used to be, potatoes and cauliflower... now farming's after the fancy money; avocados and truffles.'

She nodded. 'Really? So, have you been here all your life?'

'Yes. I was born in the room I now sleep in. Of course,' he explained, 'It was my parents' bedroom back then. Surrounded by the forest on all sides. Cleared it for crops.'

'The trees would have been something.' Cass often imagined what the region would have been like before colonisation.

He gave a heavy sigh. 'They were. Cold axes hit trees so big'n old and heavy that they smashed to bits when they hit the ground. Tractors and chains to rip out the roots. The noise was wretched,' His voice broke, raw with regret.

Astonished. Cass took a second look at the man. He was a wraith dressed in ill-fitting clothes. She could feel the waves of guilt emanate from where paper-thin flesh slipped from the bone. He was giving her his confession. She replied, 'That's a shame. I've seen photos of the old trees at the Town Park. They were massive.'

'Ah, the Museum of Death. They were so big it took half a dozen men to embrace them. Ha! Some tree-huggers we were! Went crazy! Cutting everything down. Even trees so big, trucks couldn't carry them out of the valleys. We left 'em lying where they fell. It used to look like that moon in the Star Wars movie, you know the one? You could *feel* the energy.'

Cass knew which film. Thinking of Ewoks and the Star Tree and mantis orchids, she wanted to say, *'Oh, I know,'* but she didn't. Instead, she looked into the grim, wrinkled face. Time creates human maps, the journeys of our lives, and this one was etched with deep lines of regret. Cass had no absolution to offer, no words of comfort. 'That's very sad,' was all she could muster. It didn't matter. Her words fell on deaf ears. The old man was not looking at this physical world. He was floating through a portal to the land of the leafy giants. Too late to change anything.

He croaked, flicking tears from his eyes. 'There used to be magic in the forest. Tree killers will always feel tormented by what we've done.'

'Good morning!' Tara sang out as she opened the door and fetched the spud farmer back to present-day Muckemup. Cass helped him stand, allowing him to enter the post office first. She was in no hurry, wanting to update Tara on Rovello and Sandra's latest tirades. She saw the school bus driver had also been waiting.

'Hey, Miro!' Tara waved while giving Cass the subtlest nod of acknowledgment. But, little passed by the bus driver.

'How long have you been there?' asked Cass.

He tipped his wide-brimmed hat above a narrow face, hollowed under those prominent cheekbones was an expression as tough as old biltong. 'Long 'nuf to hear old voices tell a desolate tale.'

CHAPTER 42

The publican postponed the local government edition of Politics at the Pub. There had been a murder in the district, and the victim and the alleged perpetrator both came from families of the local aristocracy.

People spoke in subdued tones while queueing at the post office. 'But it was one of our own!'

'One of our own taken by one of our own,' was the incredulous reply.

'A terrible thing all around,' murmured another.

'Did you hear the council refused to pay for the snake gaiters?'

'Well, it's not really council business, is it?'

'No, I guess not, but the CEO seems happy splashing out loyalty cash to the staff. I'd rather keep our boys safe while they're looking for their mate.'

A troubled hush settled upon the district. It stretched for a couple of weeks while search parties looked for the body. Folk said little after the initial shock. The old families closed themselves off from the outside world. But, plenty of old and new locals speculated to each other through private internet conversations; for with the Major Crimes Squad came decent broadband coverage.

On the rescheduled date of the event, Tara relayed the snippets of gossip while she and Cass sat in the beer garden of the Cattleman's Hotel waiting for the debate to start.

The publican had scored a pulpit from Facebook Marketplace since the last event. 'It used to belong to the

Jehovah's Witnesses,' he said, proudly rubbing his hand over the timber trim as they took three seats near the front; Liz Calder would be late.

'I love it! You could start regular Soapbox Sessions, like Hyde Park in London,' suggested Cass, laughing before she leaned in towards Tara. 'None of that surprises me. Did you read some of the online comments a few days beforehand? There was a post that said, "Whoever told Robbie that I've been ripping off his avocados, knock it off!" They went on about Robbie being a good friend. Yada, yada. There'd been some argument. I noticed the post is gone.'

Tara twisted around in her chair to speak close to Cass's ear while she scoped the room behind her. 'Hmm... both families go way back. That's the *we look after our own"* mentality. I'd say whoever wrote that post got a tap on the shoulder.'

The space was filling, a few councillors who were not up for re-election and reps from various community groups like Rotary and the CWA were present. The farmers were out in force and plenty of family and friends of the candidates. This time Aconaday's wife was not in the front row. She was in the city, tucking her grandees into bed.

'If shooting someone over avocados is a private business, I'm relieved!' said Cass.

'What?—Why?'

'It takes the target off my back. Two murders within a few months would be too much.'

'Cass, what's wrong with you? One murder is too much!'

'Oh, yeah, of course! You're right.' Cass was humbled enough to feel contrite.

'What it *does* show is we've never completely turned off the tap for violence. Someone...' Tara nodded towards the empty panel waiting for the candidates to arrive, 'Just needs to give the nod to a few of the attack dogs, and we're back to the tinderbox situation of the 90s.'

'I can feel it, eh? Something dark just waiting for permission to be unleashed.'

'Interesting how *"death threats"* recently got bandied about on the radio, then supposedly Rovello received one too.'

'What? Really?'

'Yep, at the loggers' rally. He claims he found a bullet casing in the back of his ute, which is code. But, really?' Tara pulled her lips tight. 'It's almost like the actual message is *from* them.'

'What happened in the 90s?'

'A new Regional Forestry Agreement was due; they're every ten years. Things got heated, and the thugs were out with baseball bats. A few choice words is like taking a match to straw, many old hatreds ready to fuel a new fire.'

'Yeah, I've noticed one in particular—'

The moderator took to the podium and cut short any further talk. He announced the event was about to start. He was also an outsider, hired for the event and supposedly without bias. The format for the night was the same as the debate for the State Election. This time, however, only some candidates were in attendance. One was standing unopposed for their ward, and another was on holiday. Those who came introduced themselves and spoke of their values and vision for Muckemup, and then there was a break. Campaigning continued over a drink or two, topping up with Dutch courage to parry questions from the audience. The lineup was the mayor, the deputy, the former mayor, the numbat fan Chip Smith, a woman called Charlotte Diamante who was part of Farnham's water security collective and Graeme Mantel, a long-time resident who now headed the ministerially appointed Dilbanup River Rural Strategy Group.

Liz arrived during the interval. 'It took Graeme almost a decade to get on that committee. For a while, he was the only greenie in the village.'

'Ha! You make him sound like the only gay in the village,' said Cass.

Tara snorted and choked on her drink. 'That's what he was like!'

Liz thumped Tara on the back. 'Where's Marion?'

Spluttering, she pulled a handkerchief out of her bag, wiping the wine off her chin. 'Mum offered to watch the girls. I'll fill her in later.'

Romeo Aconaday brought two booklets with him and now rubbed his hand back and forth on their covers as if they contained a genie. One was the State Water Act, and the other was the council's Indigenous People's Strategy.

It didn't take long for things to heat up. Adam Calhoun, the brains behind *"A Clear Vote"* had questions about the Irrigation Scheme. Snake had not returned his questionnaire and refused to answer him now.

'You're involved with that Mu-Muck Up Unrivalled!' stammered Aconaday. The name didn't taste good on his lips; he wanted to spit it out. He'd finally drawn the battle lines and officially declared Muck Unrivalled the enemy. Cass's face remained passive, but choppy waters picked up under an arching brown.

'Umm…No, I'm not—' said Adam.

A woman jumped up from across the aisle. 'For crying out loud. Enough about the water! We want to know about the candidates.'

'Hang on!' replied Adam, taken aback by the interruption. 'I want to know about the water. That's why I emailed all the candidates those questions. That's why I'm here!'

'That's Graeme Mantel's ex-wife,' Tara murmured to Cass.

'Oh, is that why she looks like she is supporting his opponent?' Cass whispered back.

There were a few special interest questions from the art group and the local community health sector, with each candidate giving appropriately supportive answers. Tara looked behind her. Sitting at the back, next to Big Dave, on the Farnham's team, was the pub's resident barfly, Stanley White. He had a few under his belt and was giving Big Dave a running commentary under his breath. Every time Serena Benchley spoke, he mumbled louder than usual.

'Bissshh! Look at her..' he slurred, 'Pfft, that's a stu... stupid bissshh answer.'

'We've only got time for one last question this evening,' announced the moderator. 'Let's wrap it up with tonight's youngest audience member. After all, it's their future. Have you got a question, young man? Is this your first election?'

'That's Graeme's kid. He must be just eighteen,' said Tara.

'Oh, okay. I think the emcee's laying it on a bit thick.'

The virgin voter answered, 'I'd like to know how the candidates would work to include Indigenous Australians in the community and on council?'

Aconaday answered first, picking up the booklet he'd brought, waving it high and speaking with the authority of a salesman. Then came Logan Rovello, followed by Serena Benchley. The deputy mayor was mid-speech when Stanley White stood up and started talking loudly over the top of her. She trailed off at the interruption and everyone turned to the commotion at the back of the room.

'I'm a veteran and.. of this bransshh..' his words were unclear.

As if watching a game of tennis, the audience looked at the moderator to umpire the match. He respectfully nodded. 'Let him talk.'

But ol' self-medicating Stan hadn't waited for permission. 'I'm a veteran and fought in Vietnam beside

Abo... Aboriginal men..but if their flai..their flai... I WILL QUIT IF THEY RAISE THEIR FLAGGH NEXT TO OURS ON ANZAC DAY!' shouted Stan to a stunned room. Before his spray of vitriol landed, he turned and staggered towards the front bar. For a moment, the room was silent. Tara and Cass looked at each other in shock.

'Well, that's that sorted then,' said Tara.

'Who was that?'

'President of our Soldiers League.'

Cass's jaw sagged even further. 'You're kidding?'

Liz leaned over and said in a loud stage whisper, 'We should find a flag!'

Aconaday bowed his head, shaking it like Stan was a hopeless case. But he couldn't stop himself from laughing at the performance.

CHAPTER 43

Cass wrote a formal complaint to the Soldiers League, followed by another to the Anti-Corruption Commission about the mayor using unreported death threats for political gain. She headed off to work to find the owner of one of the Airbnbs had hung a giant framed Bintang Beer poster above the king-sized bed in the main bedroom.

'How romantic!' Tara chuckled as Cass shared the story.

They'd met for a BYO lunch at Marri Lake, Cockemup. The forest was a green backdrop on the far side of the lake. Before Cockemup's mill shut, it supplied water to the tiny satellite workers' village fifty kilometres south of Muckemup. Decades ago, the council opposed any further development citing bushfire risk, but the developer took his case to the State government and had the decision overturned. The community was small, now mostly retirees escaping the city and wealthier waterfront holiday houses where townies retreat for summer weekends to enjoy views of a glassy bedazzled blue reflected on the serene face of the lake there was still a *"No Swimming"* sign in place, even though they'd been trucking potable water in since the sale of the town twenty-plus years ago.

'I can't unsee it! Imagine if you will, a beautiful home, truly gorgeous.' Cass spoke with words and her hands. 'Bedroom on the mezzanine floor with treetop views, fresh white linen, $400 a night, and he puts that crap up like it's some sorta man cave!' She shook her hands a final time in despair and took a bite of her sandwich. Still accusing while munching ' What a... a... a styletard!'

Tara laughed. 'We call them CUB's, cashed-up bogans. Money doesn't guarantee good taste, especially down here. Changing the subject, have you seen Graeme Mantel's enviro group is hosting a water conference?'

'He emailed me something... "From an Indigenous Perspective" ... sounds like a box-ticking exercise for someone. How many groups is he in?

'A few. They've already got the Traditional Owners onboard. The biggest Treaty ever, according to Miro. It was something like $1.3 billion.' Tara rubbed her finger and thumb together, the universal sign for money.

'That alone is a red flag!'

'You reckon they sold out too cheap?'

'Probably!' exclaimed Cass. 'What is that money for? When has the government ever been altruistic towards Aboriginals? Why does this make me think of Rovello and Sandra losing their shit over that carbon credit post?'

'I don't know. Maybe they're filling the gaps on the cover story for when future generations search for where it all went wrong?'

'The victors write the history. Tell me about the bus driver. He's an interesting guy. We met in the forest. Is he a Traditional Owner?'

'Miro? Nah, I think they extinguished one of the neighbouring nations as part of the agreement. Miro's the last of his tribe.'

'Rarer than pandas and numbats, eh?' Are you going to go?'

'We both should. Check out who's presenting: a lawyer specialising in water legislation, some climate guy who contributed to the IPC, and our old Friends of the River boys.'

'Ugh, really?'

'Yep. Departments of Ag and Water too.'

'Lawyers don't come cheap. Who's funding it?'

'Good question. Here! I bought us a treat from Bazza's' Tara, opened a small cardboard cake box to reveal two vanilla slices.

'Ooh, Yum! Snot blocks.'

CHAPTER 44

The political Right didn't hold the patent on backstairs shenanigans; small *"L"* liberals were also no slouches in the fabrication of intrigue. Cass had kept tabs on the *Green Dream* Facebook group since Sandra Star Tree had invited her. It wasn't the cabinet war rooms, more a hang-out space for the cheerleaders. Still, the group's administrator was the Senator who had lost her seat at the recent State Election and helped Benno and Craig establish the Friends of the River Association. Cosy enough to warrant keeping a check on. The ex-parliamentarian had been low-key since her defeat. But now she'd popped up with a cryptic hint that her Party had a candidate in the wings for next year's Federal Election. Cass scrolled through the commentary; it was mostly Forest Defender types fawning over the former politician.

"I hope it's you running, Viv!" was the common theme. Then she read, "How about Craig? I think he lives in Muckemup?"

Cass didn't know how she recognised when someone unseen was transmitting a falsehood, but she and Tara both had the gift. Reading the words several times, she thought it smelt like a segue. The Senator's initial post also reeked. Cass took the bait before anyone else commented. "Are you talking about Craig from Friends of the River?"

"Yes! They've done great work."

'Hmm.. and who are you?' She looked at the man's profile. There wasn't much to go by. He could be real or an alias; too hard to tell. 'Okay, let's see what you do?' She replied, "Sure. I hope they conduct criminal background checks for whoever the Party chooses as a candidate." Cass twisted her lips. She'd pulled the pin on a grenade.

The guy replied, "Yeah, absolutely!"

It was all benign.

'Wait.' She told herself to be patient. Within half an hour, he'd removed his comment and, therefore, the entire thread. 'Boom. Gotcha!' snapped Cass. She pressed redial on her phone. 'They know I know, and only you could have told me!'

'Woah! Well done. Imagine those two with their snouts in the trough at a Federal level?' The thought appalled Tara.

'They'd have to get in first. But things happen; Look at Morrison pulling a Stuart Bradbury back in 2019,' cracked Cass. 'It looks perfect to the inner Enviro Party circle; they've already got a solid support base in the region outside of Muckemup.'

'Ugh, I can see it.' Tara imagined the backroom conversations. 'They plan to pick up votes from locals who are against the Scheme. Our two redneck greenies are fluent in bloke-speak around the campfire. You know, the *Blokes, Beers and Bitches* stuff those farmers love!'

'So they're angling to pick some more votes there. Heck, maybe even a few Hunter Party supporters. They'd be so smug!' Cass pieced it together.

'It'd be killing Benno to turn it down. So close, he can smell it.' Tara chuckled, then turned deadly serious.

'They need to go! Because right now, they'll be hatching vengeance.' The two men would be livid.

'Don't worry. I got this. The boys will be backing out by lunchtime tomorrow.'

'Whad'ya going to do?'

'Poke the bear. Check Muck Unrivalled in the morning.

"WHAT IS CONTROLLED OPPOSITION?"

Think of it as a protest organisation led by the government or corporate agents. Nearly all governments in history have employed this technique to mislead their adversaries.

Now, imagine a small group of farmers concerned over a river with insufficient water. Several local elites have formed a cartel to privatise water from every river and creek within the region and create a water market. They all know there's not enough water, but that's irrelevant. The syndicate has government officials in their pocket, and there's money to be made. They've been working at the long game, and the strategy is in place for the next elections when the manipulated farmers will all be screaming for water.

This first group of farmers who discovered the lack of water is unaware of the *ACTUAL PLAN*, so they're scratching their heads. Why spend $80 million on something that won't work? They speak to their local MPs, the Water Regulator, their State Ministers, and the Federal Rep. Nothing! They're ignored. So, the farmers make more noise, put signs on their gates, and create a public Facebook page to inform people, but they're farmers, not social media experts.

The cartel isn't too worried; the State Seat is safe, and the local government is in on it, as are the Feds. But these elite are clever, and as hundreds of millions of dollars are at stake, it's better to be safe than sorry. They can see that out of desperation, the farmers may ally with those crazy tree-huggers. Therefore, this is the best place for the elite to introduce their agents.

Farmers need to trust the agents. A couple of "Redneck Greenies" is what's required.

As predicted, the farmers find the tree-huggers and tell them their sorry tale. So it's time for the conspirators to go out to the forest and build a makeshift barricade to impress those clean-air-loving rule-breaking hippies. They've set the honey trap.

Now for the farmers. At the greenie camp, word on the street is that concerned farmers will be at the next council meeting—the perfect place for the agents to establish a link and instigate themselves as an authority voice. Signing up members and selling calendars and stickers won't stop the Scheme. The "real work" is to ingratiate themselves into the farmers' network, the forest lovers' network, and any other political opposition channels they can.

There are a few hiccups, as there always are. Members suggest becoming incorporated to protect themselves from a well-funded capitalist juggernaut; individuals taking action, like putting in trail cameras and contacting the media. Then disaster strikes! That safe political seat doesn't look so safe anymore. The intended plan for the Controlled Opposition group to wring their hands and moan, "Sorry folks, we did all we could to save the River," is now useless. Those cunning rats go quiet and wait for further instructions.

What's next? *"Plant yourselves into the Political arm of the enviro movement"* is what they get told, so that's what they do. So well, that the greenies are considering running one for the Federal Seat next year.

The elite are pleased; they will have agents reporting *EVERYTHING* back. And when those rat agents get too big for their boots or too many people to smell the stench of their lies, the puppet masters can cut them loose and destroy the Enviro Party in the process. Check. Mate"

Cass scrolled through Google, looking for a suitable photo of two rats to put with her post. 'It's true. A picture does tell a thousand words.' She scheduled publication for 7 AM the next day.

* * *

Matt Farnham called minutes after seven. 'You need to remove that post!'

'Good morning to you too!'

'What the hell do you think you're doing?' He was riled.

'It's self-explanatory. I kept quiet during the State Election, but no more.'

'About what?'

'You know what. You may think it's okay to mislead the community for political gain, but I don't.'

'I'm not kidding, Cass!'

'Neither am I. The only authority those two cowboys have is what you handed them...on a platter! And only because it's convenient for you farmers to have a cover. You guys are being played by people with deeper pockets and way more skilled at deception.'

'What the hell are you on about?'

'Exactly! You don't have a clue what's really going on.' The pace of Cass's speech quickened just thinking about all the interconnections.

'People are right. You're mad as a cut snake!'

Cass shrugged. 'Well, if that's the consensus, you've nothing to worry about. No one will believe me. No harm, no foul. But I won't be removing the post. Let me know if you ever want to meet for a coffee.' She hung up and checked her Facebook feed. She'd dumped the post in a few groups, including the Green Dream. A message came through from Charlie Swican asking her to pull the post, and the volunteer who had installed the trail cams with Sandra Star Tree was losing her mind. Still, a few others were seeing the bigger picture.

"Wow, it's like HOUSE OF CARDS!" someone wrote.

'You're not wrong, mate.' Cass kept scrolling, 'You're not wrong!'

The Senator removed her from the Green Dream Facebook group.

'Good. Message received.' Cass RSVP'd Graeme Mantel's water conference. She would attend.

CHAPTER 45

'It's a fast-moving feast.' Tara's daughters had bailed on the dishes, pleading they had homework. Exhausted, she finally flopped onto her couch, chatting with Cass as she caught up with the online day she'd missed while at work.

'It went off like a frog in a sock! Farnham rang me, demanding I remove it, and then his boy Chuck messaged me. Hang on, I'll read what he said. *"While I have no qualms about you being in dispute with Friends of the River, bla bla. It concerns me that perceived infighting will comfort supporters of the Irrigation Scheme."*

'That doesn't sound like a farmer. Who is he?'

'Charlie Swican? I don't know? One of Farnham's team. Anyway, I told him that while I appreciated his concerns, I recommended that people do their due diligence.'

The mainstream environmentalists in Muck Unrivalled were agitated. Tara could feel them knotty and on edge in the ether as Cass's cunning rat story buoyed along the algorithms. The Forest Defender hierarchy did its best to discount the outspoken woman. Craig and Benno put on a suitable injured front. But they also backed away from being considered contenders in the Federal election, so they couldn't prove Cass wrong without a doubt. The loggers watched without comment, unaware or uncaring that they were witnessing backroom politics. They had issues of their own.

'Huh! Would ya look at that?'

'What's up?' asked Cass.

'Well, for starters, Sandra is commenting all over the place that you have mental health issues and "harvested" her friends' list.'

'Oh, dear, of course I did! All fifteen of them. I told her that months ago. I think I used that exact word — *harvested*. So what? When I created Muck Unrivalled, I knew no one. What does she think? My circle of friends over east care what's happening here? Pfft, next?'

'Okay, hmm... Serena Benchley posted about what happened at the pub and how racism is a cancer that eats at communities.'

'I saw that... and a bunch of the responses. Oh, brother!' Cass suddenly shivered as if someone had walked over her grave. 'The tribalism down here is off the wall. It's all footy and racism — the rednecks' biggest quandary is which one to kick first!'

'That's the water we swim in. We have been isolated for so long that people think it's perfectly normal.'

'Not everyone, thankfully. A few others messaged me. They've also formally complained about Stan. I saw the emcee comment on the *Tutelage* page, saying it was all lies, and ol' Stan said nothing racist... I don't know what event he reckons he presided over. My recollection is Chip Smith spoke directly after Stan left and said how offensive it was. So much for bringing in an unbiased moderator. The whole thing stinks!'

'It does. Chip's wife is Aboriginal.' said Tara.

'Oh God, just when you think it can't get any worse.'

'I know, right? You might've met her; she works at the thrift shop with Liz. Convenient Mantel's kids asking that question, and Snake just happened to have the Indigenous policy with him.'

'That post will probably nail Serena's coffin shut. But at the end of the day, you've gotta be able to live with yourself.'

'I wonder if her husband recommended she create the post or tried talking her out of it?' pondered Tara.

'They'd have discussed it for sure. The doc is very much her campaign manager, isn't he? Did you see him filming her at the debate? Do you reckon they lie in bed at night, replaying it?'

'Ew, Cass! That's gross!'

'I bet they do!' Cass laughed. 'Doctors have their own special brand of freak... God complexes' n all that.'

'True.' said Tara.

'What's the go with the Regional Forestry Agreement? I can't believe the Forest Defenders are publicly supporting MacGovern before reading the fine print.'

'It's interesting, eh? A couple I know from Cockemup came into work today. You'd like them. They're both arty-farties; he's been here since the 1970s photojournalist background. Documented a lot of the logging carnage through to the 2000s. I'll see if I can organise for us to visit.'

'Sounds good.'

'Matthew Farnham also came in.'

'Oh yeah? What'd he have to say for himself?'

'Oh, just the usual... you're out of control, a conspiracy theorist. I tried asking what he thought about the logging, but he wouldn't touch it.;

'So, no surprises.' That ties nicely with Sandra's narrative.

'That's how to do it. Build a story from multiple angles and sources until it's perceived as *"must be true"*. Works every time.'

It wasn't until just before the election that Tara introduced Cass to local artists, Raven and Jack. She'd extracted a dinner invite, and they drove together under a waxing moon. Cass had Brahms Quintet in F minor, filling the car as they followed the thin dark serpent of road winding its way to the village of Cockemup. There were roadworks in progress, and they crawled along slowly. Tara shook her head at Cass's eccentric driving.

'What? You don't like it. What's wrong with you? Brahms dedicated this to a princess! Listen... this music stands at a junction — looking both back and forward.

Tara rolled her eyes. 'A place of the *Everywhen?*'

'I like that.'

'I'll let Mum know.'

'Smart woman is Marion. Schubert's my favourite,' Cass, sat forward on the steering wheel in concentration. 'Despite him being short and fat and an alcoholic.'

'Sounds as if you're describing Stanley White,' laughed Tara.

'Huh, so it does!' The realisation hit Cass. 'Whatever happened to drunks? They used to compose songs like Ava Maria; now all we get is ... well, Stanley!'

'Ha! It's unfortunate. Booze and white supremacy will age ya like an avocado! Although, I'm sure there were ugly drunks back then, too. Wasn't the water so bad that even children drank ale?'

'Yeah, in the cities. Talking of the olden days... I can see neoliberalism morphing into neo-feudalism. One big self-perpetuating cycle and we all become peasants again. Except we now have corporate masters that will never die—'

'Just here!' Tara pointed. 'Last house on the right.'

Cass slowed down along the invisible edge of the road; there were no street lights, and they could see the faint glow of the kitchen window.

The postmistress was correct; Cass immediately hit it off with the couple as they all squeezed around the kitchen table. Like Tara, the septuagenarian artists resided in a former mill workers' cottage. Both were talented practitioners, and their tiny space teemed with creative pieces at various stages of completion. They were also a living record of the local logging protests since the late 80s.

'We knew something was up with the water, didn't we, Jack?' said Raven as she welcomed the two women into their home. She was spry and bright-eyed in her early seventies, with white hair cut short around a sharp-featured face.

'Ahh, to have a raven's knowledge,' said Cass.

'She's more djidi-djidi,' said her husband, referring to the lively, willy wagtail bird.

'It's an Irish proverb. It means to have the gift of prophecy. Ravens are the totem of Morgan Ley Fay, Queen of the dark faeries... the Trickster.' Cass twinkled her fingers and then raised them in surrender. 'No offence to you, Raven.' she clarified quickly.

'None taken. I love it!' said Raven, serving large spoonfuls of aromatic curry into deep pottery bowls.

'You can be pixie-tricksy, love!' Jack teased his wife as he grabbed the steaming dishes from her and put them on the table for their guests.

'Like Mummaries,' added Tara.

'What are they?'

'Sounds like boobies!' said Jack.

'Not mammaries, you twit! Sheesh, what is it with men and breasts?' laughed Tara. All three women rolled their eyes; his wife shot him an extra warning look. Jack opened and closed his mouth; he knew when he was beat.

Tara explained, 'They're shapeshifters in Aboriginal folklore. Small hairy figures that can grow into huge dark shadowy giants. They can change into any form. They supposedly communicate telepathically; sometimes, they might reach out, trying to get your attention for a reason; other times, they keep away. You can feel their presence when walking into certain parts of the forest. If you ever feel unwelcome, they're telling you to go away. Anyway, that's what Miro told me.'

'Oh!' gasped Cass. 'Some parts of the forest *do* give me the jeebies. You'd never get me out there at night. A guy sent me a message to check Railings Road near the Acheron Plantation. I looked at his profile and was nuh-uh.'

'Why's that?' asked Jack.

'Well, for starters, his bio said *"Pig Shooter"*, and his profile pic was him in a ghillie suit holding a shotgun with a scope mounted. Legit, I could hear a banjo playing?'

'Only one?' The three locals asked in unison. Despite being only a few hours south of the big smoke, Muckemup remained remote until recently because Australians have a habit of clinging to the coastline like limpets sticking to a rock.

'Don't tell me you wouldn't crap yourselves if you came across that?' Laughing, Cass held up her phone so they could all see the photo she was talking about.

'... or a Mummarri,' shuddered Raven.

'Miro says there are many surprises deep in the forest that would even have him running.'

'No special privileges for fairy queens or blackfellas, huh?' Jack squeezed his wife affectionately as she passed a plate of naan bread to mop up the stew.

She purposely misinterpreted him, 'None!'

It was a long night, and the conversations deepened with the hour. Tara and Cass brought the couple up to speed on the Irrigation Scheme. Jack gave his account of the situation with native forest logging and the Forest Defenders.

'Everyone, apart from me, has fallen for the same crap that was dished out in 2002. Which ran like this; the Workers Party election in '01 was based on a promise of change. However, the government's deception didn't stop the forest destruction—'

'It was all to get votes, wasn't it, Jack?' piped Raven.

'You're right, love. The then Premier promised to end all old-growth forest logging and to declare new National Park areas. But what he did was let the Forest Bureau change the definition of "old growth" to allow for the continued clearing of ancient forest—'

'They split the new definitions between high conservation value and two-tier forest. These definitions are still in use and are interchangeable.' interrupted Raven.

'What's two-tier?' asked Cass.

'A two-tier forest is a double-cross the government played back in 2001. If there was evidence of any human intervention in a forest, a sawn tree stump or a rusty ol' fence post...any disturbance from any time, for any reason, then the loggers could clear a two-hectare radius around it. In the twelve months leading up to the new Forestry Agreement, they ran all over the forest, removing random trees from all over the place for all sorts of reasons constructed to fit this clause. That meant for the next decade, the loggers could, at their leisure, take beautiful old-growth forests with one, two, and three-hundred-year-old trees and keep turning them into wood chips after they'd won the election promising to stop native forest logging.... It was the Judas Kiss of the Workers Party.' Jack's voice lowered, the final sentence dark and heavy as he remembered the fraud.

'More like a *flood* of tears than two-tier.' asserted Raven with a rush of outrage.

'And now we are going to have "ecological thinning", and once again, they're waving the bait of new National Parks when they haven't even converted the 320,000 hectares promised in the last Agreement.' said Tara.

'Yep.' Jack replied. 'Back then, the new parks consisted primarily of dry scrub and immature stands of aged karri monoculture, *regen* plantations. While scrub and peatland are important and need protection, we also need what remnants of ancient forests we've got left to enable complex ecosystems to survive—'

'Meanwhile, there was a $120 million handout and then back to business as usual!' Raven highlighted the cherry on top of the swindle.

'They're sneaky, alright. I've watched the Premier's media conference a few times now,' said Cass as she processed the revealed legal loopholes.

'Cunning as shithouse rats!' Jack winked knowingly. He rallied. 'If you look at the light in that footage, you can see both MacGovern and the Forest Defenders spokesperson were at the same venue for the media release. They staged it.'

'Can't half tell you are a photographer. I guess it makes it easier for journos to get a statement, but they look like a united front.' Cass acknowledged dryly.

'If you sleep with dogs, don't complain if you get fleas. Deception is everywhere! Like promoting aged regen plantations as a forest,' said Tara.

'Oh, indeed! We've got tourist centres complicit, promoting plantations such as Boranup while showing no interest in protecting the real native forest,' said Raven.

'You got it, love! Boranup is not a fully functioning forest and has the visual excitement of striped wallpaper.' snapped Jack.

'I call them zombie trees,' said Raven, 'Not dead, but neither properly living.'

Cass started humming, 'In your head, in your head... how do you incrementally convert a public for–est, to private ownership?' The tune was The Cranberries. She contemplated the foreseeable policymaking out loud.

Tara joined her. '... do, do, do. It's been the same old logging scene since two thousand and three. We weren't mistaken—'

Jack didn't know the song. 'I fear our current Premier's plan is far worse... and once again, it looks like the Forest Defenders are in connivance.' his words fell like a shadow, recognising the deceit that had been and more that was to come, the place of the Everywhen. The four fell silent.

Tara was the first to snap out of it. 'Here! It's getting late. I don't want to be a zombie at work tomorrow. Let us help with the dishes!'

CHAPTER 46

Voting counting began at 7 PM, an hour after the polls closed. Cass wandered to the Town Hall a short while later to witness the proceedings. Snake and his family members, his sons, daughter, and brother, were present. Cass could see they were clannish close. So, you're not a complete monster? She thought as she surveyed the room and then answered herself with; Hilter also had friends and followers, you know!

James Templar had returned from death-threat leave and was watching with interest.

Friends and accomplices, thought Cass.

Serena Benchley was also present with her husband, and behind them sat Logan Rovello.

What an assortment! She messaged Tara, "I feel like I've just walked into the viper's pit!"

"What'd you do that for?" Tara texted back.

"I want to publish it on Muck Unrivalled as soon as we get results. There's still a scrap of hope. I heard Snake was sitting at the bar alone last night, nursing a scotch and looking worried."

"I will report you missing if I don't hear from you by 9."

Cass smiled as she signed off. The piles of ballots were still being sorted. It was too early to tell.

Serena and her husband moved outside. Cass followed them to introduce herself. 'Hi, I'm Cass Leason.' She gave a friendly smile.

'I recognise you. I'm Serena Benchley, and this is my husband, John.'

Cass acknowledged the doctor before turning back to Serena. 'Good on you taking a stand against that incident at the pub. No matter what happens tonight, that sorta toxic behaviour needs to be nipped in the bud.'

'Thank you,' said Serena.

'So this is where the action is?' The Calders strode across the road, with Bob escorting Liz, her usual glamorous self. Suddenly the elderly bookseller tripped on the curb; without missing a beat, Liz's manicured hand stretched out and caught her husband, remaining a hold even after he regained his balance.

'What's the score?' As the words left Bob's lips, Rovello appeared stone-faced. Ignoring them, he stormed up the street to his car, burning rubber as he sped off.

'I'd say South Ward's decided,' said Cass.

'Oh yes! Looks like it.' Liz sounded delighted.

'I wonder if it went to Graeme Mantel or the incumbent?' mulled Bob.

'Go check, darl!'

'I'll join you,' said Serena, accompanying Bob inside. Her physician husband stayed.

'So, what brought you to Muckemup, Cass?'

'Clearly, the need called her here!' deflected Liz, fixing the doctor's gaze.

Cass laughed. Liz Calder was formidable. She changed the subject. 'How's Serena faring? I've read most of the haters' comments on her post.' The doctor was in his prime, mid-thirties. He and his wife were upwardly mobile — a power couple.

'She's doing alright.'

'Good. It's nearly over. I'm sure you'll be relieved when it's all done, no matter how the chips fall.'

'Yes, I'm torn. I work with one and sleep with the other,' joked John Prescott, but it fell flat on his audience.

'That young man is a *no-brainer!*' Liz gave him a haughty stare, employing a buzzword they knew she'd stolen from the mayor as she dramatically swept past him to go inside.

Cass pulled an *"Oh, dear"* face at the doctor and followed her friend.

All the incumbents kept their seats except for Serena Benchley. Charlotte Diamante, Matthew Farnham's girl, replaced her. Aconaday was returned by the skin of his teeth, but that was all he needed. Liz and Cass watched with fascination as Snake grabbed the Electoral Officer, firing questions. The public servant, aware of an audience, disentangled himself and replied that everyone would have to wait until the Electoral Office made the official announcement in a few days.

'Seems overly keen for someone who's been at this game for forty-plus years.' whispered Liz.

'That's desperation you can smell. Anyway, I'm off home. I'll drop by during the week.' They exchanged air kisses. Cass shook hands with Serena and congratulated Charlotte, the newest councillor, before exiting onto the empty street where darkness had fallen like an eyelid on the world. There was no moon and only one streetlight buzzing outside the Town Hall. It was the perfect location for a psychological thriller. As soon as Serena went against Aconaday, her days were numbered.

Cass messaged Tara. "Rural folk like their politics raw as hooch!" It was a stupid thing to do because, like Bob earlier, Cass stumbled on the curb. But the artist had no quick responding wife to save her. Her ankle rolled, with the full force of her weight collapsing on top of it. 'FAARK!' she cried.

Everyone in the Town Hall heard her. All except Liz mistook the meaning. Snake's grin slanted sideways. He could feel his mother beside him.

'*Cui cerca, trova; cui sècuta, vinci. Who seeks, finds; who perseveres, wins.*'

PART THREE - EARTH

This little piggy went to market;
this little piggy stayed home;
this little piggy had roast beef;
this little piggy built a mine
and this little piggy went wee, wee, wee....

CHAPTER 47

'Holy guacamole!' Cass's words galloped down the phone as she hurried through the Town Park with its landscaped brook and clusters of edible reeds providing refuge for wildlife. The halo of a full moon illuminated a lunar chart showing the way forward. Fate searched for a golden thread, and the racket of humming, hooting and motorbike frogs called to the rain gods, forcing Cass to raise her voice just to hear herself.

'It's more like *Unholy* guacamole down here!' joked Tara, but she felt the urge to cross herself against bad news. 'How was the meeting?'

'You won't believe it. No, actually. *You* will believe it! As we anticipated, Snake submitted a bid for mayor. Only one councillor ran against him, and I think that was for show because there was no dog in that fight. Poor guy!'

'What story did Snake come up with this time?'

'Oh, you know him so well. You're gonna love this. He said, and I quote, "We've had three mining companies contact us, and in the interest of business continuity, I must keep the position" Blah, blah...Sorry, I stopped listening after he mentioned mining.'

'Did you find out which ones?'

'No. He didn't go into detail, and the public only gets two questions each at the start of the meeting. Mine was, why hadn't the council issued a media statement and updated its website to show they no longer supported the Irrigation Scheme? Praise be to former Councillor Benchley!'

'What did they say to that?'

'Nothing. But they'll need to record it in the Minutes, and that's part of bearing witness. I'll have to wait until next month to poke the bear with mining questions.' said Cass.

'Is that what we're doing? Bearing witness.'

'I'm afraid so. We need to create a paper trail.'

'Okay, so in the meantime, we look. He kept the mining news real quiet during his campaign.'

'Didn't he just? I tried to pin down Templar after the meeting. He looked at me as if I was something he'd trodden in.' Cass's grin was bitter. 'He claimed it wasn't council business, and they'd received a form 21.'

'What's that?'

'A clue, Scooby-Doo! It's a clue,' said Cass in her silliest Shaggy accent.

* * *

It was late. The newly sworn-in officials had finished their monthly post-meeting, ratepayer-funded dinner. Snake and Templar headed back to the office on foot.

'What were you thinking? That hag will be on social media telling everyone!' Templar couldn't fathom his boss sometimes. Romeo would always get the top position; there was no need to bring up mining.

'What can she do? Mining owns this State. The wood hicks will become pit workers, and logging will remain as mining clears the land.'

'Who knows what she is capable of? Look where Moriarty is, and now we've got one of Farnham's crew on the council.'

'Don't worry. I know Charlotte's type. She just wants to be one of the boys. The legislation recognises extraction in the Forestry Agreement. It now falls under Federal jurisdiction. We're untouchable!'

Templar stared at the seasoned politician, unconvinced. The Earth itself contracted, curling with disdain like a wave on the ocean. For a second, James pictured himself standing on the deck of the Titanic.

Aconaday tittered. 'Muckemup will go from a food bowl to digging holes... I think we should change the name of the town.' He'd had a few celebratory whiskeys with dinner and felt a warm liquid confidence leak outward from his gut. 'Trust me, the shanty boys will sort her out soon enough if she keeps running her mouth. Farmers can either get with the program or go broke!'

Aconoday may have positioned himself as the statesman of the region. But with his own agenda, Templar was the grunt behind the fancy footwork. Cassandra Leason had thrown a curveball, requiring them to respond accordingly. James and his trusted inner circle, including Rovello, strategised at length. As the woman had arrogantly pointed out in one of her posts, legal proceedings would give her greater access to documents under disclosure laws. Instead, they devised fluid contrivances that were rudimentary but effective — beginning with an assault on freedom of the press by emailing the local journalist. Templar threatened withdrawal of all council advertising if the Tutelage published any more of her letters. He then employed a smear campaign, ensuring everyone he talked to knew he thought she was a paid activist from over east. He changed the council's Standing Orders so that public questions were required to include one's residential address, which was then recorded in the Minutes. Cass's home address was now accessible to all. They'd made her vulnerable with no blowback on themselves. It was, in part, a psychological weapon designed to intimidate her. But it would have nothing to do with them if her car caught fire one night while she slept in her bed or if someone took offence at her online antics and saw fit to tune her up. That was the way of the world. Like the colonisers responding to resistance from the natives, the proven solution for time immemorial was to crush dissent. Take one sheep — wipe out the tribe; don't have enough grain to pay the lord — raze the entire village to the ground; woman dares to speak the truth — lock her up in Bedlam!

Meanwhile, the CEO performed Olympic qualifying gymnastics to help big business wherever possible. He twisted the rules, awarded peppercorn rents and backdated documents. He used the council to underwrite private contracts and incrementally altered any application to achieve his desired outcomes. All conveniently hidden under the banner of commercial-in-confidence to shield from community backlash. James Templar hoped he was impressive enough to one day soon escape this jerkwater.

He was finally shaking off his deep inferiority complex. He saw a bigger future for himself as a member of the upper echelons of private industry.

He pinched the bridge of his nose. 'I think we should move on to the hotel project.'

'Good idea,' Snake asserted. 'Get in touch with the Indian tomorrow, see if he's finally ready... I think I'll take the back roads home.' Romeo swung his keys on the end of his finger. He was triumphant, having kept his crown — *the King of Muckemup.*

James Templar slowly escorted his boss out to his car. He'd walked to work and would return the same way, following the path along the disused train line under the full moon. He waved as Snake pulled away, muttering, 'Veni, Vedi, Vici... I'm *going* to conquer.'

Old sins make long shadows, and the silver-lit darkness witnessed the CEO manifest his unintentional hex. At that moment, Templar suddenly felt certain; the words *"So it shall be"* resounded in his head. He headed homeward with a sneer on his lips and a jaunt in his step.

CHAPTER 48

'You awake?' asked Tara

'Yeah, I got a bunch of messages from the Airbnb I clean.'

'Who, the Bintang bloke?'

'No, the other one. You'll never guess why.'

'You missed scrubbing some poo?'

'Ha-ha, hilari-*arse*. No. Towel Art!'

'What?' asked Tara.

'That's what I said too! That crazy woman must have been on Pinterest, scrolling through cabin porn. Sending me pictures at 6 AM, as if I cared too?' Cass padded around the kitchen. 'Lord, give me strength. I'm reading instructions on how to fold towels into fucking swans!'

'Well, stop doing that! Can we catch up?'

'Yes! Pleeeease rescue me!'

'I've found two of Snake's mine sites. One is near the lake.'

'Oh no!' Cass felt her heart sink.

'Afraid so. I'll give it an hour, then call Raven. Do you want to meet afterwards?'

'Can you give me two? I need to run a vacuum over this joint.'

'Sure, I'll be around then. We need staff!'

'Imagine how dangerous we'd be with staff... an office... and some funding!' Cass marvelled, the thought exciting her.

* * *

They sat together in front of Cass's clunky old laptop. Like everything she owned, it had paint smears covering it. Art was the one constant in her life. The Mines Department website showed most of Muckemup covered in a mosaic of mining tenements.

Cass whistled between her teeth. 'Would you look at that?'

'Spent the other night studying them. This restless legs thing is a killer. I woke up at two and couldn't sleep again.'

Cass commiserated. 'Oh, I remember menopause. My hot flushes were so bad I thought I was causing global warming!'

'I haven't had those yet. But my girls are seventeen and thirteen. Between the three of us, the hormones in my house could crack concrete. I slept more with two toddlers than I do now.'

'Hang in there! It's great when you get to the other side. A veil is lifted, and no fucks are given.'

'You promise? I reckon things will kick off here real soon. Tara pointed at the screen. 'It's these two. Marri Lake to the south, and the other's just north of Muckemup.'

'I promise. As you stop being eye candy, you become soul food.'

Tara recoiled in horror. 'Oh, I don't want a man!'

Cass laughed. 'I think you're pretty safe around here. Soul food is rich. Gives most men indigestion. What are they after?' she nodded at the screen.

'Silica down at Cockemup. The other is near the old Ruskin place. Remember the farm Reid bought?'

Cass certainly remembered. 'It took about seven shelf companies to track Reid's new partners to Nimbostratus Water Assets.'

'Oh yeah? Hmm... shelf companies? Well, that one is looking for lithium.'

'Right. Rare minerals. The bullshit *New Green Deal*. Do you see how close they are to water sources?'

'I noticed. So, like Acheron, Reid's avos are also a front?' surmised Tara. 'Mining doesn't care about salinity problems as much as agriculture does. I looked at Marri Lake. It's just a short distance from the Proja River — six kilometres through the State Forest, which explains our original pipeline question. Both are six k's from the nearest rivers, as the crow flies.'

'Do you think that's the sweet spot before it becomes too expensive?' Because the Irrigation Scheme pipeline doesn't run directly to any of the mines, it looks like the mining companies will pick up the tab for that one. Three mines by six kilometres, 666.... The devil's number.

'They'll get an infrastructure grant. I don't know the whereabouts of the third mine. But there's not enough surface water for mining. In a few years, they'll demand to tap into the aquifer.'

'Then they'd better pull out those regen trees. The water table has dropped significantly because of planta—Shit! That reminds me, I got notes on this stuff somewhere; hang on!' Cass disappeared into her bedroom. 'Did you speak with Raven?' she shouted, rifling through her desk.

'She doesn't get it. They had a Community Association meeting last week. She told me it will have to wait until next month.' Tara stood, stretching her limbs, and wandered outside.

'Here it is!' Cass followed her. 'Remember when I went through all the old council Minutes? I took notes. The "No Swimming" sign triggered me the other day.'

'What've you got?'

'Let me see.' Cass put on her glasses and thumbed through her notebook. *"The Water Department offered the council to lease the lake for a peppercorn rent in 2017. They go back and forth about maintenance of the dam wall, etcetera. Councillors drag their feet... wanting to avoid the added burden of ongoing costs, blah, blah. The Department then returns with a generous proposal to be responsible for all the upkeep. So, the council moves to accept the lease."* Looking at it now, it reads like theatre.'

'And then?' Tara looked at Cass expectantly.

Cass shrugged. 'And then, nothing. The sign pinged me when we had lunch there. If we can't swim, it still belongs to the Water Department, meaning there's no lease.'

'Hmm. I wonder if that's because they need to alter the drinking water catchment legislation at the State level or because they don't want the locals getting too attached to what they've earmarked as a mine's water supply?' Tara chewed on her lip, flicking cigarette ash into the garden.

'It would be great if Raven and Jack convinced their neighbours to be proactive. Get the Association to write some pointed questions on letterhead. I mean, it's their properties at stake. I'll ask questions about this lease.'

'Agreed, but I have no time next week. Can you do it?'

'Give me their number, and I'll invite Raven for a coffee under the pretext of talking art.'

Cass didn't need subterfuge. Raven sent her a Facebook message the following day asking if Jack and she could drop by after they finished their errands in town.

"We'll bring cake!" the Queen of the dark faeries texted.

CHAPTER 49

Cass published her account of the council meeting, and Aconaday was again voted mayor. She also dropped the mining bomb. As expected, it went off. Over the next few days, the comments varied from loggers blaming the conservationists for making things worse.

"See what you hippy fuckers have done? At least with logging, there was regen and forest management. All your fucking protesting has done is make things worse!"

While the environmentalists maintained outright denial, "Cass, you sound more and more like a conspiracy theorist. There have always been mining tenements here; nothing will happen."

'This town is a tough nut to crack. Can't they see they're *all* getting played by the elite?' Cass lay flat on her rug, staring at the stained ceiling. She could hear the western ringtail possum scratching and getting ready to go out for the night. It's like living with a 20-year-old night-clubber, thought Cass while doing pelvic floor exercises and listening to Tara on her phone.

'If you're brainwashed long enough, you reject any evidence of the deception. We're no longer interested in the truth. Both sides are as bad as each other. How'd you go with Raven?' After working all day and feeding her family, Tara was ironed out with just enough energy to lift her cup of tea to her mouth.

'They understand the urgency. Raven will shake down their President tomorrow. She also told me the council has a lease on the lake because it gave their community group the money to buy a pontoon.'

'Well, that's something... I have a serious question for you.'

'Okay, hit me. What's up?'

'Should we stop? Here in the west, mining is a never-ending search-and-destroy mission. Look at what happened after the destruction of Juukan Gorge. Next to nothing!'

Cass lifted her hips. 'That was a classic move. Don't ask for permission; build the fine into the costing and just do it. Then beg forgiveness .... I've thought of giving up a few times. It's like peeling an onion; the never-ending layers make me wanna cry! The way I see it, we have two choices. We keep going, knowing there will never be a ta-da we've won! Let's have a forest fiesta moment. Like those Forest Defender turkeys are trying to sell to everyone. Or—'

'Or we buy mining shares?'

'Ha, yeah!' snorted Cass. 'Or water shares.... What a fucking mess! I get why Jack speaks with the viscosity of thongs on wet tar. It's depressing.'

'I hope you mean foot thongs! I'm okay with just being a stick in the wheel, but let's have some fun where possible.' Tara was a quick-witted woman whose talents were wasted working in a country town post office.

'Definitely foot thongs!' Cass grinned and lowered her bottom to the floor. 'You're right. Let's find something to sharpen our teeth on. Just because the globalist demons will probably win doesn't mean we need to make it easy for them.'

'We'll feel better about it, and that's something—Oh, check it!' Tarra interrupted herself. 'Talking of Forest Defenders. Their grand poobah has commented on the thread where you're arguing with their pet beekeeper about mining. Catchy line, by the way: *"Credibility is all you've got."*

'It's the truth. Let me look.' Cass rolled over onto her stomach and checked her notifications. There it was,

"@Cass, I'm not sure I know what you are implying."

'Is it me, or does that sound condescending?'

'Not you.' confirmed Tara.

'I tell you! That beekeeper is a piece of work. Mansplaining to me that mining is not gonna happen. Gimme a break!'

'You know, he made his money working in the mines? When he first bought his property here, he worked loading logs onto the trucks.'

'You're kidding. He was a logger?'

'Yep. Those boys didn't like him even before he became a born-again environmentalist. His wife started beekeeping as a hobby with one hive. She fell pregnant and outgrew her beekeeper's suit, so he took over. Next thing you know, he's bought more hives, started a business, and had an epiphany that cutting down trees would impact his bottom line; only then did he make noise. I discussed the water with him and warned him about the Dilbanup boys. He didn't care, no comprehension that trees and bees require water.'

'Ah, there's nothing like a good ol' dose of hypocrisy with a side of cognitive dissonance. How muddy does that water get when one manipulative player meets another?' asked Cass.

'Oh, the partnership between him and the Forest Defenders is *all* about mutual benefits - they're forever looking for new recruits.' said Tara.

'He's pretty good at the game if he's leveraged to become their poster boy, but where are they now? I don't see them standing in the trenches to save the forest out the back of his place, or *any* forest south of Polcoa, for that matter.'

'Hmm, I wonder why that is?'

'Who knows? Anyway, I've no bandwidth for her tonight; she can wait until tomorrow. I'm off to bed. Night,'

'Yeah, good idea. Sleep on it.'

* * *

"I beat you to it!" Tara signed off with a smiling emoji, belying that she'd been up all night digging like a numbat through Forest Defender documents.

Cass woke late. She watched a New Holland honeyeater sipping morning nectar from a showy red bottlebrush outside her bedroom window, a flash of yellow on its black and white wings and whiskers under its beak.

'You're just like me!' She plucked at the thick hairs on her chin as she scrolled through Muck Unrivalled until she found Tara's response. She choked as she read her friend's closing statement.

"Some greenies are greener than others, huh? Just like some are more forthcoming than others."

She then went over all the contents; it was a long one.

'Whoa!' Cass whistled under her breath, struggling to pull herself into a sitting position as she woke up properly. Tara had found the Forest Defenders' business plan.

"Forest protection and fair, beneficial transition through farm forestry,"

'Those idiots!' Cass couldn't believe what she was reading.

"We understand that the industry is driving for more pine plantations, and we believe that pine and hardwood gums can coexist... our proposal is mutually beneficial. The program aims to establish 350,000 hectares of pine plantation and encourage 100,000 new farm forestry plantings...."

'Oh, would you look at that! They even use the term *mutually beneficial*. Good God! Establish and *encourage*? They've sold out!' Disbelief mounted as she read on.

Tara had nailed it when she wrote. "It looks like you guys want to move from forest activism to being the master controller."

From activism into corporatism under the guise of effective altruism... 'Gahh, what the—?'

"The Forest Defenders Farm Forestry plan will only be successful if it can access markets for carbon reduction through offsets. We will pursue two key pathways: The Emissions Reduction Fund and the Standard Certification Scheme."

The penny dropped. 'No wonder Sandra got worked up over that BlackMore Investment post... they want to trade in the carbon market!' Cass raced to find the original article she'd posted a few weeks ago that had set off Sandra and Rovello. She'd written about avocados being the vehicle for corporations into the water market. 'What else did I post? Ah, here it is!'

"Are pine trees the vehicle for corporations into the Carbon Market?" attached with a quote from the national broadsheet:

"Chairman of BlackMore Investments speaks with the persuasiveness of a $US10 trillion investment platform when he says the climate transition is a historic money-making opportunity."

Cass scrolled through the comments. A local had added a news article from New Zealand.

"The Carbon Group now owns most of New Zealand's agricultural land... The company removed the house and other structures when they purchased the farms and re-classified the land as non-productive farmland. The

Valuation Act excluded trees from the land's rateable value. Plantations are replacing the farmland, and the local government has to lower their rates, leaving the rest of the population to bear the burden. As the carbon price rises, agriculture won't be able to compete."

Cass recalled the loggers' protest and Snake talking to the television reporter. At the time of the event, the Premier had announced a $350 million proposal to buy farmland as part of his end of the Native Forest Logging package. The farmers laughed at the news. They wouldn't be laughing for much longer.

She scrolled through the current news. A media release from Minister Julia McDonald offered funds for southern farmers to join with research bodies to establish how the farmers could cash in on the carbon credits boom. She needed coffee.

It's a pyramid scheme! Thought Cass, checking the kitchen clock. Tara would be on her way to work. Cass cut and pasted her friend's response to the Forest Defenders' and made it a stand-alone post with all of Tara's evidence, attaching a scathing header.

"ARE FOREST DEFENDERS PART OF THE PROBLEM?"

She'd pushed the greenies too far this time. In between jobs, Cass spent her day removing the green waste from Muck Unrivalled. *Green waste* was the moniker she'd given the environmental traitors who were losing it over her post. Anger swelled as she thought toxic blooms of green scum weren't confined to rivers. The

Forest Defenders media officer brought in the big guns. The Director of a peak conservation group accused her of spreading conspiracies. Still, he didn't offer evidence to counter what Tara had outlined from their own business plan dated 2018.

'You greenies aren't delusional. You're fucking *COLLUSIONAL*!' Cass shouted as she removed him from the group, along with the others. She then noticed that Sandra Star Tree was conspicuously quiet. 'Yeah, you! I can see you there.'

CHAPTER 50

Cass sat across from Snake and Templar, among other old guard members, at the Indigenous Water Forum. She was a couple of rows behind Tara. Hearing about her great green purge from the Forest Defenders, Graeme Mantel, the organiser, sat beside her to avoid any issues.

'I thought your group had no rules.' he whispered loudly.

'I'm a graduate of the Water Department's School of Deportment.'

'Eh?' He didn't follow.

'I'm making it up as I go along!' Cass gave him a pointed look that made it clear she wasn't interested in discussing trivialities like the rules of a rough-and-tumble Facebook group.

Tara sat in the second row from the front, behind the guest speakers. She peered over the climate scientist's shoulder as he scrolled through his phone with a bored expression. He checked his emails, then Twitter, then Facebook. Inspired, she Googled his company creds while waiting for the event to start.

"It's laid out with good transparency. Unlike some, his operation appears financially sustainable with minimum government funding!"

Cass glanced to her right, smothering a laugh.

"Grant whores, you reckon? I'm curious how much $$ it took to convince Mr Climate to drive 4 hours from the city, and who paid?"

An environmentalist and academic introduced everyone to the program.

"Good question. I'll check this woman out too. If you take notes."

"Deal. Except for our fake greenies," replied Cass.

Tara looked around at the packed room; at least fifty people, including the Dilbanup boys, were in attendance. "I see them. I won't make it through the day."

The event was opened by an indigenous elder with town links, although not a Traditional Owner. She acknowledged the Country as per protocols without actually welcoming the audience.

"$1.3 billion treaty and still can't find a T.O to open a show?" texted Cass

"Elite would prefer no Traditional Owners."

"Doubt much of that money will reach those in need."

"Or maybe you want to choose them; handpick the anointed ones" In a single sentence, Tara revealed how easy it was to create a top-down hierarchy on which you could fan the flames of discontent for decades.

The Climate Scientist's 15-minute presentation followed a public servant from the Ag Department who talked of glasshouses being the future of farming. It was almost like he picked a speech arbitrarily while leaving the office. The farmers looked at him as if he had tinned spaghetti for brains.

Mr Climate opened by saying he'd tried to find river data from the Water Department just as Cass had on the fateful night she'd created Muck Unrivalled. She felt vindicated that he'd had no luck either. He questioned the tense-looking departmental staff why there wasn't anything available. They didn't respond. He asked three times, assessing their reticence with a knowing flicker.

'Seems it's worthwhile commissioning a CSIRO review. In the meantime, I've sourced figures from various other sources.' It was a pointed statement, letting the department jockeys know that someone at his level had the ways and means around their obstacles. The scientist gestured to a PowerPoint. 'This graph is from a 2017 report showing rainfall decline and land use impacts, like regen plantations, on run-off from catchments in the south. You can see here...' he hovered the cursor over the graph. 'The summer water flow in the Dilbanup River has steadily declined, effectively stopping around 2010. The underlying reason for this has ramifications for the amount of rainfall reaching the river in winter. Groundwater levels have also declined and disconnected from the river bed, so now, when it rains, it does not immediately result in a flow in the river. In 1975, the water table was half a metre underground; by 2017, it's 18 metres, and that's where the available data stops!'

Cass hurriedly typed notes into her phone.

'Rainfall has declined around 20 percent since the 1960s, and run-off into dams and aquifers has fallen by a massive 80 percent! The forests, aquifers, fauna, farmers, etcetera cannot take any more cuts. In this part of the world, you can only create reasonable quantities of potable water with a billion-plus dollars in desalination plants. De-growth, not expansion, will help the status quo, but science tells us that rainfall will continue to decline in this region. The status quo is an ongoing disaster. We're headed towards the most expensive water in the world. We must change how we allocate water to manage this crisis. Believe me when I say the political pressure will be enormous. I encourage the people of the south to give water traders all the encouragement they need to leave!'

'Okaaay. That's all the time we've got! Thank you... for that sobering analysis. Do we have any questions?' The facilitator searched the room for raised hands. There were none.

"I can't bear it anymore!" Tara messaged Cass soon after the scientists finished painting a bleak future.

"No probs, go! I'm staying. Catch you on the flip side."

"Let's meet up for a swim at Marri Lake tomorrow."

"Sounds good, 2 PM."

The artist searched for the Aboriginal woman when they broke for lunch; she'd seen they were Facebook friends. She found the Elder deep in conversation with Benno and Craig. Cass pulled a face and did an about-turn towards the buffet. Standing across from her was a pair of CEOs. The one for the Irrigation Scheme looked nervous. Graeme Mantel had told her he'd received an email from him that morning, saying as much. He was good-looking, a face with "*frontman*" written all over it and a curtain of shiny brown hair flopping into his eyes. The other was Templar. He looked smitten.

Cass watched with interest as she piled sandwiches onto her plate. The men were chalk and cheese. Oh, hun, you're never going to be one of them. You don't spend your weekend doing exciting enough, borderline dangerous sports, thought Cass. Suddenly, she felt she was being watched and looked around to find Sandra Star Tree's gaze intently focused on her. Cass had piled enough food on her plate for three people, stepping away from the word '*SPY! SPY! SPY!*' shouted in her head.

The event was long but insightful. Cass asked the law professor about the springs he'd mentioned in his presentation. He informed her they kept the original map of the springs under lock and key in the Water Department's head office. In return, she shared her discovery of Gio's Crown land lease not being listed at the Land Office.

Her revelation surprised him. 'Sounds like you need a lawyer to dig around.'

After lunch, one of the Ag Minister's pretty boys manoeuvred to sit beside Cass, clearly missioned with reconnaissance.

'Did you draw the short straw?'

He missed her jibe and rattled on about how unfair her online commentary was and how underfunded the department was. Cass made all the right sympathetic sounds while thinking about how she'd earned herself a bucket of wine after getting through today.

* * *

'Look here, lady, we don't like this stone-throwing! We did everything with the best of intentions.'

Cass saw a man bee-lining for her while she filled a doggy bag for her dinner. Chardonnay with cold sausage rolls was on the dinner menu. 'Ah, best of intentions! How many times do we need saving from those?' In a bored tone, she took a bite of smoked salmon and cream cheese blini. It was too early for avocados.

'I don't know what you mean.'

He looked familiar. But old white guys all looked the same. 'Stolen Generation doesn't ring a bell?' she asked.

'This is different.' he argued.

'Hardly. You're still trying to take something that doesn't belong to you. What's your name?'

'Silas Rosetti,'

'Oh right, one of the Scheme Directors. I rest my case.' Cass flicked her thick hair with contempt and was about to walk away when something stopped her. Remorse was scribed into the man's features; she'd seen that aged face somewhere before.'

'Silas? Really? Your name's Silas, as in "man of the forest"?'

'I know what it means,' he replied gruffly.

'Oh, good. I'm glad. Do you also know that we've met before, old man of the forest?'

Silas Rosetti peered closer at the woman opposite him. He wasn't familiar with this agitator. 'I don't think so,' he said coolly.

'Oh yes, we have!' Cass waved her pancake at him. 'Outside the post office one morning. Don't you remember? Born in your bedroom, farmed potatoes. That's right! I recall it now, the tractors and chains... the cries that trees make when they hit the ground.' Cass watched the colour drain as Silas flinched. He turned his grey head away, but he couldn't move. Rooted like a stone, she cornered him and was prepared to finish what he'd begun.

'Ah, I see you do remember! Well, well. Chance isn't a blind man, after all, Silas of the forest.'

'We didn't know' Silas's throat tightened, and he bowed his head.

Her glare held him trapped, almost hypnotised. 'You can't fool me. I heard your confession, remember? What are you doing, old man? You have more than enough money. Is this the legacy you want? Destroying the trees isn't a sufficient burden for you? You want to carry the guilt of the water too?' Her disgust drilled into him with the accuracy of a dentist.

He glanced sideways at the woman; Silas hadn't recognised earlier, because she'd covered her hair the morning they'd met. He didn't dare analyse what compelled him to share with her then. But now her hair was free like albino snakes on Medusa hissing at him, *"LIES! LIES! LIES!"* Terrified by the vision, Silas pushed past her and scuttled away like a crab.

CHAPTER 51

'How was it?' Tara dipped her toes into the cold water.

'Long. The Dilbanup boys prattled on about desal being the solution. They looked like idiots following your climate guru. He'd just finished spelling out desal is at least a billion-dollar exercise.'

'What? Eighty million isn't enough for them?'

'Probably not. I don't think it will be sufficient for the current Irrigation Scheme, let alone building a bunch of desalination plants. While investigating the lease on this lake, I found an article from 2012. Back then, it cost $30 million for a 50-kilometre pipeline to top up the domestic supply dams.'

'Yeah, we had a drought. Water was piped in from Bellenup.' said Tara.

'Well, when the Ag Department tries to convince us in 2022 they'll build 250 kilometres of pipeline for $80 million, I call bullshit. A decade ago, it would have cost $140 million!' Cass threw her towel on a bench. The council had given the locals a beach load of sand as well as the pontoon. She noticed the *"No Swimming"* sign was still in place.

'Well, we don't know because Julia MacDonald has her fat bum on the business plan. Pfft, commercial-in-confidence! What competitors? The Feds gave them a million bucks for that alone. What do you reckon that buys you?'

'Good question. I'd almost screw my way to seeing those business plans, all three of them! My guess is it shows they intend to separate water from land.'

'Oh! The water's fresh. When we get to the pontoon, I'll tell you my news!' Tara was wearing boardies and an ebony rash vest. She was already in the water, melding into the glowing, almost black-green liquid. Cass was in a blue one-piece. She made her way to the shallows.

'Whoa! Fresh?' Cass convulsed in alarm. 'It's frigging Wim Hof!'

Tara laughed and duck-dived to reappear further out. 'MacDonald's now talking about rolling the scheme out in stages as funding becomes available. I'll race you out there!'

The pontoon was floating across the far side of the lake after unmooring from its anchor overnight.

'That's so they can hide the cost blow-out!' It's their third bloody business plan in five years!' Cass shouted back. She stepped gingerly through the water until thigh-deep. Holding her nose, she plunged below. Silver bubbles ran upwards over her body and face. The world blurred, dark and ghostly. Cass unfurled and swam as far as she could, her lungs burning before she broke the surface for air.

Tara had already reached the raft and was lying flat in the sunshine.

'So what did you find?' Cass hauled her dripping self next to her friend. She was cold, wet but felt refreshed.

Tara didn't open her eyes. 'You took your time.'

'I'm unfit. Sadly, shit-posting on Facebook isn't a workout.' her Celtic skin goose-bumped, and her extremities turned blue-white.

'Ha! You'd have a six-pack by now if it were! So, I checked who funded Mantel's event.'

'Oh yeah? Who was it? They over-catered. I took home a mountain of leftovers.'

'A Trust Fund coughed up the cash, and the only Trustee I could find is the woman who was yesterday's facilitator.' Tara teased, her voice a lazy drawl.

Cass turned toward her friend, lifting her hand to shield her eyes. 'Oh? And would she have any connection to our Forest Defender friends?'

'You're no fun! She does... and has experience creating the type of forest farms we read about in their business plan.'

Cass sat up. 'Enough suspense. Tell me!'

Tara laughed. 'Alright, I'll put you out of your misery. Here's what I've got; it's fascinating. She's an environmental consultant, recently resigned from the Forestry Board and is a Trustee, the *only* one I could find, of a fund called Hookemup Trust, which has its finger in many pies. But I couldn't find them listed with the Securities Commission or the Tax Office.'

'How's that work? Based overseas, maybe? By many pies, how many are we talking about?'

'More than a baker's dozen! Hookemup has been involved with shaping environmental policy in Western Australia for the last twenty years and not just WA, but all of Australia. From the blue gum, managed investments back in 09—'

'Holy Cow, I read about that!' spluttered Cass. 'A four billion dollar Ponzi scheme! That's how I connected MacGovern's $350 million for buying prime ag land for pine plantations... the only other plantations I'd seen down here were regen karri and blue gums. Digging into that is what threw up carbon credits — the next rort! Except for this time, they won't collapse because they've got the Federal Clean Energy Regulator to underwrite it... to the tune of billions!'

'Yep, billions. In the double digits. A green energy wet dream! Within a decade, carbon credits will make the blue-gum-managed investments look like child's play. This time, the stakes are higher. While it can't fail financially, we got stupidity like virtual carbon credits being issued without even digging a hole and clearing permits granted to remove 20 acres of trees on 500 hectares to replant malee gums for carbon offsets. What we've got is a recipe for disaster because the biosphere is the only thing left to collapse!'

'Don't worry. I reckon we'll be killing each other before then!'

Capitalism was brilliant at co-opting anything that resisted it. Like much of the broader environmental movement, carbon credits and "green" energy weren't immune. Globalisation enabled business as usual on a massive scale, and it had finally caught up with this insular corner of the world. Muckemup, with its rustic population and remnants of timeworn magic still living deep in the forest, were under attack, and neither would survive for much longer, for greed and self-interest had trapped them all. While the two swimmers sunned themselves like lizards, a gentle breeze overheard their conversation as it dried the moisture from their skin. Swirling free, the water-soaked air absorbed their gossip and passed the news back to the lake. The wildlife fell silent to listen. Trees rasped, and the water trembled. A deliberate current rippled outwards from the raft. Only from a bird's-eye view was the movement visible. This was the real bush telegraph, and unlike humans, nature would not go quietly.

* * *

'Oi! Can't you read?'

'Huh? What?' Tara looked at the worker dressed in long pants and a hi-vis shirt, shouting at them as she emerged from the shallows like a shiny black seal.

'The sign says no swimming. That's a $200 fine' The man put his arm into the sleeve of petty authority and pulled out his infringement book.

'Yeah? Then why's there a pontoon?' Cass stood on the waters edge wringing her hair, and jumping on one foot to remove the water trapped in her ear.

Tara wasn't in the mood for random men throwing their weight around. 'You got some identification on you, please?'

'I work for the council.'

'Then you'll have ID and probably know the council paid for the pontoon and the beach you're standing on. So, if swimming is prohibited, and yet here we have an untethered pontoon. It sounds like the council has a public liability problem.'

Cass took the baton from the postmistress. 'Uh-huh, that's right! I'm sure there'd be a maximum distance on those things, so kids don't drown trying to reach it.'

Tara nodded. 'I'd imagine so, Cass.' Cold water dripped from her blonde spikes as she confronted the intruder. 'Did you install that pontoon? Because we're debating on writing a formal complaint.'

He looked from one woman to the other, trying to comprehend what was happening. A pair of snapping turtles wasn't what he expected. He pointed at Cass. 'I know you!' His bravado slipped; the council worker didn't get paid enough to take on a woman who had mastered the verbal shovel hook, let alone two of them.

'Maybe I should write a post about it.' Cass added maliciously, giving him an *"I dare you"* face as the women sauntered past to grab their towels with casual confidence. Righteous satisfaction squirmed on their lips.

Tara watched the man's stiff strides as he retreated without another word. 'Looks like the council lied to Raven, and there is no lease.'

'I could go a cup of tea. Let's visit and ask... and see if they know anything about this Hookemup Trust.'

CHAPTER 52

Weekends go too fast, thought Tara, peering into the bathroom mirror first thing Monday morning. She patted concealer over the worst of the violet shadows under her eyes and a couple of hormonal spots on her chin.

War paint was a perceptive description of makeup. Indigenous Americans once painted their faces to rally themselves for battle and to frighten enemies. Some people think women use cosmetics as a weapon to get men's attention and more privileges. Maybe when she was younger, Tara had unwittingly done the same. But as she grew, she'd found she developed a thing she called standards. Makeup was now used as camouflage to fit into societal norms to prevent raising the alarm of her dissent. For two types of women stood out when the male gaze inspected the low-security prisoners in their patriarchal system. Those who were subjectively attractive and those who rejected the efforts of feminine accoutrements. Like many women, Tara's first action when arriving home from work was to remove her bra. Sometimes the urge to escape was so strong that she took off the offending constraint while walking through the front door. She regarded her relationship with her lingerie the same way she considered her relationship with her boss. In short, she put up with it.

Life stretched thin as a rake between navigating an increasingly erratic boss, caring for kids, checking on her mother and moonlighting with Cass as Muckemup's version of Erin Brockovich.

The logistics of being a single parent are complex. Juggling work with after-school activities and organising lifts for the kids. Weekends full of chores, washing, cooking, car repairs, cleaning and gardening until exhausted but ready to start again with a new week. Tara often collapsed into bed physically beat, to find her mind had clocked on for overtime with doubts and mother guilt preventing sleep. Researching policy management plans became a relaxing distraction.

She critically assessed her facial features in the bright morning light, applied a lashing of Revlon's Rum Raisin and blew herself a kiss. 'You'll do!'

* * *

'I saw ol' Camel Tow hooking up Andy's car out on Barker Road the other morning. It didn'a look real good. Is he okay?' Miro had stopped to chat while collecting his mail.

'He was lucky, walked away—a few bruises and shook up, but fine.' Tara was sorting shelves in the mid-morning lull. The post office provided various services beyond mail. They also refilled gas bottles and sold hardware. Not Bunnings, but a good enough selection that often saved locals a 200-kilometre round trip to the coast. There was plenty of flotsam, and dusting was a Sisyphean task, like painting Sydney Harbour Bridge.

'Woz he comin' back from the city?'

Tara knew Miro picked up more than most. She stopped cleaning and turned to the bus driver 'Universe, giving him a gentle tap, tap. You know how it is, Uncle.'

He grunted, then said, 'Yer wanna have lunch? Something I wanna run past yer. Meet at Bazza's in an hour?'

'Sounds good. Andy should be in soon.' Tara said as Miro left, squeezing past Pam Diaz.

The woman enquired about the Makita chainsaw special. Despite the offer finishing a few weeks ago and there being no Makitas in stock, Andy had kept the promotion up, saying it encouraged the punters to ask questions.

Tara nodded. 'I know what the poster says, but can you see it here? It also says, available until 30th September; today is the 21st of October.' she pointed to the fine print. Pam didn't care. Tara bit her inner cheek in frustration, thinking the woman was as dumb as a box of hammers. 'Ah, here's Andy! Can you please help Mrs Diaz? Maybe you can recommend something similar since we don't have any specials left in stock.' With relief, Tara handed the customer over, giving her boss a knowing look. A few people were waiting patiently at the service counter. Fifteen minutes later, she found Andy standing in the back.

'Heya, would you like a coffee?' she offered while packing away the duster.

He spat at her from the other side of the cupboard. 'I should kick you in the cunt!'

Stunned, she closed the door, noting a spray of foaming sputter on the beige laminate. 'I beg your pardon?'

Andy's pupils were empty black holes. His lips cracked, and white spiders' eggs of spittle were trapped in the corners of his mouth. Tara could smell his tumorous breath. Her eyes widened, and the hair on the back of her neck stiffened. She carefully took a step back.

'You foisted that fucking retard onto me on purpose.'

The postmistress gauged how far gone he was, feigning a calm she wasn't feeling. 'Do you mean a customer, Andy? Yes, so you could help her... I'd explained the offer was over...remember, you said leaving the promotion up would encourage punters to buy other things.'

He wasn't listening. *'IN THE FUCKING CUNT!'*

Fear prickled down her spine, and adrenaline pulsed through her, making her palms clammy and overstimulating her saliva glands. She swallowed. He was cooked! Tara's heart started thumping, and her jaw tingled as if someone was driving ice picks into her back teeth. She registered the message; it was fight or flight.

The door buzzed, and she heard it urgently calling her, *'Ding, Dong! Run, girl. Run!'* She backed away, not taking her eyes off him for a second until she reached the shop front. A couple approached the service desk, unaware of the hostilities just metres away. Tara moved quickly, greeting them without seeing. Her face was ashen underneath her tan.

'Andy will be out to serve you in a minute.' She smiled tightly, grabbed her handbag from below the counter, and fled.

* * *

'He did *what?*' Horrified, Cass steered Tara into her house and plopped her onto the crying couch. 'Take a seat. Let me put the kettle on. Are you okay?'

Tara's voice quivered. 'Yeah... No... I need to message Miro. We were 'sposed to meet for lunch.' She shook with emotion. Now that she knew she was safe, she could no longer bear the wincing burn of held-back tears and burst into hot, angry sobs.

Cass recognised the signs of aftershock and raced to her room, grabbing a woollen throw off the end of her bed to wrap around her friend's shoulders. 'Here, give me your phone. I'll message Miro and let him know you're here. Do you want me to invite him over? I could scrape a ploughman's platter together.'

Tara's chest heaved, and a wave of nausea swept over her. She shook her head weakly, handing Cass the phone.

CHAPTER 53

Cass wound down the car's back window, and her loose hair swished into her face. 'I explained to my gallery owners what it's like down here. They said the only two things they'd heard about Muckemup were meth and incest.'

They were bouncing along the dirt roads west of Muckemup with Miro at the wheel of his rust-beaten Jeep. he hadn't caught up with Tara the day she left the Post Office, leaving the two women alone to convict Andy for his offences. He examined her at the bus stop the next day but didn't ask questions. No one in town did. They didn't need to.

A few weeks later, soon after Minister MacDonald finally released the damming CSIRO review of the Dilbanup River, Miro rang her. 'Tara, I wanna show yer something. Bring your feather-footed friend.'

He now glanced at Cass through the rearview mirror. 'There must be some drawbacks, too.'

'What about when the cops used to be the dealers?' added Tara from the front seat.

Miro veered onto a narrow unmarked track off Big Ben road, and the forest closed over them.

'Let me guess. Was Logan mayor? I never tire of these views. The colours smell of peppermint and mushrooms.' Cass breathed in the spicy earthiness.

Miro pulled over, and they all got out, following him into the forest. They silently walked a distance before he halted at a clearing by a creek and gave instructions. 'My sound is Yingarda Miro Kalinga. Use your name; first, grab a touch of earth.' He showed, picking up a handful of the ancestor-rich soil. 'Rub it under your arm and throw it into the water. This is calling out. Notifying the spirit of the place that you're here... you're asking for permission, not sneaking about. The land thinks you're up to no good if you don't tell it you're there.'

They took a handful of dirt and reached under their shirts to rub it in their armpits.

'Tara Diara Laurel.'

'Seriously, Tara Diara?' Cass giggled as Tara tossed her soil into the steam. They all watched the brown crumbs of dirt hit the lethargic soak of dark water.

'I know, right? It was a thing down here in the seventies, along with fondue parties and being able to buy a house for ten grand. I went to school with five sisters, each called Belle, or a version of it. Belle, Isabelle, Annabelle, Rosabelle, and something like Trixibelle. I can't remember now?' She squatted and washed her hand in the creek, wiping it dry on her jeans.

'You don't need to; just call her Belle.' That's hilarious! Like George Foreman. Sorry, Miro—'

Miro's face had stiffened to stone; he shook his head. 'No man ever teaches you birds' respect?' Under his perfectly feathered brows, thick as crows wings, his eyes glittered cold and dark as an onyx talisman.

Cass was still laughing. 'Afraid not! My granny raised me with an Irish contempt for most men... Cassandra

Leason of Muckemup.' She threw the earth she'd been rubbing into her hands while talking, inoculating herself and infusing her essence for the land to recognise her.

Miro grunted in a language older than legend and led them along the creek. The only path through the long grass was the ones their boots made, leaving their wake like a flotilla of vessels in still water.

'Isn't this out by the back of Acheron Avocados?' asked Tara.

'I'm gonna show yers.' said Miro.

The forest ended abruptly. Before them was a wall of dirt stretching for kilometres on either side and reaching over twenty metres high.

Tara gasped. 'What the—?'

'Hidden in plain sight' They both stared in awe. 'Have you climbed up to see what's over on the other side?' Cass asked their guide.

'Of course. They're terraforming for that dam. Two years of planning to this stage. Now there are helicopters in and out at all hours.'

'Hang on. We've just had the CSIRO confirm there's no water.' Tara clambered up the hill. 'I want to see it!'

The old horse-whisperer clipped a chuckle as the pair clumsily heaved themselves up the ridge. His voice dropped lower than a tawny frogmouth. 'Yeah, I know they're Wadjella Earth Sisters. Desperate times, Boodja.'

'Get down!' Tara tugged urgently on Cass's trousers as she reached the top. Lying on their bellies, they dragged themselves up to the crest. It looked like a construction site, abuzz with activity. The workers had cleared trees and scraped the topsoil back to the bare red earth far as the eye could see. A massive concrete pipeline ran directly below them. Tara pulled a small pair of binoculars from her top pocket and trained them onto an excavator to their right.

'They're unearthing springs. There's water everywhere. Check it!' She handed the lenses to Cass, who was filming the scene on her phone.'

'Jeez, you're geared up like the SAS?'

'Meh, I was bird watching this morning.' replied Tara.

'Unemployment suits you.' They watched the scene until Miro's whistle called them. 'I forgot about him.'

Tara shook her head. 'He only brought us here! C'mon, let's go!' They slid back down on their bottoms. The dirt mountain was steep; staying low kept them out of sight and prevented them from falling head-first down the hill.

Miro gave a rundown of what he knew on the way home. 'The rodeo bull is trying to get back into the gate. Mega-dam. That river report ain't gonna stop 'em.' They're after that underground spring that feeds Fount'n Pool.'

'That creek they were digging up looked spring-fed. How many bores did you count, Tara?' asked Cass, looking over the footage on her phone.

'I think that's Three-mile creek. About five. Don't they need EPA approval for something this size?'

'Refer by self-assessment,' said Miro.

'That's insane! Who's going to refer themselves?'

'Remember that law professor I spoke with at Graeme Mantel's talkfest? The one who showed us how to see water lines on the satellite maps?'

'Nah, I'd left by then.'

'Okay. Well, he also mentioned that the Water Department has an original map of all the springs in the area. It's on microfiche, kept in a vault at the Head Office.'

'Yer? Mayor Snake woulda seen that map.'

'Miro, you're a genius! Of course, that's it! Who used to be the Water Minister?' asked Tara.

'And ran around the bush down here shooting anything that moved.' Miro glanced across at her, they exchanged a look. 'The spring doesn't start at Fount'ns but comes out of a hill across the road. I did some work for the old farmer there once, long ago. He told me they wanted to buy his land, and he would'na sell. Nice bloke, a quiet man... not a redneck. It was a long time ago. I remember him saying four megs of water passed through a day,'

'Not anymore.' replied Tara.

'True dat. I gotta go to the end of the pool to listen to the water.' Their seatbelts safely trapped them all in the moment as Miro swerved past trees. 'Mining companies like this, too, disturbing acid sulphate in the soil relieves heavy metals and all this drainage into underground water to wash away contaminates. Twonk is definitely not happy about water contamination. I must look at yer Irrigation Scheme map.'

'Who's Twonk? You're welcome anytime. I've got the original ones Tara's mum lent us.' replied Cass.

'Twonk, he frog bruther. Eh, good on Marion! She'd know all the creeks. Taught me, son, too... that was a long, *long* time ago.' Miro drawled. 'She knows one of the most important aspects of biological water stability in science and in our Lore. It's time that people in power treat cultural custodians as the first scientists, not just tokenistic knowledge holders.' Tom Cochrane's classic "Life is a Highway" came on the radio, and Miro smiled. The world liked to joke with him even when life wasn't funny. 'I think about two waters. They'll want one for ripping off farmers and a different one for mining. Who controls the water, controls the mining. One dam to rule 'em all!'

'One river to bring them, and in its depths bind them...' Cass chanted in Tolkienesque tones from the backseat.

Tara glanced over her shoulder and rolled her eyes, then dialled up the volume on the radio.

CHAPTER 54

The elite were not used to public scrutiny. Corruption was so commonplace that covering their tracks or arses never crossed their minds as they built their many interconnected empires — no need for a formal conspiracy when interests converge. What outcomes do you expect when the same key players are involved in every committee and club, and have the same interests?

'I see that two-bit slum lord has unblocked me.'

'Which one is that?' Tara was wiping her kitchen down with bleach, her phone nestled in the crook of her neck.

'That farm manager with his 13 Pacific Islanders squeezed into a two-bedroom dump,' said Cass.

'I didn't know he'd blocked you. Funny, I've noticed he and Pat Murphy have been more active online recently. Talking up Murf's expansion into the composting business at the old mill.'

'Yeah? He got on his high horse about that meme I posted after Prince Phillip died. As if dying at 99 is some great tragedy. Jeez, for his last six months, the footmen propped up the old bugger like *Weekend at Bernie's*.'

'Oh, that's right! I remember. You set off all the closet royalists.' Tara laughed. 'I wonder why he has unblocked you after all this time? They're connecting for self-gain. It looks like Murphy is taking his farm waste.'

'Pfft... sorted the wheat from the chaff. That little man spoke as if he spent all his childhood Christmases at

Balmoral! I thought the mill was contaminated and not functional for years.'

'Yeah, it is. They used to treat wood with arsenic and pentachlorophenol. Murphy must have asked the owners. The timing's weird. He's sticking his head above the parapet like he wants us all to know he's there.'

'Penta-chloro-what-all?' asked Cass.

'Chlorophenol. PCP dioxins are worse than arsenic. They treated the logs by soaking them in baths of an oil and PCP mixture. Infusing it into the wood with heat and pressure. For thirty years, the onsite furnace cooked the preservative deep into the grain of the logs. I remember Snake making a song and dance about how it was a sad day when they turned off the furnace.'

'That's messed up. Back east, I used to be part of a community garden. They organised a "War Against Waste" excursion a few years back. Visited a recycling plant and compost business. Commercialisation involves jumping through many hoops. No way the government will let you set up shop somewhere full of arsenic and shit. Tell 'em they're dreamin'.'

'I'm not telling him anything. He's a hard case.'

'Oh, right, *that* kind of Irish. He and Farmboy will make a charming pair then.'

'Hmm... it certainly smells like they're cooking more than compost.'

'Speaking of over east. I've found a Federal Senator to table Irrigation Scheme questions for us. We just need to write them.'

Tara screwed the lid back on the bleach bottle. 'Done!'

CHAPTER 55

Liz watched the Acheron video on Cass's phone. 'Is Matt Farnham aware of this?'

'I don't know. I haven't spoken to him since the CSIRO review. The farmers are basking in the glory of vindication. Should we send it to him?' asked Cass.

'Why not? Won't be so easy to write that footage off as a rant from a crazy woman. What do we know about Acheron?' asked Tara.

The three women set themselves around Cass's table with their laptops open. Cass and Tara had taped Marion's maps to the wall. They now had 250 kilometres of pipeline pinned with coloured yarn and a patchwork of mining concessions marked in different coloured highlighter pens.

'It's interesting which properties don't have tenements over them,' Liz traced her ruby-tipped finger along the black line of the highway to a block of land near the old Ruskin farm that she and Bob had called home for thirty years. After the mayor spilled the beans in the council chambers, she'd done her own investigations and had discovered an exploration licence sitting over the top of her property, too. She was in the same boat as the residents of Cockemup.

'It's hard to ignore that there's nothing over Snake's joint, although that's probably all that's keeping Mum's place safe,' said Tara.

'For now... Acheron is six kilometres from the Dilbanup and another six from Gio Luciano's place, with his unlawful water title. I see our local member, Alice Kennedy, is to head another bloody community reference group since the CSIRO has confirmed there's no water.' Cass called out as she organised refreshments.

'Remind me again, how is it illegal?' asked Liz.

'You can only own as much water as your dams can store. Luciano has a licence for 1,000 meg and a dam that only holds about half that! I wonder how the Water Department worked that one out?' answered Cass.

'That's how you separate water from land — create carryover water and water banking. Remember, just after the CSIRO review, Farnham's lot posted about the Department of Ag and Water having a *"secret meeting"* out at Acheron.' said Tara.

'Yep. I don't envy Alice one bit. MacGovern will want to use farmers to push it ahead despite what that review says.' shouted Cass, still fluffing in the kitchen.

'The latest gossip is that Gio and Worm have resigned from the Irrigation Scheme Board, claiming someone tricked them,' said Liz.

'Puhleeze, who tricked them, his dad? I don't believe it for a second. What's the bet they're now in cahoots with Acheron?' I tried to find Gio's Crown land lease on the Land Office records, but no joy. So, I called them and listened to this rubbish... The woman tells me it's not digitised because it's historical and, therefore, not considered relevant. But for $150 per hour, they can search for it.' Cass placed a coffee plunger and plate of brownies on the table.

'I'd have thought any current lease would be relevant. I couldn't believe it when I read that Matt Farnham wrote "There's room for both farming and mining." said Tara.

'Matt doesn't know shit from apple sauce! And Gio's lease is not from the last decade, let alone last century.'

'They're pirates! It's near impossible to keep up with all the threads of deception, let alone stop them. I can't believe none of the councillors warned us.'

They all heard the catch in Liz's throat. She sniffed hard and blinked to prevent the tears that threatened to flow. Her property backed onto State Forest, where the bush she deeply loved was struggling. It hadn't been a very dry winter, but even the Balgas now languished. That meant the mycelium fungus, an essential part of the grass trees' life support system, was drying out and becoming dormant. Nature was unravelling, and it was breaking her heart.

'Oh Liz, I know it's shitty! Here, have one of my special choccy slices. It will make you feel better.' Cass proffered forward the plate of treats.

'I think only two councillors knew, and both have shares in the Scheme.' Tara raised an eyebrow, 'Here we go! Talking of special, it says, "Acheron is a *Special Purpose Vehicle*, they're leasing—'

'What's that mean?' Having composed herself, Liz took a slice.

'It's business-speak for creating a private consortium for a specific project. Like building an airport. They subcontract builders, plumbers, sparkies, etcetera.

Guaranteed every time a few subbies go to the wall, but by the time they'd even consider taking legal action, the job's over, and the corporation is dissolved. There's no one left to sue.'

'Not that the smaller players could afford to sue, anyway; they're bankrupt. So, Acheron reckons they've got access to about 11 gigs, separate from the Regent Brook dam.' Tara stood up to push down the plunger and poured everyone coffee. 'Mmm... yum Cass!' her mouth was full of cake.

'Well, that differs a fair bit from the water register. It has them here at three gigs from a catchment, with only two and a half available. They need to employ some new number-crunchers in that joint!'

Tara scanned Acheron's website. 'They've also got a contract with the landowner for half a gig from his orchard next door.'

'That's Ricco Conti's farm. One of the largest growers in the State! Why would he give them over sixty percent of his water?' asked Liz, looking at the screen of her old hand-me-down Apple laptop her kids had passed on when the cursor broke. It irritated her every time she used it, which thankfully wasn't often, so she made do. Life was a sticky wicket, full of make-dos.

'Maybe he fell for the investors' bait of 300 hectares of avocados, thinking he'd profit no matter what. They default. He takes the land back with the orchard?' Cass reasoned.

'Then what? They convince him to pay a million plus for the dam by letting him sell the gravel they dig out.

All the best cons offer you something upfront.... to pull you in. I don't know? Look here. It says they only need to grow 50 hectares to meet the lease agreement.' added Tara.

'Then I reckon it's more likely that he is in on it one hundred percent. I'll ask Farnham when I send him the video.'

'Ha-ha. He thought he'd stitch them up when they're pulling one over on him.' Liz giggled.

Tara slanted her head shrewdly. 'You can't con an honest man. Nothing better than having a company his size screaming for water before the next election. *Especially* after everyone rejected their Regent Brook angle by voting out Moriarty, oh, jeez—!' She exclaimed, chuckling too.

'What is it?' asked Cass and Liz in concert.

'They've recruited Stamos Price onto some Board of Advisors they've put together.'

'Who's that?' asked Cass.

'They call him the *Great White Pointer.*' Tara laughed harder as if the appointment was funny.

'What's so amusing about that? He's one of Australia's wealthiest men. This is terrible!' Liz was horrified but also still half giggling.

'Uh-huh, we got the apex predators circling— I don't know. Wh-what's in those brownies, Cass?' Tara wiped her face. She felt weirdly euphoric.

A wicked smile grew on their host's lips as she took another bite of her cake. 'The ingredient that makes them special is just a smidge of mull butter.' Cass squeezed her forefinger and thumb together. 'I thought we could use the mood lift. We obviously aren't going to beat these guys with money. So, we need to tap into our creativity and outwit them!'

'Y-you what?' Tara's mouth formed an "O" of astonishment as she looked from Cass to Liz, unsure of what to do, but her brain felt a pleasant buzz and looking at Liz's shocked face, she again launched into laughter.

'Nooo?' Liz's hand flew to her mouth, and her eyes wide, making her look like a Pekingese dog before she too burst into a fit of hysterics.

'They can have beers, bongs and bitches. We got coffee, cookies and witches!'

'That's *Blokes,* Beers and Bitches.' Tara clarified between guffaws.

Cass shrugged. 'Whatever. Ours is better! I'm visualising us as the three Fates in Shakespeare, but instead of a caldron, we mix our spells on the internet. Eye of newt and toe of frog....'

'Oh dear, you *are* nuts! I haven't been stoned since I was at university. But I agree it's time we held the Talking Stick for a while. Oh dear, I need to stop laughing, or I'll wet myself.' Liz clutched her pearls and disappeared down the hall, cackling like an enchantress.

'Good thing Bob is picking her up', Tara, gave Cass an admonishing look.

'What? You told me you wanted to have some fun! We need to use our strengths and make some magic.'

'Getting wasted wasn't what I had in mind. I don't believe in that hokum, Talking Stick! Hmpff... what will we do, lecture them into oblivion?'

'Wash your mouth out! There's a good reason older women are feared. We can see the truth. Art is magic. The same goes for anything creative, poetry... writing. It's the science of manipulating words or images to change people's consciousness, and that's the ultimate goal of our posts. Soft power. I mean, look at that video of the dam they're building... it just needs context so people understand.'

'Well, we certainly need to find a way to do power differently. Imperialism is *soo* has been.' Liz returned, cheerfully swivelling her hands and weaving her hips like a belly dancer. 'How about a song?'

'Music definitely counts! Arrgh, how about a sea shanty for them thar pirates, Liz?' joked Cass.

'Oh, that's perfect! Just a minute.' Liz held up a manicured finger, then fumbled about in her handbag and produced a small black box, which she brandished theatrically while waving her free hand above it like a magician with a wand over a tophat so that her audience of two half-expected her to produce a white rabbit out of thin air. She slowly opened the box and, with a hooker's knack for burlesque, revealed a harmonica. She blew into the mouthpiece.

Surprised, Cass clapped her hands. 'Oh, you're a musician. Yes! Yes! Go, girl!'

Liz warmed up the mouth organ by inhaling and exhaling a mournful, tinny vibration and bent the notes as best she could. Then she hit on a folk ballad.

Tara tapped her foot for rhythm and then suddenly jumped up. 'I got it!' She began clicking her fingers. *Hey, ho! The name of the ship was the I.S.C .... There was no water for the barrel. Farmers, greenies, frowns on furrows. Three business cases along the way, ten million dollars still to pay! Nothing for the trees!'*

Liz picked up the melody and quickened her tempo.

'Hey, ho. Things in motion, state of play, keep the money anyway. Hey, ho! The name is dead, but we'll keep intent instead. Minister MacDonald can stay in bed. Now it's all on Kennedy's head. Hey, ho! No EPA, too much trouble on the verges, they say—'

'Oh my! You two are naturals!' Cass's face beamed with delight, and she picked up a teaspoon to tap on the table's edge. *'Hey, ho! We'll give farmers a meter, so they'll think the numbers are neater!'*

'...Count for every millimetre! Hey, ho! Suck the streams dry. Drought-proofing scams, no rain from the sky.' Tara was in fine form, slapping her thigh and belting out her improvised lyrics.

Liz's eyes shimmered with laughter as music spilled from her jaws. She played with gusto, and sound surged and frothed around the room like water, remembering where it came from.

Again, Tara took the cue. Her voice was honey and hemlock. *'The water's just goods and chattel. File yer form at the Shire chapel. Hey, ho! It's on Alice's head when rich farmers are in bed. Selling water, no avo's in the shed. When the forest is dry and dead... Hey, ho! Couldn't make this shit up. No standing there with your cup. We'll be wanting more for the trees. The forest and the fucking bees! Hey, ho! How does this fit—?'*

'Well, it doesn't when the environment's shit!' Cass was now dancing around the tale. The three women creased up and flopped into their chairs, high-fiving each other.

Liz gasped for breath. 'Holy moly! Put those brownies away! We need to get these Senate questions done!'

CHAPTER 56

A poster, "Cockemup–Too Magic To Mine", appeared on the noticeboard at the small townships community centre. Raven and Jack were busy hand-delivering letters to all 130 properties in the small township, inviting everyone to an urgent public meeting to discuss the silica mine planned for the State Forest on the far side of the lake. Cass had raised the alarm across Facebook, and Tara led the research. She'd distilled 75 pages of information on the proposed mine down to seven that would be easier for the average Joe to comprehend.

The Cockemup Association President emailed a copy to all the members. He now opened the meeting. 'Thank you, everyone, for coming, and I understand thanks also goes to our mayor for bringing mining in the region to everyone's attention.'

Tara summarised her findings to her friends and neighbours in the old one-room schoolhouse while passing around a map showing the tenement. It covered half the lake, the State Forest behind it, and five houses on the reservoir's left-hand corner.

'Anu Sands plans to put an open-pit mine that will output 20 to 40 million tonnes over thirty years just north of the lake. Let me explain to you what that looks like for us. That's a sixty-tonne double semi-trailer on the road 46 times a day, 24 hours a day, seven days a week for thirty years!'

'It's our forest being cleared. Our orchid trail gone, no home for possums or peacock spiders and the paleo-channels contaminated.' added Jack.

Cass spoke. 'I was at the council meeting when Aconaday raised mining, and I've reviewed the previous minutes. While the council insists it's outside their jurisdiction and they have no formal position. I'd suggest not informing residents when they've received notifications of tenements *is* a position. Widening the road and leasing the lake is clearly for the mine, which is also a position.'

A few members of the audience began protesting. 'Oh, that's a bit over the top. We're long overdue for repairing the road.'

'That's right...and locals will have exclusive use of the lake.'

Cass couldn't believe it and sneered. 'Is that what the council told you?'

Hackles rose. 'Yes! That's what James Templar told us!'

'Ha! I'm not at this meeting to protect a gated community. Wake up, people! It sounds to me like the CEO was pandering to some grandiose delusions. The fact is, mines need water, and you've got a mine wanting to be on your doorstep. You do the maths!'

The room fell silent. Cass was right, but her tone didn't endear her to the group.

Raven recognised her frustration but knew better how to approach the bourgeois fantasies of some of her neighbours. 'Silica needs to be kept damp to prevent dust. I'm sure we've all heard of silicosis.'

'Has anyone contacted Anu Sands?' asked a woman sitting beside Tara.

'No. This information was collated from the company's website and the Departments of Mines and Water.'

'Well, Felicity from the bowls club *did* contact them, and they're happy to come and talk to us. Maybe before going down rabbit holes, we should ask them.' suggested the woman.

The President spoke, his tone conciliatory. 'Is that what everyone would like to do? Because I can send an email requesting a meeting.'

Half the room began nodding and murmuring in agreement.

Tara replied. 'Sure, we can do that. But keep in mind that engaging with any party is a double-edged sword. For Anu Sands, that would count as public consultation. It will not necessarily be an exchange of ideas in a friendly discussion. In the future, you may be required to validate your point of view or provide legal arguments. Did Anu reach out to anyone here, offering to share their plans before the alarm was raised?'

Silence. Cass ghosted a smirk watching people physically recoil as they began to understand the need to be strategic. The woman next to Tara sat stiff and frosty, her mouth closed tight as if she'd sucked on a lemon. Tara turned to Cass raising her eyebrows and discretely leaning her head towards the ice queen.

Cass shrugged and mouthed, *'No idea?'*

Jack took the floor. 'When MacGovern promised to end native forest logging, he rang the bells of doom, which everyone ignored. Remember when the Premier said mining was exempt from the ban? He knew *exactly* how many tenements existed down here. It was all just to get the votes, and it worked. Once again, the public fell for the lies!'

'You're right, Jack. The other day, the Mining Minister described this region as the Southern Mineral Field. What does that tell you all? He didn't mention the forest or food bowl. *Southern. Mineral. Field.*' Cass noted the last three words as if they were absolute proof. 'I recommend everyone download MineralTracker and look at the situation for yourselves, and if you know a farmer, have the conversation with them too. Because the miners have used them to get access to the water, just the same as you, with this "private lake" palava.'

'Thanks, Cass....Look guys, we've all got skin in the game.' soothed Tara, 'For Cockemup, that means a million tonnes a year of silica sand being extracted and processed on-site five hundred metres from the nearest residential property. This will lower your property values—' She'd found the magic button. No environmental group on the planet has the motivation of a handful of homeowners with their equity on the line. Everyone, except the ice queen and the President, squared up in their seats. Tara continued. 'I've included the link to MineralTracker in my email handout. It shows all the tenements. Proposals are blue, and approved are green. Luckily, Anu is still at the proposal stage, so we have time to lodge an objection in the warden's court.'

The small community formed a steering group with a fortuitous mix of connections. A couple of FIFO miners living in Cockemup. They were conflicted men, in denial of being NIMBYs while sharing a fount of industry knowledge; a teacher who dreamt of being a graphic designer, a city-based publicist and a woman who was married to a solicitor who agreed to represent the group pro-bono. Tara joined them. She could fast-track the team and keep in the loop with what they were facing.

Cass declined. She had no patience for decision-making by committee. But she gave everyone a starting point for action. 'You want to create a petition formatted per parliamentary requirements, don't use a change dot org form. And two letters, one from the Association with questions on notice for next week's council meeting and the other, which we can all do individually, write to our local member Alice Kennedy.'

CHAPTER 57

Liz helped Cass flick through clothes racks, like a couple of bowerbirds looking for things in blue. 'Have you asked Graeme Mantel about this Hookemup Trust?'

Cass laughed. 'No. He's a nice guy but about as sharp as a bowling ball. He told me it took him 13 years to get onto the Dilbanup River Board. You know that's only because they've now got the funding for the Irrigation Scheme and can leave it sitting in caretaker mode. He's the glorified babysitter!'

'Here, how about this one?' Liz pulled out a floral shirt.

Reaching out to rub the paisley fabric between her fingers, Cass shook her head. 'Nah, it needs to be cotton. When I first posted about mining, he was happy to tell me how wrong I was, then informed me how he'd won a court case against a bauxite mine years ago. So, I looked it up. They won by default.'

'A win is a win, Cass.'

'Pfft. That's what he said, too. They were just lucky that the mining company had failed its due diligence. The judge had no choice but to rule in their favour. It was just dumb luck.'

'I think I might ask him about the Trust.'

'What?' Cass jerked her head up to scrutinise Liz. She wore a hot pink and black silk kimono over a plain mid-pink shift, a black velvet fez fitted snug on her head, and a single-strand necklace of large turquoise beads extended to her waist.

'Why would you do that? If I wanted that, I would have asked him myself!'

Liz defiantly jutted her jaw and rattled her bead. 'We should find out. I want to know.'

'Ugh, Liz and do what? What's your plan?'

'I don't know. We need to do something!'

'We *are* doing something. Don't cherry-pick information I give you and then shoot your mouth off and mess things up.'

Liz gave Cass an offended look. 'But—'

'But nothing! I'm serious, Liz. Think about it.' Cass tapped her forehead. 'He's already selling carbon credits through one of his groups. So, either he's knowingly part of their bigger plot, or he's drunk the Kool-Aid and doing as he is told. But sure as eggs, if you go blabbing, he'll unwittingly tip them off. I've been watching him; Aconaday plays him like a fiddle. So, I'm pretty sure the Forest Defenders can do the same! You've seen him yourself at council meetings. And his kids asking that last question that triggered Stanley off at the pub? That doesn't sit right.'

'But maybe they can help us.'

'God, Liz, what are you doing? Don't you think if they had any intentions of helping, they'd have started already? How long has that tenement been over your place? Did Graeme call you to tell you about it? No! Look around. Do you see the Forest Defenders down here? Not even for the beekeeper!'

'I know...but...' Liz plucked nervously at the coathangers before her.

Anger choked Cass, and she spoke between a half-whisper and a growl. 'You still need convincing? Are they posting anything about what is really going on? Did you take a look at their business plan? It was from fucking 2018! You could argue gross incompetence, except they took out full-page ads in how many newspapers to support MacGoverns new Forestry Agreement? I'm telling you, they've been hand in glove with the government the whole time. Heck! That's why the group was formed in the first place, and you want to blunder in and tell them we know about their secret stash of money?'

'I understand.' Liz let loose a high sigh, wishing Cass would shut up.

'Do you? 'Cause it sounds to me like you think they're going to help us. What do you think they're going to say? Dang, Liz, you got us! We're really paid opposition, but we'll go straight now. This isn't a kid's game, Liz. Are you aware, like really cognizant, how much money is in it for them too?'

'I know, I know.' Liz gave a sidelong glance under her lashes. Unconsciously taking on a stubborn look, her mouth firm.

'Then what are you talking about? *I'm going to ask Graeme*, Sheesh, Liz!' Cass's desire to shop or stay any longer in Liz's presence vanished. 'I've gotta go.'

CHAPTER 58

'I come bearing gifts...they created a change dot org petition.' Tara entered Cass's house with her arm outstretched, swinging a bottle of wine.

Cass sighed. 'Of course they did! It's useless. I warned them... Parliament won't accept it. But I'll accept this, thanks.' She took the bottle.

'Yeah, Alice Kennedy told them. They're now whining that they've lost three hundred signatures.'

'Some people won't be told. Wine?' She grabbed two glasses.

Tara nodded. 'Yes, please. How was last night's meeting?'

'Templar refused to accept the Cockemup Community questions on notice but tabled them in Councillor Questions at the End of Business. Apparently, the ward rep owns shares and has a conflict of interest. The Director of Regulations had prepared a written response... it just covers the usual. Limitations of local government power with mining being outside their jurisdiction, blah, blah.'

'They don't want the community's dissent on show. Did you ask about the lake?'

'That's precisely what they're trying to cover up, amongst other things. And that's why, where we can't influence action, we want to leave the breadcrumbs for Hansel and Gretal and a future Royal Commission. Yeah, I asked about the lake. According to the CEO, there's a lease. Also, they voted in favour of an application to downgrade a four-star hotel proposal. It must have gone through before my time. I don't remember reading about it, but honestly, I wasn't looking for that kind of thing.' Cass handed Tara a glass of wine and opened her computer to show the hotel's new building specs.

Tara took a sip of wine. 'Hmm, they look like dongas. What the hell? This is a mining camp, slap, bang in the centre of town!'

'Yep, and the restaurant is now a *"clubhouse"*, Templar's words.' They peered at the architectural drawing attached to the council's agenda. Cass read. *"Not open to the public"*. It's definitely a mining camp. But it gets better.'

'Gawd, this sounds like a two-bottle of wine conversation.'

'Ha! We'd be stonkered if we measured the corruption with alcohol consumption.'

'True, I can't wait till they livestream the meetings. We can watch with a glass of wine in the comfort of our homes and commentate like we're on Gogglebox.'

'That would be hilarious. Get the whole town involved in a monthly Council Bingo drinking game. Everyone has to take a shot each time the mayor says, *time immemorial*. You see that land they're putting the dongas on?'

'I vaguely remember something about the council buying it from the State, on the proviso it's used for tourism.'

'That's maybe why it's only being rented to the developer, not sold. Which proves mining dongas were the plan from the get-go.'

'I remember seeing a *"FOR SALE"* sign before they tore down all the trees. Mum was furious. They have been home to Carnaby Cockatoos since we were kids.'

'Did you ever see a *"SOLD"* sticker? I promise you, it's only leased, and for peanuts, I bet, too. I asked a councillor to check it out.'

'Okay. Well, we had our first Cockemup Stakeholders meeting.'

'Oh, yeah. How did that go?'

'About as good as you'd expect. It's easier herding wombats down a tunnel.'

Cass burst into laughter.

'However, they've managed to organise network news coverage. Hopefully, it goes live next week, and Alice Kennedy came down; we loaded her with questions for the Mining Minister.'

'Wow, that's great! There's hope yet.'

'Yeah, if you ignore Jack hassling people for voice-overs to his film footage and the graphic designer insists on making the promotional material look like the CWA discovered Canva.'

'Let them live the dream.'

Tara rolled her eyes. 'Meanwhile, I've been researching sand mining. They intend to strip mine. It's so straightforward that they call it the kindergarten of mining. And ol' Jack's right about the paleochannels;

it will cut off a major tributary to the lake and disrupt groundwater flow. A mine would eliminate a considerable portion of the total catchment and contaminate the aquifers downstream.'

'The lake isn't enough to supply the industrial amount of water needed for processing a million tonnes of sand a year. And that explains the Irrigation Scheme pipeline going down the Proja River. Again, proof of the conspiracy to introduce a water market for mining.' said Cass.

'Pro- *ya*,' corrected Tara.

'Pro-*Yaa*. No mixing of the good gear is necessary. Anu Sands won't care about the salt content to wash and dampen down silica. But that pipeline now tells us they know there's not enough water in the river to supply the lake. They'll be pumping from Acheron. Guess what the distance is between the river and the lake?'

'Six kilometres?' Tara guessed drily, checking the time on her phone. 'I better get going; I promised the girls I'd pick up Chinese for dinner.'

'Yes. Six kilometres!' Cass stood on her porch, waving as Tara reversed out of the driveway. For an instant, she saw it clearly in the garden, and then it flittered into the shadows. She froze, as the blacker-than-black shapes shifted in the corner of her eye. She closed her lids tight, Mummaries! 'Are you eavesdropping? Do you want to tell me something?' She whispered calmly and waited for an answer but received no telepathic message. She opened her eyes and stared into the garden, it was empty. She went back inside telling herself she'd imagined it.

PART FOUR: FIRE

Tyger Tyger, burning bright,
In the forests of the night;
What immortal hand or eye,
Could frame thy fearful symmetry?
-William Blake

CHAPTER 59

Paintings and rough studies filled Cass's house. Trees she talked with daily imprinted onto canvases and her home now resembled a wild fairytale forest. They were her children; she'd miss them when they left for the gallery, but that was life.

Cass could tell the birth season of each painting by sight. In May, white stars of native clematis woven over Kahlo-blue hovea, and flurries of orchids with names like leaping spider, pink fairy and flying duck flowered from July. Lorax-inspiring tassel plants exploded with purple buds in August, and old man Banksia came out for the summer. She turned on Beethoven's Piano Concerto No. 5 for motivation and opened the mail collected on the way home from her hike, imagining if she owned rather than rented, she would paint the forest onto every wall. But ownership tied you to a place.

Her phone buzzed with a text from Tara. "Listen to the radio now!"

'The Premier has requested my resignation to allow more women in leadership roles.'

'Woah! Here comes the switcheroo!' Dropping her letter on the table, Cass bent double, with her ears cocked for the details. Two weeks ago, Julia MacDonald had retired not even halfway through her term, and now Lipshut was leaving the Water and Forestry portfolios for the backbench.

Cass rang Tara when the interview ended. 'More female representation?' Her indignation was palpable.

'Puhleeze! Meanwhile, they replaced MacDonald with a bloke fined for breaching restraining orders. He should probably be in jail, not Parliament. This has collusion written all over it.'

Tara agreed. 'Remember Liz telling us about Snake's strange speech out of nowhere, emphasising the value of women in the region at the last Business Chamber meeting?'

'Almost as if they're exchanging notes! "Let'ss run with death threatsss" one week. "Women are useful political leverssss" the next.' Cass was an uncanny mimic, sounding just like Aconaday despite him having outgrown his lisp.

Tara chuckled. 'Mainstream media has us primed to accept the story. Repeating it a few weeks apart embeds the idea into the public consciousness. Remember when Muckemup had its own Bioela moment? First, a family of Sri Lankan refugees makes national headlines. The local brain's trust views it as an opportunity to roll out an Italian barista with a visa sob story of spending two grand a year on migration lawyers while *not* in offshore detention!'

'And you don't believe in casting spells? Do we have a shortage of cappuccino makers?'

'Pfft! More likely, using a nice "whitey" refugee to introduce the concept before we're inundated with Pacific Islanders. Brown skin isn't as palatable for sympathy amongst the landed gentry. It's about drip-feeding for the long game,' explained Tara. 'Then, when folks complain because all the labour jobs are under contract to lower-paid foreigners living in work camps, you remind them they were fine when it was Luigi. Few people embrace the label of racist, even if they are one.

'I've noticed.' Cass picked up the letter she'd opened. 'Remember when Snake banged on about death threats towards the CEO in that radio interview just before the local elections?'

'There's a perfect example! Rovello claimed he'd also received a threat. Who knows if he did or not, but it legitimises the story. Wash and repeat a few weeks later with the Premier running a similar narrative.'

'Well, I wrote to the Anti-Corruption Commission regarding that stunt. They've responded. Listen to this crap, "Miss Leason, we've investigated your complaint blah, blah...find no evidence of Mr Aconaday manufacturing death threats against himself." That's the Triple C owned! I distinctly said he was referring to the CEO.' Cass screwed up the letter and lobbed it across the room.

'Sorry, but no surprises there. Add it to the bearing witness file.... I keep thinking about twenty years ago when MacGovern was a lowly media officer in the Premier's office. He's seen it all before. It's a template. Find loopholes in the Forestry Agreement, tick. Managed investments scam reincarnates as climate profiteering with carbon credits, tick. Model the water market on the shitshow over east, tick.'

'Don't forget, with the same key players! None of this is new.' Frustrated, Cass pulled out two blank canvases and then searched the freezer for one of her special brownies. Today she needed to escape, no matter what was happening with the government and its minions. She shut the door on the world and painted as if possessed.

CHAPTER 60

Tara saw the fresh plume of dark smoke billowing grey and powdery into the pastel morning sky while waiting at the bus stop with her girls.

'It's from the mill,' said Miro as Ivy and Chloe climbed aboard to sit with their friends.

Tara hadn't heard the shrill sirens just after 5 AM. She raised her eyebrows. 'The mill's on fire? The day after the Forestry Minister resigns?'

'Limited opportunities before the fire season starts. You don't wanna risk the Emergency Service boys getting caught short.'

'You're a cynic, my friend.'

'Yer knows as good as me. Pay enough to the arson squad and they'll declare whatever you want. I gotta go, or these kids will be late for school 'n we can't have that. Eh, you mob?' Miro shouted at his charges, winking in the rearview mirror as they all groaned on cue. A grin split his lips as he shut the doors. Lifting a forefinger in farewell, he swung the bus onto the road.

When Tara arrived home, she checked Facebook. Murphy had raised the alarm, and Cass, being an early riser, had already shared it. Emergency Services advised residents to close their windows and not drink from their rainwater tanks because of the mill's asbestos roof. She checked the Bureau of Meteorology's 10-day weather forecast, then grabbed a ladder muttering to herself, 'I'd say the problem is more than an asbestos roof if there's no rain coming.'

Meanwhile, having finished her hike, Cass dropped yesterday's Airbnb laundry off at the town's linen service. The business shut at midday, which meant she often picked up fresh sheets on the way to work and returned the following day after she'd stripped the beds and cleaned bathrooms. The owners, Sharon and Trevor were amongst the most hospitable locals she'd met. Cass had become cautious when meeting people in this small town, unsure if they were friends or foe. There were occasional threats and the ugliest cohort had publicly called for a witch hunt. She and the young journalist often exchanged horror stories. He had the unenvious position of the court reporter and frequently upset undesirable elements of the community.

Sharon had asked for her contact details at their first meeting, pen poised over her order book.

'Cass Leason 049—'

The laundress looked up with a jerk. '*You're* Cass Leason?' Then she turned her head towards the back of the warehouse and shouted at the top of her voice. 'Trev, Trev. *TREV-VOR!* Guess who's here?'

Responding to his wife, Trev recognised Cass and grabbed an old plastic Coke bottle from behind the reception desk. 'You see this?' He plonked the bottle on the counter. It was full of sediment-infused water, the colour of dirty tin.

'Yeeaah...' Cass worded hesitantly, unsure what was coming. 'What is it?'

'That's from our old premises. Used to be on Main Street, next to the old chainsaw shop.'

'What chainsaw shop?'

'Before you arrived. It's now that fancy restaurant. This was the tap water there. How can I wash sheets in this muck?'

Cass screwed up her nose. 'Eww, is that how the town got its name? *Muck*—em up?'

Trevor didn't smile.

'Sorry, not funny. You're right, that doesn't look good.'

'No, it's bloody not! The council, the State government and the Development Board all fobbed us off. We were told we'd have to move. Guess what's there now?'

'Isn't it a cafe next to the restaurant?' Cass mapped the street in her mind's eyes.

'That's right!' Trevor shook the bottle. 'Old asbestos pipes disintegrating...not safe enough for washing sheets in, but fine for making lattes!'

During that first meeting, Sharon helped her carry the fresh linen out to the car. They threw two large duffle bags into the boot, and Cass shut the lid. Turning to say thank you, Sharon could no longer contain herself, and with a massive grin, she hugged Cass 'Call me Shazaa. I *LOVE* that you're a cleaner!'

* * *

The morning of the mill fire, Cass called out her usual greeting as she headed back to her car for the second bag of laundry.

Shazza followed. 'Heya Cass! How are yer today? Have you seen the news? Of course, you have! We found out from you, ha-ha. Well, you and the sirens.' She laughed cheerfully while helping lift a bag full of damp towels.

'The fire?' Yeah, it's all action around here. Ministers resigning to the back bench, mills burning down. I wonder what's next?'

'I want to know how they worked out so fast that it isn't suspicious?'

'Is that what they're saying? Do you think our council has the collection plate ready for the State to pick up the cleaning tab while the mill owners take their end-of-logging handout and disappear for a while?' asked Cass.

Trev joined them. 'Radio said it was a disaster waiting to happen. After seven years, how does a fire *"accidentally"* break out on a decommissioned and unused site?'

'I don't know. But it wasn't unused. Patrick Murphy started making compost there a few weeks ago; he was posting about it on faceache. Maybe spontaneous combustion? I wonder how Work-Safe feels about the leasing of sites deemed disasters waiting to happen?' mused Cass. 'Anyway, I gotta keep moving. I don't have a guest bump in until next Wednesday, so I'll see you then.'

'Sure thing, Cass! Have a great weekend, and keep the bastards honest!'

Cass always felt like a working-class hero after visiting Shazza. With her ego recharged, she returned home to find a queue of requests to enter Muck Unrivalled. No loggers this time, just a mix of locals, including Pat Murphy's wife.

'Uh-oh, now what?' She scrolled through the community's main group, noticing the farm manager's comment about the fire under Murphy's original post.

"Don't worry, Murf. Those clowns in Muck Unrivalled don't have a clue about your business model."

'What are you gibbering about, little man?' Cass accepted most of the requests. 'Sorry folks, you're going to be disappointed. There are no controversial attacks on Mr Murphy in my group.' She paused, grey eyes narrowing as she ruminated over the farm manager recently unblocking her and the subsequent commentary between the two men. 'He wants me to see what he is posting.' Cass could smell the bait, like bacon spitting in grease for a Sunday morning fry-up.

'Okay, I'll take a wee nibble, but just remember you started this.' Instead of responding to his comment, she stuck both men's names into the search bar and took screenshots of their posts in the lead-up to the fire.

A few weeks ago Murphy had posted a video of himself standing in front of a pop-up caravan inside a massive warehouse, kicking an empty can on the ground, and complaining about supposed squatters. "Look what we have to put up with!"

'Setting the scene nicely there, Irish.' Cass listened to his rhetoric, shaking her head at the show. 'Now why would someone risk squatting in a filthy mill on the main street when there's plenty of beautiful forest to camp in? And why wouldn't you just tell them they're trespassing or report it to the police, instead of this performance. Good grief, you'd think you're at the Abbey Theatre!' She laughed, they just couldn't help themselves.

'Sounds like trying to point the bony finger of blame at a phantom.' Was Tara's assessment a few days later when Cass told her what had transpired.

'You couldn't make this stuff up! I've received a few messages. One said the mill owners have been relocating equipment onto that site for the last six months, which means at least one truckie knows something.'

'They're astute enough to keep their mouths shut. What are the odds of the Forestry Minister stepping down and the mill catching fire the very next day?' asked Tara.

'Handy! It's now in public service no-man's-land. The absence of a minister in office renders them unaccountable for any future inquests. Can't answer incriminating questions because they don't know; not during their tenure. That Department will be a hive of activity right now, all the drones making things happen before a new queen arrives. And let's not forget the $80 million end of native logging money sloshing about. You may as well get that light industrial wishlist item sorted while the State government has its wallet open.'

'They'll just dig a giant hole, bury it all and put a concrete slab over the top,' said Tara.

'Probably. Meanwhile, the mill company has a cleanout and can now claim worthless equipment on their insurance? Nice and tidy.'

'How many workers came into contact with poisons during each processing stage?'

'Huh, what?' Cass lost the thread of the conversation.

'I'm thinking how they'd have stored drums of PCP onsite. Spillage and dripping solutions. Sludge removal from the tanks. Every time they opened the cylinder, a burst of air and contaminants were released.' Tara explained how they had to clear debris and release condensate after every batch.

'Sounds like you've been working on a new project?'

'I started digging around when Murphy first popped his head up. PCP furnace oil mixtures considered too contaminated were piped to waste ponds across the road; you can see their outline in the field next to the bowling club.'

'Oh, yeah? I've seen that patch of grass with the indentations. Doesn't Gio's creek run past there?'

'Yep, Mokine Creek. Gio is further upstream.' Tara continued. "Sludge too thick with sawdust to be piped was thrown back into the furnace to burn along with the mill waste. As was all other contaminated waste on site. Smoke from the furnace continuously graced Muckemup from the first time it was lit in 1919 until the late 1980s.'

As she listened to Tara, Cass imagined thick tendrils of acrid smoke hanging in the low-lying valley like cobwebs, pervading every nook and cranny of the town.

Wood smoke naturally contains dioxins, but timber mills engaged in chemical preservation and onsite waste disposal included cocktails of much greater significance.

'In the early days, they mixed arsenic, molasses and creosote, a known carcinogen. Then in the 60s, they added Pentachlorophenol mixed with furnace oil and later chromium to the ingredient list.'

'I remember you saying, what does that do?'

'PCP? It's a pesticide. Stops bugs from eating the wood, but it's also highly toxic. Exposure harms the liver, kidneys, lungs, nervous system, gastric tract, blood, and immune system—'

'So, just the whole body! Does the EPA or Water Department test that creek?'

'I found some data from when the mill first closed. The Water Department said it was fine.

'I bet they did! But would you trust them after the CSIRO report?'

'Not to pour piss out of a boot, if the instructions were on the heel!' replied Tara.

CHAPTER 61

A small crowd formed at the opposite end of Main Street from the mill's burnt-out shell to witness the hotel delivery. Smiling, Aconaday parked in a no-standing zone and joined them. People fell back, letting the mayor through. A few men mumbled acknowledgement.

'What's all this then, Romeo?' one asked

Before he could answer, a voice said, 'Looks like dongas to me!'

If anyone still doubted the commentary on Muck Unrivalled, a crane lifting the bright yellow accommodation pods into place confirmed mining was indeed the master plan being imposed onto the community. The group's mood swiftly changed as the people cottoned on. Decades in the political arena attuned Aconaday to such nuance shifts. He felt an itch of uneasiness spread through him as realisation and distrust mushroomed through the congregation.

'Thought this was 'sposed to be a four-star hotel, Romeo?'

'Umm..' Snake faltered for a moment, gathering his thoughts.

'Yeah, what the hell is this?'

'It's nothing to do with me,' Aconaday countered. 'I haven't spoken with the developer for over six months. James is overseeing this project, and you know full well George, that councillors can't interfere with day-to-day council business. It's gotta be tabled at a meeting.'

Emboldened by his peers, George wasn't buying it. 'Whad'ya talking 'bout? I remember the four-star idea being put out for public feedback—'

'And it said nothing about banana boxes!'

'This land was for tourist use, not mine workers.'

'Now calm down, everyone. The land still belongs to us.' Aconaday raised his hands and switched his voice. 'My understanding is the land is only being leased.'

'Oh yeah? What's the rent then?' asked a big, roughly hewn fellow with wide-set brown eyes and a mullet reaching his collar.

Snake looked up into his face, shaking his head. 'Now Stevo, I can't tell you that either. The CEO has put all council leases as commercial in confidence.'

'Really? To have such power of words, that you can make the entire world believe a piece of pineapple on a pizza is a miraculous joy!' A woman's mocking voice spoke closely behind him. Romeo turned to find himself face-to-face with a figure backlit by the morning sun.

'You!' He gulped his loathing.

Placing a hand on her chest, 'Moi? This...' Cass waved at the building site. 'Has nothing to do with me. I wouldn't be putting a mining camp in the centre of town, but I tried to tell you all.' she shrugged.

'Your unwarranted attacks on my family are beneath contempt.' Aconaday snapped. He intended to own the moral high ground in this exchange. It was essential to appear reasonable while portraying her as unstable, maybe even work towards having her sectioned under the mental health act. Yes! His eyes sparkled as the idea occurred to him.

Cass lifted her hands, mirroring the mayor's cavalier dismissal of accountability. 'I'm not attacking anyone. I'm just curating the evidence available in the public domain... and connecting the dots.' The spectators lost interest in the dongas and quietly closed in on the pair, not believing their luck at witnessing the confrontation first-hand.

Cass continued. 'I guess there's no out-of-pocket expense involved in approving a mining camp under the guise of a hotel and then tweaking it down the track. Just like using Regent Brook to pay for the Scheme's pipeline. Clever. I'm sure we'd all be interested to know what changes will be flanking your son's State Forest lease.'

Snake's eyes shifted, noting the avid onlookers were awaiting his next move. He pressed his lips tight and fixed his gaze to look at a point just to the right of Cass's head.

'Nothing?... Oh, and don't want to make eye contact either?' She laughed. 'I don't recall reading that trick in Machiavelli's Prince.'

Romeo sneered. 'What do you know about politics? I was a Minister?' He couldn't help himself. She had some nerve and he clearly needed to remind everyone who he was. He let the statement sink in, reasserting his authority and buying himself time to prepare a cunning response. To trap her in her own territory. 'It'ss not illegal, and you know it!' a soft lisp crept into his voice, 'But as you're sso fond of books, here's a quote for you. Aconaday paused briefly for effect and to regain control of his treacherous tongue, 'The best way to find out if you can trust s-someone is to trust them.'

He calculated wrong. It was Cass's turn to have a twinkle in her eye. 'Hemingway? Oh, he's a favourite! But I prefer his lines, "I don't recall having met a nastier-looking man... he has the demeanour of an unsuccessful rapist!" Cass paraphrased the punchline like a pro boxer landing an undercut. She noted her opponent's face go white then red and then apoplectic purple. Direct hit! She smiled, licked her index finger and sketched a tally, awarding herself a point.

People audibly gasped, and a handful of the brave sniggered. Snake was stunned by her effrontery. He scowled at the background laughter, instantly shutting them up before narrowing his eyes towards her dangerously. But Cass was done. She'd won the round, if not the war.

'Y'all have a nice day now. See you on Facebook!' she raised her hand and exited the throng. The show was over.

Matthew Farnham had watched the exchange and pulled away from the crowd to follow her. 'Cass!'

She turned towards the voice, and he jogged to catch up.

'I'm Matt Farnham.' The farmer introduced himself, shifting his weight from one foot to the other.

'Yeah, we've met— the Friends of the River meeting.'

'That's right! I wasn't sure if you'd recognise me; it's sometimes hard between online and real life. You're going to get shot talking like that to Snake.'

Cass glanced across at the group with a lopsided grin. Aconaday was still there, in damage control. 'Not on the main street in broad daylight, I'm not! Anyway, I've been told he is a crap shot.'

Farnham laughed. 'Yer... he is. Nor does he like getting his hands dirty.'

'Who does? I've been meaning to message you. Have you seen what they're doing out at Acheron?'

'Not seen, but heard. There was a big meeting out there with all the Department boffins after the CSIRO review slammed their Regent Brook plans.'

'I read the post you guys put up about that on your page. Here, look at the substitute Regent brook dam. Just three kilometres from the original site.' Cass pulled out her phone and handed it to Farnham, showing the video she'd taken with Tara and Miro. 'Watch this and tell me if you still think farming and mining can coexist.'

Matt's eyes widened. 'That's a lot of pipeline.'

'Isn't it? I'd say it's paid for with one of the Ag Minister's so-called *"drought-proofing"* grants that she was yammering about before she quit! I'm telling you, you farmers, *are* the Special-Purpose-Vehicle. That pipe stretched for about three kilometres and we saw five springs tapped with bores.'

'Can you send me a copy of this?'

'Sure, I'll do it now.' Cass took her phone back. 'Also have you seen the questions tabled at a Federal Estimates Hearing?'

'No, but I can tell you who did that.'

'Oh yeah, who?'

'Senator Drummond-Willoughby. We met with him, Dicky and a few others in Tollie a few months back.'

'Oh, right. Well done, they were interesting answers... and questions.' she said obliquely.

'Thanks, I better get back to work. That was an entertaining way to start the day. You should be careful, though.'

'And enlightening. Don't worry, I will!'

As Cass waved Matt off, an Aboriginal woman approached her. 'Hey, you're the new woman!' It was more a statement, than a question.

'Hi, Cass Leason.' The woman shook hands 'I've been here almost a year now. How long before I stop being new?'

'I'm Athena Papadopoulos, Traditional Owner. Youse all new compared to us.'

' Touché,' Cass conceded. 'Your name sounds Greek.'

'My father's Greek, but my mother's line is here. She was the local Elder, it's now me. Have you seen the interpretive signs out at Bush Park? Me mum did that!'

'I have, it's a cool story. So where are you guys on the water? I haven't seen or heard any T.O comments.'

'I been livin' up the city. My brother says to stay clear of you. Yer a shit stirrer.'

Cass laughed. 'I guess that tells me.'

'Nar, gammon. Mining means jobs. It provides money for projects that help my people.'

Cass took stock of the woman before her. She was stunning in her early thirties, with long, thick black hair, hazel eyes and skin the colour of milk coffee, but the artist knew that beauty was only ever skin deep no matter what colour. 'Athena. It's a good name. The Greek Fates liked Athena.' she wondered if this Athena was favoured too.

'I scout for mining companies. While the council is bending over backwards for outsiders,' she pointed across to the camp still being unloaded. 'There is no focus on opportunities for locals.'

'Athena, I'm going to tell you straight; mining is the dildo of destiny that rarely comes lubed. I heard the Treaty was a billion dollars. That may seem like a lot of mon— of course, it's a lot of money!' Cass adjusted her comment because a billion dollars was a hell of a lot of money in anyone's language. 'But I doubt you guys will see much of it. And where do you draw the line? Because mining involves creating a water market, they won't do it any other way. A billion dollars for all the trees and all the water. What use is money going to be when everything is gone?'

Athena pouted. 'That deal ruined everything, and soon people will point blame fingers. Yer knows the Director of the Indigenous Council signed up with the government without many of our people's consent. He's also good friends with Snake. Athena nodded her head towards the building site. 'They've known each other a long time.'

'That doesn't surprise me. I read the Indigenous Council is to be no more. I guess their job is done.'

The woman frowned. 'That Council is a joke. The mob on country will run the show once we set up the regional corporations. We have four regional directors that were signed up last Saturday. Hopefully, the government will choose our group as the entity to collaborate with on the new spring rights and Forestry Agreement'

Cass rubbed her forehead. 'I reckon you'll find the government chooses whoever does what they're told. Do you know why there's an even number of groups? Four, not five or three to create a majority decision? It sounds to me like they're setting you guys up for future in-fighting.' She watched for a reaction. Nothing. 'I also notice that the Treaty moved borders. It now goes straight through the middle of Muckemup, just like the British did with India and Pakistan...it's textbook stuff.'

'A cuz has a High Court challenge. That's why as a Traditional Owner I want support. My connection with Muckemup is strong. I would fight for all resources pumped into our community for my people and the pioneers. I need Wadjella to recognise my goal as T.O to protect my country. I don't need money. I just love my country sis. Will you help me?'

Cass gave a half snort.'Pioneers? I know things happen slowly down here, but I'm pretty sure Muckemup has crossed the threshold into this century. I can't support... *won't* support anything that means yes to water trading. You may also want to look at the Forestry Agreement plans for your mum's park. MacGovern intends to transfer it from *"other recreational" to* State Forest, which means they can log it.' On that note, Cass said farewell and headed home.

PART FOUR: FIRE

CHAPTER 62

Up in arms, Cockemup locals versus Anu Sands dominated the evening news, and the Manager Director of the mining company came away from the exchange second best.

'I laughed so hard watching. Imagine coming across crazier than the Cockemupians? His face was wild!' Cass hooted.

'I know, right? That leer made me shudder.' Tara shivered as she helped Cass bubble-wrap her painting for shipping the day after the segment aired.

'With laughter, I hope. I'm so impressed with that little community!'

'No. That was one creepy expression. They did alright, eh? Alice Kennedy sent a letter to the steering committee. Anu is withdrawing their tenement application for that site.'

'Really? That's a win. I wonder who's going to short-sell on that information?'

'What do you mean?'

'Imagine you're mister Anu Sands and you've got four tenements with pending exploration licences all over the district.' Cass made a ripping sound as she pulled a length of packing tape.

'Five.' corrected Tara.

Okay, five tenements and only one is near a population... who start making noise about a potential mine in their backyards. Then you get the heads up from

269

the Mines Department, or the Minister's office telling you they're going to refuse the Cockemup project because the unwanted attention jeopardises all the other shifty projects they have happening, so you'd be wise to remove the application, quietly... say, in two weeks, this gives you time. Maths isn't my strong suit, so let's make it easy. You borrow a hundred shares from your broker at today's prices. I don't know, $5 a share and sell them to another investor on the stock market. You're now a hundred shares *"short"*. When the price drops in two weeks, as you know it will be because you've got to declare the withdrawal of a $25 million project to the ASX and all your shareholders. Then you buy another hundred shares at a reduced rate to return what you borrowed. Let's say the announcement drops the price to $3 each. The difference between the selling price, $5 and your buying price, $3 is your profit. In this case, $2. Multiplied by the hundred shares is a $200 gain, ta-da! Borrow ten thousand instead of a hundred; you've made a lazy twenty grand. Not bad money for receiving a phone call.'

'How do you know this?... What about those' Tara pointed to a pair of large canvases making a two-metre diptych.

'No, leave them. I once dated a trust fund kid.'

'Lucky you!'

'Not really. He was an arsehole.'

Tara laughed. 'Talking of which, I heard Templar is in hospital.'

CHAPTER 63

Friday's walk home from the office was a terrible end to an arduous week for the Muckemup CEO. The yellow dongas in the town centre were unmissable. As expected, Snake dumped it in Templar's lap and their true intentions were now obvious, even to those who were marginally smarter than a mossy rock. Initially, Templar thought managing the peasants would be simple. After all, he'd been doing it for almost 25 years.

But the reality was exhausting. He'd been fielding calls from farmers and irate townsfolk for two weeks, and since laying everything bare, they needed to hurry and get the other 600 beds online. Templar had awarded an Indian developer a peppercorn lease to accommodate 80 beds, 160 if you hot-bedded. The businessman then committed and bought more land around town; across from the supermarket, behind the supply yard, and a large block near the public servants' enclave. Thirty houses for mining management would go there, furthering the suburb's middle-class exclusivity, increasing property values and ensuring police officers, teachers and nurses remained complicit. The farmers would be trickier, but Templar hoped to be gone soon. He had a couple of pots on the boil. James walked along the bike path in the half-light of dusk with his head down, thinking of one pot in particular, the nightclub. He'd convinced the councillors to underwrite the renovation. Suddenly, something solid clipped his shoulder, almost knocking him to the ground.

'Hey, watch it!' Momentarily stunned, Templar shouted at the passing figure that had bumped him. Twilight made it difficult to see, and he'd been miles away pondering liquor licences and burlesque shows. James squinted, his flesh crawled as if strange fingertips were stroking it. The silhouette of a tall man spun around, broad across the shoulder with big straight hair, standing on end... or was it? Templar couldn't make out a face. Strangely, the form got darker and bigger the closer it stumbled towards him.

'BANG!' He heard an explosion. But not from outside; something blew up in his skull like a balloon popping. Dizziness overcame him, his body began shaking, and he felt himself break out into a cold sweat. A tiny spot in his brain became searing hot, and a moist warmth oozed outwards. Templar thought it was probably a burst blood vessel causing internal bleeding. Then the pain hit. His body seemed to cave in while also exploding outward. He gasped without air.

Am I having an aneurysm? Was the second to last question that formed in the CEO's injured mind, as from an odd angle with his face smashed into the pavement, a guttural, unearthly voice boomed inside his head *"Veni, Vidi, Vici"*. Unable to move, he watched the enormous black and hairy clawed feet of his shadowy assailant shrink into the night before darkness engulfed him.

CHAPTER 64

The Romeo's, Junior and Senior, and their fellow Irrigation Scheme Directors sat in the leather semi-circular booth of Muckemup's newest nightclub. It was Monday lunchtime, and all were keen to conduct urgent business in the luxury venue.

The downstairs restaurateur, who'd cut a deal with the club owner, had been rushed to hospital with heart failure, meaning catering would need to be supplied from elsewhere. Snake couldn't believe the run of bad luck they'd recently had. Hopefully after today, things would turn around. He brought a box of Cuban cigars from his office, anticipating a positive meeting. Acheron and department bigwigs were due in an hour.

'Our time has come, boys!' Are you all set, Gio?' Aconaday rubbed his hands together and his tone promised the group that everything would be okay.

Gio threw a folder onto the table. 'The paperwork is ready.' His property was about to be listed for sale. His father was an estate agent and would handle the transaction, keeping the commission in the family. The buyer was Acheron. It was all pre-organised, but they would advertise on the open market to look impartial.

'We're getting out too," said the Scheme's Treasurer. 'The missus wants to wake up to ocean views.' Alex Crooks, like Lenny, had married into Muckemup's elite circle. His father-in-law and Silas Rosetti were cousins. His wife's dad had mentored the former forester, guiding the couple to farm on the inside track. They inherited the farm and, in the past ten years, had built their property portfolio to almost two thousand acres around Muckemup. Alex followed Muckemup Unrivalled and like the artful dodger, he had wisely remained out of sight. His holdings all had springs, keeping his details off the public record. During the last eight months, Gio's old man was selling his properties as well, all except for two blocks.

Real estate agents aren't kidding when they say location is everything. One block Alex intended to keep was 150 hectares with a small river running through the middle. They'd hold on to that parcel until the water market was established, then they'd sell the land but keep the water entitlement, assigning Acheron to manage assets worth an estimated $50 million.

'Where are you moving to, Sullivans?' asked Lenny, referring to the exclusive seaside township a hundred kilometres west, full of mining executives and corporate lawyers.

'No, the south coast. We've found a place, settlements in ten weeks.' The other block Alex Crooks was holding onto had been earmarked for a biomass plant back in 2006.

Back when Sullivan's Beach and the neighbouring districts rejected the proposal because its pollution would damage their pristine image of wine and food production. Rovello and Aconaday welcomed the proponents. *"Over here, boys, pick Muckemup!"*

Fortunately, the Global Financial Crisis of '08 and the near collapse of the US company behind the project killed the idea. Sadly, not dead enough. Local council and EPA permits had been on a rolling approval for 15 years. Eventually, the world markets recovered, and the economic climate was again favourable. The bailed-out corporation signed a lease for Alex's land at the top of Sapphire Brook, spanning across two catchments and a 5-year deal to buy his water for the facility. Eucalyptus would be the fuel stock; Alex's place was conveniently a kilometre north of the mill yard, where plantation karri was turned to wood chips for the Japanese market. If things went according to plan, construction would begin next year, and the plant would be commercially operational within a couple of years.

'Okay, getting to business, we need a few of us in MacGoverns Irrigation Reference Group; he's trying out Alice Kennedy. What say you, Silas?'

'Sure.' The old man said dully. Silas was as powerless as the loggers, with brittle bones he was a leaf to be blown. As he'd aged, life had shown how self-interest allowed him to be manipulated by friends and misled by chasing financial gains at a price that exceeded a pound of flesh. Guilt and profound loneliness had made the farmer sick, removing his strength to even take the simple step of ridding himself of the lie. Rossetti was a prisoner of his own making, and his punishment was to live the rest of his days in possession of that knowledge.

'What about me, Dad?'

'No. It's best if you keep low. I'll get Larry Wolfe and Uncle Angelo onboard.' Romeo referred to one of his younger brothers, 'Also, let's train up Charlotte.'

The men's dirty smirks were a collective knowing. They would pull the newest councillor into their web, lulled by self-importance. They would encourage and honour her with minor achievements and soften her for future use. Everyone could see she was an easy target for Snake to exact revenge upon Matt Farnham.

* * *

The Premier hitched a ride with Stamos Price for the short flight to Muckemup. Their entourage included top-level senior public servants, who escorted the two leaders as they disembarked from the eight-seater Learjet. Their primary aim was to visit the Acheron dam site and witness the progress up close. MacGovern had remained silent as a mardoo on the matter of water, leaving it for his ministers to wrangle. When they failed, he appointed new office bearers. His focus was on establishing the water market. He'd taken on the role of State Treasurer to guarantee smooth financing, even if it required unorthodox methods. Price was in alliance, but even his clout and industry knowledge wasn't enough to prevent the new Federal government from conducting a snap audit and withdrawing the National Water Initiative funding of $40 million. Three deficient business plans, a damming CSIRO review and Senate Estimates questions had created a paper trail that white-anted their initial plans.

The Irrigation Scheme failed the Pub Test. There was no clear definition of the project's finances, it ebbed and flowed like the tide. The Scheme's own figures contained an $11 million deficit; Farnham's group thought it was a miscalculation. But the elite intended the shortfall as a segue for Acheron to enter the Co-op later and exert power through their voting rights. An announcement on the Fed's decision would be made public in a couple of months, providing the State with sufficient latitude to investigate alternatives, but the noose was tightening.

Soon after the agreed time, MacGovern and Price climbed the stairs to the club. The decor, tacky in the daylight, looked gentleman-dungeon-like. Still, an improvement on earlier venues the Premier had attended in this backwater. He assessed the moody steel-blue walls and smiled. The owner had decorated the premises with symbolic paraphernalia that any Scottish Rite Mason would recognise.

'Good afternoon, gentlemen,' said Magovern as everyone stood to greet him. 'Shall we get down to it.'

'Absolutely! Here make yourselves comfortable.' Lenny Reid moved along the couch to make room for the various staff. The Executive Directors of Strategy from three Departments — Mining, Forestry and Water were in attendance and would take notes to ensure agency alignment.

MacGovern launched into the details. 'We'll introduce new mining legislation next week, removing public objections until after any mineral explorations are completed. Giving us five years, with extension for another five if needed.'

'Yes, let's see what we've got down there first, eh?' said Price. The man oozed success. He displayed his wealth through discreet details like his Richard Mille watch and bespoke Italian leather shoes.

'That's a marvellous idea.' Romeo stated. 'The financial outlay on exploration will strengthen any argument if it does go before the Warden's Court.'

MacGovern concurred. 'It's also something the Mineral Council can openly lobby for, companies already dedicating millions. Expenditure increases ownership. Scotty was fast-tracking the removal of red tape at the Federal level before the election.'

'Ha! Well, he was the backseat Minister of Mining!' Joked Worm, referring to the recent discovery that the outgoing Prime Minister held multiple secret ministerial roles, shockingly signed in by the Governor General. MacGovern and Price raised their eyes to look at the mayor's son. Snake made a slight frown of disapproval. Romeo Junior fell silent for the rest of the meeting.

'We'll pass it through the Upper House next week.' continued one of the public servants. The legislation would be easily adopted; the Workers' Party held the majority vote in both levels of the Parliament.

'What about the RFA?' Aconaday was acknowledged as the expert on forestry matters.

'Right now we're still taking mostly jarrah, from Johnson's block and the Doyle State Park to meet Polcoa's needs. If a mining tenement is present, protection under the Regional Forestry Agreement isn't possible. It falls under Federal legislation…So, that gets us off the hook there. What we're focusing on is *"ecological thinning"*, said another one of the yes men, or in this case, yes women as she was the only female present.

Aconaday nodded. 'Nice of the greenies to give us that term. I've seen you're transporting the logs in cattle trucks. Smart move, less obvious.'

'Thank you, sir. The design of the RFA is all about us controlling the water. We'll strategically target the removal of 8000 hectares of old growth per year to increase catchment flow through the systems. This will create new water.'

'Can you explain it to us?' asked Lenny. Any ministerial discretion on *where* to clear?'

'Absolutely!' said Stamos Price. 'They'll be doing the back of Acheron, for example. We've got a third of a 13 gig coming from springs. The rest we've modelled and coined the term *hydro silva-harvesting*. It's the same concept as flood-plain harvesting on the Murray, but following the contours of the land, clearing to get as much water as required. The Forestry Department will remove trees to specifically create a catchment flow or runoff. *At* the minister's discretion, of course!'

They all laughed. Stamos Price had been recently quoted as saying he believed fresh water was an under-utilised asset that would become a political imperative for the Western Australian government to develop a water market. However, what he hadn't shared with the journalist, was the manipulation he was engaged in to make it so. Price simply viewed Western Australia's severely drying future as a wealth opportunity, reminiscent of California 30 years ago.

MacGovern continued. 'Loggers will also clear regen based on the land's topography. But we'll introduce broad-scale unlimited trials when replanting.'

'What's that mean?' asked Gio.

Alex Crook responded. 'It means they won't replant heavily in key locations. *CBC*, clear, burn and keep clear to gain as much water as possible.'

'This *new* water will allow for the continued take from licenced locations.' explained Aconaday.

'That should shut your farmers up! Can't complain, if they're still getting plenty of water.' said MacGovern.

'Fantastic. Between that, and of course, the mining tenements' ability to clear at will...how many shares you got in that lithium project next door Price?'

'Enough.' laughed Stamos tapping his nose.

'That's useful, we'll soon be cooking with gas!'

'Don't you mean biomass, Dad?' Junior smirked as the food arrived.

MacGoverns's office had rung ahead asking for a light lunch, just finger foods. The Premier had scheduled dinner with the pub owner and his newest team member, Alice Kennedy. He wanted room for one of the hotel's famous Angus steaks. This day would end with pub grub and PR, a few beers and touching base with the common folk; talking up the $80 million transition funding. Not that native forest logging would end, because ecological thinning would keep it business as usual. Then they'd declare an over-cut or glut, making it necessary to find new markets for the extra regen karri and this would herald the installation of the biomass plant.

'What about your renegade Facebook group? Do you need help sorting that one out? Our rates are competitive.' Price winked.

Aconaday looked at the businessman; he knew what he meant. 'We can manage, thanks," he said brusquely. The last thing the mayor needed was another police investigation in the district. Aconaday intended for the whole town to see an example of what happens to radicals.

'Okay, let us know if you change your mind. Montecristos?' Stamos pointed to the box of cigars.

CHAPTER 65

It was a cool but clear day for the Cockemup Annual Fair. Cass arrived late to find Raven's famous curry had sold out and Tara wandering around in her Wellington boots with a neighbour carrying a massive axe like a modern-day Viking.

'You're a dangersome-looking pair!' She greeted her friend.

'Aargh, we are! The mayor gave us a wide berth. Not sure if he was concerned about the axe Tony won on the chocolate wheel or the possibility of me having a stab about Sapphire Brook.'

'Oh, Sapphire Brook would terrify him. Hi Tony, score on the axe.' Cass introduced herself. 'Are you girls here too?'

'They've met up with friends. Let's sit under the trees by the playground. That's where I told them to meet me when they're done, but they'll be going until stumps,' said Tara.

'First, I've got to smooth things with Liz. Do you know where her stall is?'

'Last tent on the left. Good luck. Ivy found a great vintage leather jacket.'

They went their separate ways. Cass passed Ivy hanging with a bunch of schoolgirls. The teenager was wearing her new chocolate-brown jacket.

'Looks good.' Cass mouthed and gave her a small OK sign. Ivy returned a clean, bright smile with dimples and a discreet thumbs up.

'Hey, Liz!' Cass called out as she entered the marquee. She hoped they could have a private chat.

Liz acknowledged her with a nod and her manicured finger across her lips. 'Shhh.'

Jack was holding court with his wife and the refined shopkeeper. 'Now, do you remember how the timber industry silenced the thylacine extinction in the jarrah forests?'

'What's this about a thylacine?' Cass joined the conversation, sending an air kiss to Liz. It was a white flag, for she could see this would not be the time or the place to have that talk.

Jack nodded greetings. 'The Bellenup Tiger is more than a myth. But getting information is like trying to catch a skink by its tail. Old Frank Gehry wrote a book about them, that his heirs were 'sposed to publish after his death; he told me about it. Then he popped his clogs and silence.'

'Very disappointing,' agreed his wife. 'A bit like the Forest Defenders, hey love? We dared to question the Great One's celebration of the so-called end of logging, and we haven't seen hide nor hair of 'em since.' Raven was an old-school, working-class Socialist through and through.

'Maybe he specified not to publish for 20 years after his death?' suggested Liz before rushing off to assist browsers.

'Yeah?... Hilma Klint did that with her art. The Forest Defenders won't touch Muckemup. With the changes to State election laws and no more regional seats, they'll want to be close to where the numbers are... the city voters. The turmeric latte set with their Teslas.

'The Forest Defenders are fast becoming the propaganda arm of the Enviro Party.' said Raven.

'I guess they thought if it's good enough to do it for the Workers Party, then why not?' Jack also wore his contempt openly.

'It's convergence.' Miro sauntered into their circle. He'd followed Cass into the stall and his ears pricked at the mention of a thylacine.

'Huh?' the group turned towards him.

'Where all the roads are meeting. Forest Defenders are the pathway for making money off carbon credits.'

The women smiled at Miro as a welcome, and Jack nodded again. 'Hullo, mate! That'd explain all those awards given to her. Environmentalist of the Year, made up by themselves! Then, the Women's Hall of Fame. What the hell is that?'

'I saw that one!' exclaimed Cass. 'Her acceptance speech was a "vote for me" spiel. Someone's polishing that turd for a run at a Parliamentary Seat.'

'The turds being gold-plated—'

'With the Workers Party blessing! How could you trust them?' Raven finished off her husband's grumblings.

'You couldn't, love. You'd have to have a camera on each corner of their mouth to figure out which side they were lying out of!'

'But Miro's right about the carbon credits.' Cass twisted one of the strong, white hairs the tweezers missed on her chin. 'No way the Conservatives will recover by the next election. It'd be convenient for MacGovern's lot... and legitimise their carbon Ponzi scheme to have the Enviro Party via the Forest Defenders selling it for them, literally!'

'My uncle, he saw the swamp dog.'

Cass gave Miro a quizzical look.

'Thylacine.' whispered Liz, returning to the chat. Her eyes peeled for potential sales.

'So?... What? Did the loggers say they were extinct?'

'There was no proof it ever existed,' said Jack. 'But fossil remains exist across the Nullabor, which would link to the western woodlands and into the southern for—'

'It existed!' interrupted Miro. 'Documented in Sid Slee's book, The Haunt of the Marsupial Wolf. My unc and him tried to tell the Forestry Department that logging was destroying their habitat. They got a photo back in the 80s. Before mobile phones, so not clear.'

'Yeah? Wow! I'd love to see it!' said Cass.

'The swamp dog is shy, cunning and don't like headlights, not like roos. But if you ever see headless roadkill, that's 'em. They crunch their heads off!' Miro snarled like he was tearing meat from the bone, eyes sparking.

Cass listened in awe, trying to decide if he was serious or just messing with her. The others already knew about the thylacine's macabre habit of decapitating kangaroos as part of its mating ritual. Roo heads became gifts to attract females, the way birds collect buttons and bling to impress potential partners.

'My uncle, he died a broken man. The Forestry boys and the public ridiculed him, saying picture'n his story were a hoax. It threw him into a reclusive state, and poof!' Miro blew on his fingers, 'Like dust in the wind, he vanished!'

'Oh, Miro. I'm sorry that happened to your uncle.' Liz touched Miro's arm.

'He was my hero. Taught me all I know 'bout the bush.'

'What a sad story.' agreed Raven, reaching out to pat the old cowboy.

'I don't know what to say.' Cass added awkwardly.

'Well, that's a first!' spluttered Jack.

* * *

Maybe the big bang was a giant burst of laughter, where nobody knows the cosmic joke. The group left Liz to serve customers and went looking for Tara. She was still with her axe-wielding neighbour and a few other locals, including the wife of the lawyer who'd agreed to represent Cockemup in the Warden's Court should it come to that. They were all sitting at a picnic table and the conversation revolved around mining. Days after Anu Sands withdrew, another company moved in and laid claim to a massive 20,000-hectare tenement.

'They're never going to give up,' groaned Jack.

'This lot is after lithium.'

'So, under the sand?' asked Cass.

'Would that make silicon a by-product?' asked Raven.

They all raised their eyebrows at the petite woman.

'My next question then, would that also make it tax-free like they've done with the crude all extracted from the gas fields up north?' asked Cass.

'I think gas and petroleum fall into a different category from minerals,' said Tara.

Raven looked up the market prices on her phone. 'Oil is $130 a barrel; the equivalent in gas looks to be about $50.'

'Which amount would you rather pay tax on?' asked Jack gruffly. 'It's like death by a thousand paper-cuts. Every election cycle, they promise to only cut ten percent. How often can you do that before it equals one hundred percent? How many slices of cake can yer take before the plate is empty?' He was almost 80, an old man who had witnessed the forest destroyed over decades by a seemingly unstoppable force.

'I got an idea,' said Miro. Typical of his culture, he was usually a man of few words, but when he spoke, it meant something. The group gathered around the bus driver, and the last of an ancient lineage that had only survived through guerilla tactics and a dose of good luck shared what had been visiting him in his dreams.

CHAPTER 66

Tara refused to go anywhere near the Post Office since the day she walked out. Andy had rung several times, leaving messages asking her to return that sounded more like veiled threats. She ignored him and now organised her grocery shopping for when the local paper hit the stands and picked up a copy from the supermarket.

On the front of the week's edition of the Tutelage was their Federal MP, one of the few Conservative Party members still standing, holding a bucket and imploring the Federal Water Minister to let the Irrigation Scheme keep the money despite the CSIRO report.

'There's a hole in my bucket, dear minister, dear minister.' Tara sang as she read the article. It confirmed there wasn't enough water in the Dilbanup to extract more than 1.5 gigs, let alone 12. There was a rebuttal from Matt Farnham, for he was regarded as the resident expert against the Scheme.

'Lord help us!' Tara groaned, tucking the paper under her arm and closing the car boot.

Unbeknownst to the women, Farnham's Water Security Group had referred Acheron to the Environmental Protection Agency three months ago and had followed up a few times, to be given the run-around. The Water Department held off the farmers, giving Acheron as much time as they could before the end of summer and dam-building season. Matt Farnham had recently sent another email. This time he attached Cass's video with his demands for an investigation. The EPA had no choice but to respond, which they did by opening a two-week public consultation period on whether they should act on the original referral they'd received. This would allow for at least another month, because it would require collating the feedback before presenting to the board.

Charlie shared the call for submissions on the Don't Dam the Dilbanup Facebook page, and Cass copied it from there into her group. She finally published the video she'd taken that day with Tara and Miro to guarantee the post got traction.

A sharp knock on her passenger window snapped Tara out of deep thought. Cass pulled a face before sliding into the seat next to her, lifting the newspaper to read the headlines before folding it onto the dashboard. 'Hey there! Are you okay?'

'Yeah, just telling myself I should check my mailbox while I'm in town and thinking about how much is happening; mining camps, mill fires, water markets...'

'Give me your key, and I'll do it for you now. Farnham messaged me this morning before Charlie's post went up asking for submissions. I told him to hit up his mates. Get Benno and Craig to rally the Forest Defender troops. Guess what he told me?'

'I don't know, what?'

'That the Friends of the River are no more? They've folded. So, I checked and sure enough, their Facebook page is gone. Five thousand followers disappeared into the ether!' Cass twinkled her fingers. 'Now why would those boys do something like that?'

'You're kidding! What about their website?' Tara's bright blue eyes were incredulous.

Cass pointed her index finger at Tara, cocking her thumb as if firing a pistol. 'Great minds! Facebook requires two weeks' notice before deleting a page, in case you change your mind. So that tells us their decision wasn't a spur of the moment, and they acted not long after Farnham's complaint would have been received by the EPA. Also, they haven't completely closed the shop. The website is still live, as is the business number. What does that tell you?'

'They want to keep the bank account.'

'You're too good! They didn't register for tax-deductible donations, so whose radar will that account be on? Not the Tax Offices, that's for sure!' Farnham's other problem is that his group has dissent in the ranks.'

'How so?' Tara was considering why those two reprobates would quit now. Not that they were ever really in it, other than for self-interest, she reminded herself.

'I'm not sure, he wouldn't elaborate. Just said that my cunning rat-controlled opposition story targeted the wrong group. The publican has sold up the hotel and resigned from their Water Security Group. He's supposedly been seconded to a working party for the Workers Party. Ha! It's like an episode of *Yes Minister,* he's a worker on a working party for the Workers Party. I can just hear Humphey's voice. 'Anyhoo...' Cass put on a posh British accent. 'It would be unseemly for him to be involved with a group that is criticising a Minister.'

'I didn't know he was on Farnham's team.'

'Neither did I, but it explains the motivation behind Politics at the Pub events. According to Matt, they've now weighted his group with paid-up members of the Workers Party. Think about that concept against the backdrop of Benno's wife being a staffer in Minister Macdonald's office!'

'I think we're coming to the endgame... If you don't mind grabbing my mail, that'd be great.' Tara passed her keys.

'No probs. It feels like the end is nigh, doesn't it? Oh, and what-his-face there.' Cass pointed to the newspaper. 'I think now is the right time to give that MP a red-hot poke. Let's publish those Senate questions with the answers, and reveal the true authors. I don't know about you, but I'm tired of the blatant misogyny around here. How often have we told those farmers it's not the State legislation, but Federal laws that are dictating things.'

'Only about a million times.'

'No shit!' Cass shook her head and then gave a really bad Schwarzenegger impression, 'I'll be back.' before leaving Tara alone again with her thoughts.

Tara grabbed the paper, and created a post to share on Muck Unrivalled, along with their official correspondence from the Senate Hearing. With some amusement, she decided the salient point had to be with the National Water Grid Fund's continued commitment to the Irrigation Scheme despite it being based on false data.

CHAPTER 67

251 submissions requested the EPA investigate the Acheron Dam, and seven thought it unnecessary. The EPA sided with the seven, referring the proponent back to the Water Department to reassess their water take. The next step was to file an appeal.

'It just goes on and on.' sighed Liz as Cass helped her tie the red and white *"SALE"* banner to the front verandah of the shop.

'If they can't knock you down, they'll grind you down. I think their next step is that the Department will cut the cloth to fit the suit.'

'The catchment is fully allocated. Are you going to file an appeal?'

'Can't. Don't want to risk being gagged from posting about it. But in the original clearing permit, the owner, our old mate Ricco Cont, ticked the box that he would self-refer. Matt Farnham's an idiot if he still thinks Conti got stitched up. Farmers are the only ones being played here.

'I'll put one in. Can you email me that clearing permit? Did you hear about Templar being assaulted?'

'That'd be great. Yeah, Tara told me. Do they know who did it?' Cass wanted to discuss their argument about Graeme Mantel and Hookemup Trust, but knew to bide her time. Social convention demanded that idle gossip precede those sorts of conversations.

'No, just a random attack.' Liz's voice dropped to a stage whisper. 'Two black eyes, broken ribs and three days in the hospital.'

Cass smirked. If they find out who did it, I'll buy them a beer.'

Liz's tongue clicked. 'Oh, Cass! That's not very charitable.'

'Oh, Cass, nothing! That man got what he deserved. You forget he changed the council's Standing Orders, especially so they could publish my address for all and sundry?'

'Oh, that's right. I had forgotten.' Liz admitted. Today she was channelling fashion icon Zandra Rhodes. Her short hair rinsed a temporary hot pink. She wore red slacks with a crepe blouse printed with watercolour blooms of pink, orange and purple, a chunky costume gold necklace, and matching ballet slippers. A large, Paspaley pearl ring glowed on her finger. 'He's in the market for a new job.'

'I imagine so. Although that was already on the cards, what with his recent plays.' Cass counted off on her fingers. 'Irrigation Schemes approved, the pretence of four-star hotels, courting foreign developers, underwriting nightclub renovations, buying property on Main Street for a motorcycle club!' and they're just what we can see via the public record.'

Liz shook her head with disdain as they stepped into the shop. 'Zhushing up a resume to leap from public servant to private industry.'

'He wishes!' Cass got down to business. 'Two things; I'm here on a mission. Raven wants half a dozen evening dresses, and I want to talk to you about our last conversation.'

Liz tilted her head, trying to recollect. 'Thylacines?'

'No Hookemup Trust and the Forest Defenders.'

'I keep the ball gowns out the back, just a minute. Don't worry about Hookemup. My lips are sealed.' Liz twisted an imaginary key over her mouth before disappearing. She returned with an armful of suit bags, piling them onto the counter. 'Why does Raven want all these dresses?'

'The Cockemup crew. They're organising a photo shoot by the lake, a la *"Priscilla Queen of the Desert"*. Expect an invitation.

'Sounds fun... Cass what you need to understand about the locals around here is we have long-standing relationships, dear... and, well, people are multifaceted.

Cass glanced sideways as she unzipped a bag, but said nothing. Gold chiffon and sequins pushed into her hand. 'These are gorgeous! To be safe, we had better take photos of each one and let Raven choose. She knows who she's dressing.'

CHAPTER 68

Early Sunday morning, Miro saw Cass sitting barefoot on the same stump where they'd first met. A wave of déjà vu swept over him. He recalled the Pheasant Coucal. Individuals with this totem were inventive and drew the energies that they needed using their willpower. Only death surpassed Cass's will in strength. He broke a branch.

Cass smiled and opened her eyes. 'Finally, you're here. I've been waiting for you. I want to discuss your plan.'

'I know, Meekah told me.'

'Who's Meekah?'

'The moon. Yesterday he left me a white ochre to find when walking home, right there by my house. The ochre is to illuminate answers. But what is the question? That is my job to find out.'

'The moon, you say?'

'Yer, in my culture, the moon is masculine. Like elsewhere, he connected with nature's rhythm of life and death. The animals are coming: cuckoo, twonk, swamp dog.'

Cass climbed down from her roost, a little more agile nowadays from regular exercise. 'Let's have a coffee at my place. I got something I want to show you.'

* * *

'Come in.' Cass invited Miro into her lounge studio and pointed at the large diptych leaning against the far wall. 'See this painting? I finished it in one day.' she held up a finger. 'Which isn't normal. I don't know why any of it's here, apart from this line...' The artist then ran her digit along a wide fluoro pink arc. 'This is the boundary tape of a proposed mining tenement. The rest of it?' she shrugged. 'It came...not from me, but through me, if that makes sense. Let me put the jug on.'

She left Miro staring at an exhausted yellow man floating on his back across the double canvas. The jaundiced figure was moving towards a dark mountain, pointing back at an astronaut with an oversized parrot on its shoulder. A full moon hung low in the sky, a black rain cloud loomed above, and a quenda gazed directly at Miro from the lower right-hand corner — the bandicoot! He knew exactly what the painting meant.

'How do you like your coffee?' Cass shouted from the kitchen?

'Hot and black, like my women!' Miro called back.

'Hardy-ha!' Cass rolled her eyes as she appeared beside the bushie, handing him a steaming mug.

'You hear about Templar?'

'Yer. Sounds like Janak got him. Thanks.' Miro took the coffee while still examining the painting.

'Who's Janak?'

'Not who, what. A powerful spirit that punishes wrong-doers of our Lore.'

'Nice one! Karma beat the living daylights out of his dogma.' joked Cass.

'Yer, or maybe shapeshifting Mummari, had enough.' Miro watched the artist out of the corner of his eye as he slurped a slow sip of coffee.

Cass felt a chill and clenched her fist in front of her heart for protection. She changed the subject. 'So, am I right?'

'Bout what?'

'That the message is for you? Because it's not for me. I held off packing it for the gallery. Not sure why? I wanted to resolve its existence before exhibiting, I guess. But when you mentioned the moon earlier, I'm thinking it's for you.'

Miro nodded his head. 'Yer, it's for me. I can't tell you what it means; men's business. But I can say Quenda teaches yer to be happy in the darkest moments. He also tells yer to scratch beneath the surface. Things aren't as they appear.' He turned to look at the middle-aged woman, her silver hair piled up in a loose topknot. 'Cryptic, I know. But yer good at solving mysteries.' he shrugged. 'I also now see what we gotta do... Thank you, Boodja Jud-ko.'

'Boodja — Earth, is ... .what?'

'It means Earth Sister,' said Miro. And at that moment there was a sense of knowing, or recognition, and a conspiracy was born.

CHAPTER 69

For a small village, Cockemup offered an extensive number of interest groups. Tai chi, mahjong, craft and, of course, the *"Stitch and Bitch"* group.

Five women had packed away their usual assortment of patchwork quilting to alter ball gowns instead.

Tara almost skipped into the old schoolroom, now a hive of activity and jewel-coloured fabrics. 'Hello, ladies!' She carried three shopping bags full of twigs, dried gum leaves, glitter and dollar shop tiaras.

Cass followed, ladened with the dresses she'd picked up from Liz. 'Looks like exploding stars in here!'

'Good job. Thank-you!' Raven's tone clipped like a veteran General's as she took the gowns from Cass, her small frame immediately buried under a rainbow of fru-fru.

'Have we got twelve scenes sorted?' Tara sat to help make wood-nymph masks.

'Almost. Chip Smith has donated a numbat photo, we'll select one from the Fair Day, we're doing a Mad Hatters tea party in the forest this weekend. Then seven of us in evening dresses on the pontoon. Are you girls good for that on Tuesday? We've got a couple of rowboats to get us out there, and Jack is getting hold of a drone for some of the shots.' said Raven.

'Oooh, that'll look amazing!' agreed Cas. 'So how many are we short?'

'Only one!' The seamstresses sang.

'How about a funny pic of some protestors?' suggested Tara. 'Get the blokes involved. Dress them up... and a few women, resembling garden gnomes. Do the photo shoot out at Gnomesville.' She referred to the farmer's folly near Kate Gill's place.

'That's a brilliant idea!' Cass got out her journal and quickly sketched up a visual concept. 'Grab some beanies, flannelette shirts, cut quilt wadding for beards.'

'Paint up protest signs, slogans like *"Too Magic To Mine"* and *"Don't Poke the Gnomes!"* said Tara.

'Anu can Fuck Offski,' offered Raaven absently as she assessed Cass's delivery of froth and shimmer.

Silence fell in the room. The group stared at the tiny birdlike woman in shock.

Raven raised her head to see what was the problem, then realised she'd spoken out loud. 'Well...' she shrugged, 'They can!'

Everyone erupted into the loud, deep laughter that builds female camaraderie.

'Now we're cooking!' Tara reached for the hot-glue gun.

CHAPTER 70.

"Are you free to talk?" The message was from Matt Farnham.

"Sure, I'm at Mother Jarrah" replied Cass. It was 7 AM and fresh, the outside air felt good on her face. She'd paused her rambling through the bush now that snakes were on the move with the weather warming up.

"Where? Can ya meet me at the bakery?"

"Gimme 10" Cass rolled her eyes at the limited boundaries of the Patriarchy, then added. "Order me a cappuccino, please."

Farnham was sitting out the back when she arrived.

'How are you?' Cass lowered herself opposite as he passed her a takeaway cup.

'Hullo. Do you take sugar?' Matt held out two sachets between his work-calloused fingers. 'I've got a problem...'

'Thanks.' Cass took the lid off and breathed in the rich aroma of real coffee. 'What's up?'

'Chuck won't post anything,' said the farmer.

She nonchalantly stirred in the sweetener. 'Who?... Oh, you mean Charlie, is he the only admin on your page?'

'Yer. I can't believe it...' Farnham sighed. '... and his name isn't Charlie; it's Phillip Giolla.'

'What?' Cass stopped stirring to stare, dumbfounded at the farmer. He was a big hunk of a man, dressed in hi-vis with a baby face and Irish blue eyes. 'Let me get this straight? First, Friends of the River removed their page, and now you're telling me you have no access to Don't Dam Dilbanup? Who the heck is Philip Giolla? Cass pulled her phone out and punched in his name. 'G-I-O-L-L-A?'

'Yer. Workers Party guy. Bought a hobby farm down here in 2018, and sold it last year. He controls our Facebook account. The farmer hesitated, unsure of how much to share with Cass.

'You may as well tell me the entire story.'

'We've got Edward Beauchamp's son too.'

She reeled in horror. 'What! Are you kidding me? As in Beauchamp, the former Attorney General?'

'Afraid so... I can't believe it,' Farnham repeated.

'I can!' Cas thought about the bandicoot in her painting; she could hear Miro's words, *"Scratch beneath the surface; things aren't as they appear."* She pressed her index finger against her forehead. 'Matt, you must understand the amount of money involved here. Over east, water prices fluctuated from $50-$60 to $700 per meg during the drought. Not just that! Speculation drove up the price. If profiteers like Acheron can carry significant quantities of water over, withholding it, then they can create demand and push the price up, obliterating you little guys. Think DeBeers and diamonds!'

She stopped, suddenly realising they'd controlled the whole enchilada from the beginning... all of it. Nothing was ever in their way... except for Muck Unrivalled. She'd inadvertently stumbled into the dragon's lair while it was fattening the goose for Christmas lunch.

Once Cass started getting serious airplay, the local arbiters took action. They portrayed her as unhinged from multiple angles, encouraging the haters to spread the narrative through the various social groups. It wasn't difficult, she'd done half their job for them by upsetting everyone from the Catholics, to the rednecks and even the greenies. Then in a move well practised by sociopaths, they tooled up the peasants with lies to join forces in the attack. They'd even press-ganged the doctor to start a clinical profile. The poor man had no choice but to follow the eccentric woman on Facebook and prepare notes. A doctor's signature could pathologise anything.

Such abhorrent sanctions instigated by powerful men are as old as Hypatia. Despite what polite society thought, Western Australia was a renegade State. Northern Regional Hospital was accustomed to receiving Aboriginal inpatients under Section 8s — particularly women trying to protect their sacred sites from mining interests. A month or two dosed up with Ketamine cocktails sorted out any further agitation against exploration companies. Eventually, with their memories wiped, they were discharged into the care of their families unfit to bother anyone.

'What have they done?' With her hand over her mouth, Cass's eyes flickered like she was watching an action replay. She reflected on her existing knowledge, both concrete and circumstantial.

'What else?' Farnham braced himself for more bad news.

'Water markets and mining go hand-in-hand. Remember my post about how Worm's State Forest lease could earn him $1.5 million. He's got a 15-year lease; that's over S25 million for turning on the fucking pump! Gio Luciano's probably the same with his Mokine Creek Lease.' Cass struggled to keep her voice calm as the chessboard moves became visible.

'Yer. All the farmers think the Irrigation Scheme is dead. Gio's put his place on the market by Tender.'

'It's not dead! What is wrong with you lot? The Devil's not even hiding anymore, and you still can't see him!' Cass clasped the sides of her head in despair. 'He's what?'

'Yeah, his old man is handling the sale.'

'Is it online? What's Charlie's wife's name?'

'Yer, real estate dot com, Paradiso Road. He wants $7 million; he's dreamin'. I can't remember her name, why?'

'No, Matt. Listen to me!' Cass put her thoughts into words slowly and clearly. 'He's not dreaming! He'll probably get it because that's the keystone property. That's why he got the Crown lease and why they hid the record in the bowels of the Land Office. It's where they'll try first to separate water ownership from the land. Look, here we go!' Cass opened the details on her phone. 'It says the sale includes a 1,000ML water licence. Let me find my post when I pinged him along with Worm's lease....' She scrolled through her old posts. 'Ah, here it is. They have two water licences on Gio's property, only adding up to 550ML. But his Crown land lease, four kilometres away, has a 450ML water licence.'

Farnham nodded, understanding where it was all going. 'Smack on the money!'

Cass barked a dry cough. 'Yep, equals a thousand meg. That's how they intend to do it. Can you see it? It's all incremental moves... Over the years, they have massaged this along.'

'Yer.' Farnham's usual ruddy face turned a ghostly shade. 'I see it.'

'Don't give up just yet. That sale is illegal. Because that's been a significant part of our problem... if it's not illegal, you can't prosecute and there's no point lodging complaints. Tenders close in a week; enough time to rattle the new Water Ministers' cage. I'll formally complain. For god's sake, keep it to yourself.'

'I will. What are we gunna do about Giolla and Ed's son?'

'I don't know. I need to think about them. How did Charlie end up with sole control of the page?'

'He created it from the outset and offered to handle it. None of us were that interested.' Farnham was sheepish. Looking back with the benefit of hindsight, he could now see where Charlie, the pub owner and the Attorney General's son, had been directing everything all along.

'That easy, huh?'

Farnham winced and confirmed with an almost imperceptible nod.

'I remember Charlie messaging me after you that morning, about my *"Controlling the Opposition"* post. You know the one about your mates Benno and Craig;

he must have laughed his head off when I told him people should do their due diligence.' Cass handed Matt her phone. It was now open on the LinkedIn profile of a Christine Giolla, Executive Director of Strategic Policy for the Water Department. 'Would this be his wife?'

'Shit! Yes, that's her. Chrissy.' Farnham felt gut-punched and dragged his hands down his face.

'Right. Let's assume the Water Department knew every move you guys would make. Did your Water Security Group file an appeal?'

'Nope, they voted against it. But I did one on the sly. This is too important.'

'Be careful. That's how they'll catch you. The laws around incorporated associations are a minefield. Just get them out of your group.'

'I'm working on it. Had to give 28 days' notice to hold a special general meeting.'

Cass checked the time as she pulled her phone back. 'I've got to go to work. I recommend you get the numbers, vote them out... and fast.'

CHAPTER 71

'I need to speak with you!' Lenny Reid ignored the youthful assistant sitting in his periphery as he stormed past her desk and into Aconaday's council office.

Romeo stood and motioned to the secretary not to worry as she jumped up to follow the old apple farmer. 'It's okay, Amy. Why don't you go to lunch, dear?' He dismissed the young woman, whose mother had been his parliamentary office manager for decades. 'What's the matter, Len?' Snaked asked as he offered his friend a seat and eased himself back behind his desk to listen, as he'd done many times before.

'My business partners, who *you* recommended!' Lenny poked a shaky finger towards his closest friend and panted, 'Have pushed us out of the Ruskin farm.'

Aconoday absently rubbed his palm back and forth across the desk to control the tremor in his own hand. 'How so?'

'I don't know! Reid brushed his words away. 'There was a clause or something in the contract. The lawyers are checking it now. But that's not all!'

'What else?' Snake asked thickly.

'We've received notice that they won't renew the lease on the storage facility we sold them.'

'Oh!' Alarm grabbed Romeo by the throat. His hand stilled as he blinked and swallowed.

'Oh! What the fuck is, oh? No packing shed means no vendor licence. No contract with Woolworths. *Oh,* means I'm screwed! Finished! What's Cronus gotta say about that?'

'Okay, Lenny, calm down. I hear you, mate.' Romeo uneasily considered his friend. 'It sounds like a misunderstanding. I'll call Ricco and sort it out. Stop worrying.... we own this town; you'll give yourself a stroke, getting upset like this. The mayor stood up. 'Want a drink?' Without waiting for an answer, he fixed two scotches.

Lenny accepted the heavy crystal glass of amber liquid as he loosened his collar. His palms were moist, and his chest felt tight. He swigged the fire water back in one gulp. At an age when he should enjoy the fruits of his labour, he was facing financial ruin.

Christa e a zita, cu 'a voli sa marita - The die is cast, and you can do nothing about it.

Aconaday glanced out of the corner of his eye. Ghosts enjoy company and his mother sat on the edge of his desk in her Sunday best. She hummed a timely lament and poured herself a marsala in one of the small gold-trimmed port glasses he remembered as a kid. Snake swallowed his drink in two mouthfuls.

* * *

Mother knows best. Senora Aconaday was correct, Leonard Reid was being shafted, and there was nothing anyone could do about it, not even the mayor. Snake had been busy trying to keep abreast of what Acheron was doing, beyond digging dams, to prevent a similar fate from happening to him. Meanwhile, Reid's partners had blindsided them.

After Lenny departed, loaded with warm whiskey and the cold comfort of Romeo's promises, Snake closed the door to his office and rang Ricco Conti.

The orchardist may have inherited his wealth, but he'd gained his poker face from years of wheeling and dealing to keep it. Conti knew when to hold his cards and when to fold 'em, so while he told Snake that the dam preparation was on schedule, he also stroked the politico's ego. 'I hear there were only five appeals to the EPA; they won't be a problem. Thanks to your ministerial foresight, locking away that original map all those years ago, looks like Acheron will tap into almost half of the 13 gigs with no one the wiser.'

'That was supposed to be under the control of the Irrigation Scheme, and what about Lenny? He's just left my office.... quite distressed. What's going on?'

'Uhh... things change, Romeo... you know that.' Conti gave an apologetic sigh. 'Quercus has bought Reid's partners out. It looks like they've got other plans.' Ricco shrugged in the Italian way. 'It's unfortunate for Lenny, but that's business. You're still fine, though.' He assured the mayor. 'You'll control water sales to the farmers as planned. We just need to ease in gently. Have you taken care of that woman yet?'

'Working on it.' Snake muttered. He knew they were ridiculing him. Maliciously suggesting he'd lost his touch — couldn't even shut up one troublesome woman.

Loathing gouged a deep chasm of hatred in him towards Cassandra Leason. *'If only she'd never come to this town!'* Snake seethed inwards. Once they had her committed, every night, she would discover that the world had teeth and there were consequences worse than death.

'Okay, well, I'm late for a meeting. Let us know when you've handled her. She's just crapped all over Gio's sale, and he's now upped the price — says he wants $8 million.'

Aconoday pushed away the phone, churning inside. He appeared younger than his seventy years. But today, he felt much older. A primal fear thinned his sap to water. He could sense the threads unravelling on the plans he'd carefully woven for over a decade.

Conti, however, shook his head and laughed, 'Dumb fuck.' He then strolled into the boardroom, for Snake had rung just as he was about to meet with the owners of Lenny's packing shed. They'd soon own all of his southern operations too, if things went well. Conti intended to sell everything, his vendor licence, packing shed and all his orchards. Better Lenny Reid get it in the neck than me, he thought as he shook hands with the suits seated around the long, polished jarrah table.

The multinational Quercus Capital Investments had made a generous offer for Conti's southern portfolio, including the property he leased to Acheron and his block next door. He'd seen it all before; they'd then stick their elbows out and pick up what remained of Lenny's empire for a song. Reid was a dead man walking without cash flow or a packing shed. After that, they'd merge or buy out Acheron. It had already changed hands once, Stamos Price and his associates taking over from the Wheatbelt cowboys who'd started the venture a decade ago.

Like a high-stakes game of passing the parcel, the elite handed Acheron around the halls of power as the weaker players dropped out. A couple more Board spills and the $8 Billion private equity firm would own most of the farmland and all the water they needed in Muckemup. The old boys, Aconaday and Reid, had nearly outlived their usefulness. They were pigs to the slaughter; Conti knew Reid would quietly disappear like a wisp of smoke after blowing out a candle. He expected Snake would scramble to install his daughter into the council, the only leverage Romeo Benito Aconoday had left at his disposal. But it didn't matter, the Anaconda's reign was almost over. Conti laughed at the thought; Yep, this is how you pulled a bloodless coup.

CHAPTER 72

James Templar reasoned that what was pitched to the town as four-star tourist lodgings, suddenly morphing into single workers' quarters, was perfectly acceptable because worker accommodation, whether miners or contracted Pacific Islanders, was what they needed.

On the council website, the project was still listed as a multi-million dollar quality hotel, and that was enough if a corporate HR Department cross-checked his CV. After the painful and embarrassing assault. Templar was desperate to escape from Muckemup. But that was proving more challenging than he'd expected. Insult followed injury, there had been no bites on his job applications, and James Templar could see the Indian developer was taking the piss on their deal, but for the moment, he was jammed in tight, and there was little he could do but wait.

Amit Sanjay was clever and aggressive in business, a rat with a gold tooth. He had numerous companies, and in 2009, the global economic collapse was a *Get Out Of Jail Free* card for entrepreneurs like Mr Sanjay. He hadn't always been so lucky. If in the beginning, Templar had bothered to make cursory investigations, he'd have discovered Amit Sanjay had spent time in New Delhi's notorious Tihar Jail, convicted of defrauding wealthy investors by selling timeshare apartments off the plan for a non-existent resort north of Geraldton. His racket had been almost perfect; most investors he dealt with didn't care that the hotel was a mirage; it was the paperwork they were purchasing and an opportunity to buy their way into Australia. But somewhere along the line, Amit had slipped. Someone was forgotten or offended and filed a complaint in retaliation. Sanjay hadn't paid enough gratuities to the political elite to save himself from jail. Being a grifter in India means ensuring the pole remains greased, and every minor official gets their cut as a bare minimum.

Another notable thing about India is they document everything in triplicate. If James had looked beyond the smooth words, he would have found Mr Amit Sanjay's criminal record digitised by the National Government of India. Instead, not only did Amit Sanjay close the Muckemup deal without spending a cent! He didn't purchase the property, but instead negotiated for a lease with the initial year rent-free, explaining he would need that time for construction. What followed was straight from the Chor Bazaar handbook. It began with the usual excuses of supply problems, then grew into a story that he'd had to buy the pre-fab building company to guarantee delivery. Three years after signing the 6-year lease, the first two accommodation pods and what appeared to be a hay shed arrived. Then work screeched to a halt. Templar wasn't a hands-on manager. Usually, he stated what needed to happen and left it to a subordinate to make sure it was completed. That wouldn't work on this occasion.

By the time warning bells sounded in Templar's office, Sanjay had leveraged off his lease, the four-star hotel documentation on the Muckemup Council website, and the Mining Department tenement maps. He used this evidence to convince off-shore investors to bankroll more of his projects, and he wouldn't allow a backwater CEO to get in his way. No siree sahib! Amit Sanjay bought blocks of land all over Muckemup. Meanwhile, in response to Templar's complaints, he paid three backyardigan contractors to build the rest of the dongas on-site in the middle of town. It was a half-arsed affair as the men only turned up a few hours a week between their other jobs.

'Sanjay, what's going on? This isn't what we agreed.' James and the property developer stretched on a lounge in the empty nightclub. The CEO now held all his confidential meetings here for added privacy. He knew someone at work was a mole, leaking information to the Leason woman. He suspected one of the councillors, but her sources were obviously more than a singular person, and he'd become risk averse these days.

'Mr Temple, don't you worry, sir.' Amit bobbed his head from side to side, in the style where one thing means another. 'This will be good for Muckemup.'

'When will you be finished?'

'Soon, soon,' Sanjay wheedled. 'If you don't mind me asking, what happened to your face, my friend?'

'Mistaken identity.' Templar raised a hand to touch his cheek. The pain subsided as Templar's bruising matured from eggplant to an ugly mustard yellow. He poured himself another whiskey and removed his tie. He was looking worse for wear these days and not just from the flogging he received; the relationship between himself and Romeo became strained as the mayor distanced himself from his CEO. James laid back on the deeply buttoned Chesterfield to stare at the ceiling. He was a conflicted man, full of malice. 'I've got to get out of this town!'

'What kind of job are you looking for?' asked Sanjay, recognising an opportunity and knowing with mules as green as those in Muckemup, it was better still to be owed favours.

'Right now, anything!'

'Can I assist? I have good connections with the panchayat...I mean, the administration of a district north of Geraldton; they are looking for a new Town Clerk. I could put in a good word.'

James swivelled his head to look at the short man, fit with dark hair. What gave away his age was brown pigmentation spots marking his face and swollen pockets of skin under his eyes as if he had just woken up from an afternoon nap. Templar sighed; he came away from every encounter with the Indian entrepreneur feeling as if it had been as useless as a safety meeting.'Yeah, sure. Thanks.'

PART FIVE –SPIRIT

Three for the Maiden,
Three for the Crone,
and Three for the Mother,
Whose target is shown.

CHAPTER 73

The photoshoot in the middle of the lake went as planned. Seven women of all ages and sizes in sneakers, strapless flowing dresses, and long chiffon scarves with red lipstick and moss and twig crowns atop their heads held each other tight upon the pontoon. The sky was overcast, and the water a mottled silver mirror. Jack rocked unsteadily in a small rowboat, fiddling about to get his camera ready. An assistant was with him, holding a large round reflector. Just as in the movies where Felicia mimes Sempre libera from Verdi's La Traviata while on top of a bus driving through the red desert; the breeze obliged to assist and lifted the models' translucent lengths of fabric. Manoeuvring to suspend the bright colours so they danced like kites, ducking and weaving — *Sempre libera, forever free.*

'Find joy in the darkest moments.' Cass's arms intertwined between Tara and Liz.

'That's very Zen of you,' said Raven. As the shortest, they squeezed her front and centre.

'It's bandicoot, actually.' replied Cass.

'Have you been hanging with Miro?' asked Tara.

'Ha! Is it that obvio—'

'Say Cheese!' called Jack from behind his camera.

'QUENDA!' cried the women, hugging each other and daring the wind as gusts strong enough to blow a sailor off your sister whipped around them.

* * *

When it was finished, and everyone returned to shore, Tara and Cass hung around, drinking cups of tea in their finery with cardigans thrown over their shoulders while waiting for Jack to put the last images onto the calendar template.

'Right, ladies.' He held out a memory stick. 'It's ready!'

'How many do we need to sell?' asked Raven.

'Minimum five hundred,' said Tara, taking the USB from Jack. 'Thanks. The Community Centre in Muckemup has agreed to print on demand.'

'Do they know what it's for?'

Cass laughed. 'Are you kidding? They've no idea, or they'd never have agreed. Adam Colhoun set us up a secure payment portal. I need to fetch a copy for him as well. I'll start pushing it on the social's tomorrow morning.'

'Roll up! Roll up! Ladies and Gentlemen, get your stocking fillers sorted with the 2023 Inaugural Collector's Edition Muck Unrivalled calendar,' announced Tara.

'Souvenir of the Fall of the Empire.' Jack bowed deep.

Cass hummed the Stormtrooper tune, then dropped her voice deep. 'In a galaxy far, far away....'

'... is a new hope!' Raven clapped, riffing off one of the *Star Wars* titles.

'And a phantom menace!' Tara's grin was wicked, looking even more so with her heavily made-up face.

'Oh dear, we could do this all day!' laughed Jack.

'We could! Let's go, Tara.' They exchanged hugs, and the women headed off to instigate the next phase of Miro's plan.

CHAPTER 74

Within a week, the small gang of wise and grizzled dissidents sold 818 calendars. With their target exceeded, they held a meeting.

'Throw a dollar in the jar. We need to brainstorm a name.' Cass said, offering a cheese platter to the group in her back garden.

'I got it, mum. What about TEFAF?' Tara pulled two dollars out of her purse.

'What's that stand for? Marion inquired.

'Too expensive for average fools.' the coin clinked a sharp ringing sound as she dropped it into the glass.

The collective chuckled.

'Is everyone here? Where's Liz?' asked Raven.

'She couldn't make it,' said Cass, directing an unspoken signal to Tara as they made eye contact.

'Should we avoid arguments and just pick one out of a hat?' suggested Tara.

'Behold the hat!' said Miro, lifting the worn Akubra from his head.

'I've been studying mining,' proclaimed Jack.

'Oh, Fark, 'ere we go!' groaned Miro.

'Hey! Hear me out first before yer start disparaging,' Jack's tone was injured but his watery eyes twinkled.

Cass played along. 'Yeah, who knows...we could even like it,'

'You might!' Jack nodded. 'As I was saying before, I was so rudely interrupted...' Unfazed, Miro popped a cheese-laden biscuit into his mouth. 'I came across a little Chinese story from the eleventh-century Song Dynasty.'

Miro gave everyone an *"I told you so"* look as they audibly sighed.

Raven giggled, 'Welcome to my world!'

Jack spoke louder 'The mountains near Changsha were rich in gold and other minerals, and many prospectors were eager to possess them. But in their wisdom, the authorities considered the place's wind and water lines as even more precious and forbade all mining.'

'I bet they've overturned that law since.'

'No, they haven't... supposedly.'

'Deadly! Like my mob. Feng Shui believers say the universe is a living organism,' said Miro.

Tara pulled out her phone. 'Google's most common question about the Song Dynasty is, "What factors within China caused the Song Dynasty to weaken and eventually fall?" Do you all want to know the answer?'

'Sure.' Cass served coffee as they listened.

'Political corruption, invasion from external tribes and civilian uprising.'

'I was wrong; that fits!' said Miro.

Jack smiled and gave everyone his *"I told you so"* face.

* * *

'What's the go with Liz? Tara helped with the dishes after the guests had left.

Cass put a plate onto the rack to drain.'I don't trust her.'

'Fair enough. So, what does she think the calendars are for?'

'Oh, to fight against mining. I haven't lied. I'm just annexing the flow of information. She set off alarms with her talk about Hookemup.'

'Have we got anything more on them?'

'Not a skerrick. The Trust could be legit, but it also could be backed by the coal industry or some crazy ASIO black ops exercise? They've got a tonne of money from somewhere, and their tree planting program reads like the template for the Conservatives' Work-For-The-Dole.'

'Undoubtedly, they've played a significant role in shaping policy over the last few decades. What about Don't Dam Dilbanup?' Cass had filled Tara in on her devastating conversation with Matthew Farnham.

'Nope, nothing there either. We seem to be the last ones standing!'

'Wow! That's something. What do you think we should do?'

'Not much we can do. Carry on with Miro's plan. MacGovern has the Regional Forestry Agreement to publish yet. He can't bypass that one with *"Departmental Guidelines"*.

'The Forest Defenders have called ecological thinning the middle-way solution.'

'Of course they did! They'll point to whatever the Premier comes up with as a win when it's guaranteed to be a bottom-line loss. People are idiots.'

'Uh-huh. Some compromise! MacGovern's talking about 400,000 hectares listed for protection, meanwhile we still have about 320,000 hectares that haven't progressed from the last RFA obligations. Including your beloved Mother Jarrah.'

'Athena Papadopoulos didn't even flinch when I handed her that grenade.'

'Yeah? Sounds like they've bought her,' said Tara.

Cass snorted. 'No need to fork out a billion dollars for that! I reckon that girl's for Team Athena!'

'Sooo,' drawled Tara, getting back to the Forestry Agreement. 'We're only gaining 80,000 hectares. They reckon they'll be *"ecologically thinning"* eight thousand hectares a year. When the term's up in 10 years, they've cleared anything we've gained.'

'And there is Jack's slice of cake theory proven. Don't forget the entire purpose for forming the Forest Defenders in the first place was to suit the government regarding the Forestry Agreement back in 2000. Imagine if the greenies hadn't bothered fighting... if they'd just said, "Meh, go for it! Don't let us stop you from tearing down four-hundred-year-old trees." It's counterintuitive, but there'd be no argument for transition funding. No $200 million from taxpayers to pretend it's over for a little while before rebranding, passing your mill on to the next generation and starting again. In a way, the environmentalists helped prop up the industry.'

'And the rest! Rip, rip woodchip subsidies. Funding to decontaminate the site—'

'Oh yeah! How are our little compost turners doing? Murphy had an online rant the other day, calling me a conspiracy theorist. Apparently, he's now the self-declared expert on environmental poisons, and according to him, there's no problem with PCPs or asbestos.'

'Making the most of his five minutes of fame. Watch yourself; he's notorious.' warned Tara.

'I remember. We went five rounds toe to toe until I snookered him by asking if he had permission to make fertiliser onsite. He then shut up and had me booted from that group.' Cass forced a grin of resignation. The skin felt tight on her face.

'Word on the street is he's in litigation with the mill owners.'

'It's dog-eat-dog out there.... *OR* just for show? To throw people off his trail. Imagine, hypothetically, if you were involved in starting a fire, and then the company that will profit from it sues you, or vice versa? Either way, it's rough, but it creates a facade of innocence, and he's already untouchable within the community.'

'You obviously heard about the horrific accident.'

'... and read. Tragic. But also a perfect foil. He brought up his charity in our argument, so I looked. Sorry, I had to laugh. Digging wells for kids in Africa while doing nothing to protect water where you live? Puhleeze! Each to their own, but yeah, I'm judging.'

'Also interesting is the council was advertising for a new enviro officer a fortnight before the fire.'

'Oh-ho, it's perfect! The site clean-up falls under local jurisdiction. The State funds it, and the council manages it by outsourcing to a mate. Wait and see! Of course, you'd want the person signing off to be a cleanskin—no pre-existing knowledge and will do as directed. Same, the journo is out.'

'Oh? What happened to him?' asked Tara.

'Well, he was sticking to it despite receiving *real* death threats ... .talk about a baptism of fire, poor kid! He was disgusted by the greed and corruption; I don't know how deep he was digging, but I reckon he may have hit a nerve. Suddenly, one of his professors checks in to see how he's doing; not too great, he replies, and the guy swings him a job out the back of Bourke.'

'What? And he took it?'

'He wasn't too keen, but they offered full-time permanent employment, and his folks put the lean on him. Those kinds of terms are unheard of at the entry level. So he's gone!'

'Wowsers. Him, two ministers, Luciano's trying to get out, and I heard Alex Crooks sold up — moving to Newport.'

'That's quite a collection of scalps. Who's he again?'

'Former Treasurer of the Irrigation Scheme.'

'Oh yeah, huh? And let's not forget the publican sold on the cusp of a mining boom when shitty motel rooms are already going for $300 a night.' Cass arched her brows.

Tara hung up her tea towel. 'It's all very convenient.'

'Well, it's got to be. Otherwise, we'd look like conspiracy theorists!'

CHAPTER 75

A bunch of Form 21s for mineral rights were piled on Templar's desk. Every tenancy application to the Mining Department also had to notify the relevant local authority in writing. There was a bigger game going on. Staking a tenement could make one incredibly wealthy. The competition was fierce as the price of lithium rose above iron ore. The Mines Department had tied one on, complaining about too many public objections clogging up the Warden's Court. They even got press coverage for their manufactured story, declaring it was a drain on taxpayer resources.

Meanwhile, mining companies failed to respond to hearings, withdrew, reapplied, and filed multiple petitions on the same pieces of land. It was a frenzied waiting game. Initially, the plan was to change spring rights legislation to access the water and create a market. However, there were inherent problems they didn't want attention brought to. Instead, the State authorities broadened the internal interpretation of the Act to be whatever they required within the Water Department. It would take a court challenge to stop them. Smallholders lacked the funds and courage for lawsuits, while corporate operators didn't need them. The changes were for their benefit.

The government would now contain the key pieces of law within the Regional Forestry Agreement; this accord was in partnership with the federal government, therefore, unavoidable. The new agreement was written to facilitate and defend water extraction for mining, well into the next decade. Premier MacGovern signed the RFA with the outgoing Prime Minister, splitting the responsibility between the two major political parties and ensuring they would both ignore calls for any future investigations when things went pear-shaped, as they surely would because of climate change.

Templar checked off each tenement, signing and placing them in his out tray. This was his last task. Most were straightforward re-applications on earlier withdrawals, except one. It was just after lunch on his final day. He was on auto-pilot and almost overlooked it. He now carefully read the document before making a copy, which he folded into an envelope and placed in his briefcase.

Amit Sanjay delivered on the promised job offer, if not finishing the hotel. Templar was beyond caring about Muckemup. He'd had enough and accepted the CEO position for the Upper Western Shire, the locale of Sanjay's resort scandal. On hearing of Templar's success, Amit insisted that James and his wife visit India as his guest. Despite Mrs Templar's lack of enthusiasm, James believed it would be rude to decline the offer or cut off future introductions and support from the Indian. A couple of weeks' holiday would give them an enjoyable break before relocating and starting a new job.

'It's also good business sense, dear.' He told his wife the morning of his last day as he brushed his teeth. Finished, he walked from the ensuite, standing before the mirror to button his shirt. 'What, with the new free trade agreement signed between Australia and India and Dicky, now the Shadow Assistant Minister for Trade, this new job could lead to more than merely a career step sideways.'

Mrs Templar had been sulking for weeks. Seeing her husband's broken face in the hospital didn't make the reality easier. 'Yes,... and our ticket out of Muckemup.' she said glumly. She'd lived in the town all her life and would miss her friends.

'We can visit the Taj Mahal, the world's second greatest monument to love.' He could see her in the mirror, sitting on the edge of their bed, staring at the carpet.

'What's the first? She questioned wearily.

Templar gave up choosing a tie and turned towards his wife. 'I'm glad you asked.' with a glint in his eye, the CEO started unbuckling his belt.

'You're going to be late for work!' she squealed.

He grinned. 'Let them fire me!'

CHAPTER 76

Aconaday had extensive experience in policy. He knew all the legislation inside out, half of it he'd written! To succeed in business, a keen memory and accurately predicting outcomes are essential. Snake knew there was always a risk of the bigger fish eating the smaller ones, including himself. But like Amit Sanjay, Romeo was a street fighter at heart. A few years before they conceived the Irrigation Scheme, he organised his brother Angelo to purchase a wedge of land in the forest. Located east of the Acheron, it joined below Gio's crown lease on Mokine Creek, nestled between land owned by the Water Department on one side and the Development Board on the other. For over a decade, Angelo Aconaday remained silent as a truffle buried in the dirt. Unlike his neighbours, he eschewed applying for a water licence. He'd secured permission to clear part of the block. That was sufficient, for now; the permit spanned eight years, and the land was the family's insurance policy, guaranteeing them a permanent seat at the table, no matter what happened between Acheron and Quercus or any other multinationals that came onto the scene.

Romeo was enjoying an apéritif on his terrace. The lingering day's heat still bearing down when he heard the hum of Templar's car down the driveway. It was the golden hour. Sunbeams of warm light stretched across his dam to fall behind the oak trees, like they did every afternoon in the season of Birak. He didn't bother going to meet the CEO. James would know where to find him, and anyway, Snake had already moved on. Templar would soon be gone, leaving a predicament for the mayor to sort out. They needed the State government to hurry up and release the funds for cleaning up the mill site; there were holes that needed filling before a new CEO took the helm.

'Mea culpa.' Romeo's involvement in causing any of the mess was irrelevant. As a parting gift, Templar had filed misconduct charges against a councillor he'd suspected was an informant. Not one, but five charges! 'Mio Dio!' Aconaday shook his head and sipped from a gold-trimmed port glass that had been his mother's. He was confident Templar was wrong. But the official had snooped into the council's financial affairs, so maybe the CEO's action was for the best. His daughter would have a better chance of getting elected if they removed him.

Templar parked out the front of his boss's place for the final time. He took a deep breath, and unlocked the briefcase on the passenger seat. This was the closure Templar had only dreamt about. After 25 years, he had his ultimate day - sex in the morning and personally delivering this note. He pushed the car door open and stretched out his legs, one polished black shoe at a time.

Aconaday was pouring a second drink when James joined him. He lifted the marsala bottle. 'For old time's sake?' he asked.

'Sure, just a quick one.' Templar accepted a glass and they toasted each other.

'Are you set to go?'

'Affirmative, keys and credit card returned to the office. Dinner tonight with the in-laws. We will head to the city tomorrow and fly out via Singapore on Sunday. Thank you... it's been quite a journey.' James threw back the last mouthful of sweet, fortified wine.

Romeo smiled, 'Yes, it has...I remember, what were you 20? Fresh out of university.' he gazed into the distance, remembering. Senora Aconaday joined them, and her son translated her words only he could hear. 'You get work from the young and advice from the old.'

James laughed, 'Indeed.' What he remembered was how Sanke had always said he could do anything, and had, because the rules were different for him. With his drink finished, he shook hands with his boss. 'Well, I better get going— Oh, I almost forgot. This came across my desk today.' He reached into his jacket and pulled out the envelope, handing it to Aconaday.

'What's this?' asked Snake, thinking maybe it was a pleasant surprise.

'It's a Form 21. I thought you'd want to be informed before it's listed Monday on the council's Antenno app.'

Aconaday opened the paper and read. 'Boschetto Holdings'

'Looks like a shelf company. They've got a tenement over *your* place. I'm afraid I've got no advice. I checked it out and it looks watertight. Anyway, I've got to run. Best of luck!' And with that, Templar strode to his car grinning from ear to spiteful ear.

CHAPTER 77

The four friends rested in Marion's handmade chairs filled with jumbles of mismatched cushions under the shade of her back verandah. Each woman had a foot in its own bucket of water sprinkled with bath salts and a glass of sparkling wine at hand.

It was the golden hour, the warm light before sunset. A kaleidoscope of rainbows shimmered under the arch of a sprinkler, doing its best to revive the already parched lawn. Behind them, the radio was playing and beyond was the forest. A screen of trees waiting.

'Did you bring your brownies?'

'Hey, ho, I did yer saucy wench! They're in the freezer. Is Bob picking you up?' Cass focused on sketching the scene in her notebook.

'Argh, he is!' Liz rolled her R's and jangled her bangles with relish. She wore a coral scarf around her neck to match her painted nails and makeup, which darkened her eyes and brightened her lips.

Tara's youngest climbed out of her grandmother's bedroom window, wearing a pair of bathers and gumboots. A pink terry-towelling sun hat covered her cornsilk-plaited hair. 'Ooh, are you all having paradox baths?' she asked, landing on the verandah with a chicken tucked in the crook of one of her arms.

'Radox... it's called a Radox bath, sweet child.' Tara scratched the chook's neck as Chloe leaned close to her mother, peeking into a foot-filled bucket.

'Oh, I don't know. Life's like a box of chocolates; you never know what you're gonna get,' Cass recited with a ridiculous Alabaman accent.

Tara laughed and took the small binoculars her mother had left hanging on a nail for bird-watching and snake-spotting.

Chloe looked over at Cass solemnly. 'Do you like chocolate? The child questioned.

'I do,' the artist replied.

The women covered their smiles, as one does when kids trip over double entendres.

'Me too!' After a pause, she asked. 'Do you like men?'

Cass glanced over at Tara. The girl's mother stopped her forest surveillance to assess her daughter with curiosity before she resumed her search, toes wiggling in the water. Schools were notorious for carrying gossip told through farmers' open doorways. Cass could hold her own.

'Not all men, Chloe.' Cass said matter-of-factly.

'Hashtag, not all men,' the girl parroted.

'That's right, hun, for example, we like that one!' Tara pointed toward the ridgeline. 'Two o'clock.' She gave directions, still spying through her lenses. Everyone squinted at the band of trees, their tapered trunks now shining gold as the sun dropped. Late afternoon rays splashed the forest with dappled light, and leaves emitted a luminescence of their own. Beneath the glowing canopy was Miro, zigzagging along the gilded edge of the grove like a stagehand. He had a homemade rope and hessian sack bag slung across his body, and hundreds of monarch butterflies rose in clouds of orange as he approached trees where they were resting. With an eerie intuition, the bus driver looked up and signalled towards the house. They all waved back, Chloe included, releasing the bird under her arm with a commotion of noise. The girl remembered her original plan and skipped to play under the sprinkler.

'Move the hose over a bit, luv!' called Marion, packing tobacco into her pipe as she watched her youngest granddaughter run through the sparkling spray.

Tara kept the binoculars focussed on Miro, then trained away from him in a straight line. 'What are you searching for, my friend?'

'Paradoxes?' suggested Liz. She was now fanning herself with a delicate Chinese fan, her feet immersed in cold water.

'Ha!' Cass laughed, only half paying attention. She was furiously drawing.

Then Tara saw it. She caught the dance of shadows, dark grey stripes drifting a short distance downwind from Miro.

'... It can't be!' She pulled the lenses away and adjusted her focus. Feeling excitement fizz like the cheap champagne in her glass, Tara zoomed in. The creature stopped and sat down, tilting its long, loping head to one side and scratching its ear with a hind leg. It seemed to await Miro's signal to move, like a dog. A swamp dog.

'Well, I'll be... Thylacine.... You're safe here, boy,' she whispered so low that only Boodja could hear her before she tore herself away and turned to her friends. Out loud, she said, 'Oh, I think Miro knows that the only certainty in life is that nothing is certain.'

'That's profound!' Marion lifted her glass.

The group followed her lead, organising refills.

'Thanks, mum. Almost as enlightening as one of Cass's brownies. Top me up, please.'

'A Muckemup Renaissance, then! Although, I think that saying's Pliny the Elder?' Liz emptied the bottle into Tara's glass.

'Ha! I want to be on your team for the next pub-trivia night.' Cass read from the Wiki blurb on her phone. 'According to Google, he died in Pompei when Vesuvius erupted,'

'That's unfortunate and ironic.... I think you should rename Muck Unrivalled to Muck-Raker!' said Liz.

They all laughed. Old lady cackles bursting forth.

'Sounds good,' agreed Cass glancing at Tara, 'I was thinking Muck Unravelled!'

The lawyer had completed everything for them and hired a third party to file the documents for their exploration licence, including the Form 21. They chose the company name by pulling it out of Miro's hat. Jack had gone with *Feng Shui,* Cass liked *Feather Puss* after Hemingway's cat, Miro decided *Karlee,* which was the Noongar word for fire, Marion inspired by Helen Reddy, came up with the acronym *HURM* "Hear Us Roar Muckemup", and Raven stuck for a name under pressure, offered to be the impartial selector pulling out the winning name, which was Tara's. The witty mother of two had written the word *Boschetto*. It was Italian, a collective noun meaning both grove and coven. *Un boschetto di streghe. A Grove of Witches.*

The name was perfect. However, it was intelligence and unpredictability that made this group a threat, not witchcraft. They now owned a tenement that stretched from Marion's place, over the forest and beyond to include all of Aconoday's farm. And thanks to MacGovern, objections couldn't be raised until Boschetto Holdings finished exploring, a process that could take ten years according to the recently passed legislation.

Tara proposed a toast. 'Here's to mining exploration in Muckemup. May it be full of uncertainties!' Everyone touched their glasses together in the golden sunshine.

The End

AFTER WORDS

Well, there you have it! It turns out I'm a writer. Within an hour of completing this manuscript, I received two emails. One from a publisher. A few months into the writing, I entered a competition hoping for editorial guidance (I didn't win, but it was a reaffirming rejection letter), and another from my real estate agent. Suddenly, the owners put my rental up for sale. I've taken it as a sign. The need for this story to be out in the world outweighs my want for time to finesse my craft. That is a luxury I hope to have for the next book. What you have read here is the manuscript edition of Muckemup, raw and flawed like my characters... like people are.

Last year I read a Facebook post by retired Professor of Sustainability, Glenn Albrecht, about hope. I replied, "Hope is addictive, we're like junkies looking for a fix!" to which he wisely said, "No Jo, it's Radical Anticipation" Dang! He's coined another term; possibly the antidote for Solastalgia. I hope this novel is read as a call to action. We have plenty of historical stories of human lives before climate change and more than enough of a dystopian future, where the chosen few get to colonise Mars, while billions of others starve to death in a nuclear winter. What we need more of are stories of now, during the climate crisis. But with positive alternate endings where we can turn things around. Stories about common folk, young and old, black, white and every other package we come in, uniting to save ourselves and this beautiful green jewel we call home.

ACKNOWLEDGEMENTS

It wouldn't have been possible to write this without the generosity of a multitude of people. Many have intersected with this project, providing resources including a physical space to work and a roof over my head, thankyou S.B., C.A and J.S. I am humbled by the heart-time, feedback, opinion and encouragement received from friends old, and new whose offerings are etched into this story. With the deepest of gratitude, I thank you all.

JH

GLOSSARY OF TERMS

'alf a mo: Slang for half a minute.

Akubra: Australian bush hat made of rabbit fur felt with wide brim.

Antabuse: Medication used to treat alcoholics, by producing unpleasant after-effects.

Antechinus: Native marsupial mouse.

Antenno app:

Arvo: Slang for afternoon.

ASX: Australian Stock Exchange.

Balgas: Balga Tree, aka Grass Tree.

Betruger: German word for cheater.

Biltong: South African word for dried meat.

Boodja: Noongar word for Land.

Bunbunbu: Ngadjon Trible name for Pheasant Coucal. Australian Cuckoo.

Climate Creep: slow and incremental shifts in average temperatures, droughts, desertification, ocean acidification, ecosystem migration, biodiversity loss and land and forest degradation.

COAG: Council of Australian Governments. Primary intergovernmental forum 1992-2020.

Cocky: Cockatoo bird; is also slang for Australian farmers.

Coolbardie/Kulbardi: Noongar word for magpie.

Coz: Slang word for 'because'.

Crapitalism: Late-stage capitalism.

CSIRO: Commonwealth Scientific and Industrial Research Organisation. Australia's peak scientific body.

Darling-Baaka River: A major branch of the Murray Darling Basin, south-eastern Australia. Baaka is the original Barkindji people's name for the Darling.

Deadly: Aboriginal English means awesome or great.

Djeran: Noongar people's name for season April—May. Cooler nights, light breezes and presence of dew on plants in the mornings.

Djidi-djidi: Noongar word for willy wagtail bird.

Djilba: Noongar season of conception. First Spring (August Sept)

EPA: Environmental Protection Agency

FIFO: Fly In Fly Out [Worker]

Gammon: Aboriginal English means fake, pathetic or to pretend.

Hi-viz: Workwear with highly luminescent properties for onsite safety.

IPCC: Intergovernmental Panel on Climate Change. Body of the United Nations to advance scientific knowledge about climate change caused by human activities. Established in 1988.

Juukan Gorge: In the Pilbara, north-west Australia. Site of two caves used by indigenous peoples for the last 46,000 years. Illegally destroyed by Rio Tinto Mining in 2020 to access higher volumes of high-grade ore.

Kali: Hindu Goddess of time and doomsday meaning "She who is Death".

Karak: Noongar word for red-tailed black cockatoo.

Knuckle draggers: Slang for large, strong and rather dim witted people.

Kurdaitcha: Indigenous shaman and executioner amongst the Arrente people, central Australia.

Machiavelli: Machiavellian means the belief that a ruler is justified in using any means to stay in power, marked by cunning and duplicity. Niccolo Machiavelli (1469-1527) author of *The Prince*, the most famous treatise on bare-knuckled politics.

Makuru: Noongar first season of heavy rains. Coldest and wettest time of the year (June-July)

Mardoo: Yellow footed Antechinus, shrew-like marsupial found in Australia.

Masso: Slang for Macedonian people.

Mio Cucciolo: Italian term of endearment, 'my pet'.

National Water Initiative: Under the NWI, all states and territories committed to prepare water plans with provisions for the environment. Achieve sustainable water use in over-allocated or stressed water systems. Introduced registers of water rights and standards of water accounting. Established 2004.

NIMBY: Not In My Back Yard

Noongar: An indigenous person of south-west Western Australia. One of the largest Aboriginal cultural blocks in Australia

Norne: Noongar word for tiger snake

Numbat: English variation of Noongar Noombat. It is one of two marsupials that are strictly active during the day. The numbat is Western Australia's mammal emblem.

Phascogale: Is a squirrel sized marsupial mouse.

Picciotto: Sicilian word for a young man, the lowest rank of the mafia hierarchy.

Porco: Italian word for pig

Proja: Macedonian word for salty, pronounced pro-*ya*

Purple circle: Elite group of people that congregate to the exclusion of others in a workplace or institution. Commonly known as bullies or the untouchables.

Quenda: Bandicoot

Quokka: Small macropod about the size of a domestic cat. Herbivore and mainly nocturnal.

Riparian zone: The area between land and a river or stream. Plant habitats and communities along the river margins and banks are called riparian vegetation, characterised by water-loving plants.

Shop Steward: Person elected as a Union representative in the workplace.

Sisyphean: Relates to a task that can never be completed. Comes from a character in Greek mythology who was punished by being forced to roll a boulder up a hill for eternity.

Snake gaiters: cover over shoes as added protection against snakes, insects, water, weather.

Solastalgia: Coined by author Glenn Albrecht, describes the emotional distress caused by environmental change.

Taking the piss: to mock someone, to say something with out intending it.

Tree hugger: Slang for environmental activists.

Twonk: Noongar word for frog.

Usnea: Bearded lichen.

Yamatji: Member of the Watjarri people from the Murchison region of Western Australia.

Youse: Slang for more than one person (two or more you's = youse)

Waalitj: Noongar word for wedgetail eagle.

What a crock: Slang meaning you think it's foolish, wrong or untrue.